*Agatha Christie*

# AGATHA CHRISTIE

◆

# THIRD GIRL

## Complete and Unabridged

# ULVERSCROFT
## Leicester

First published in Great Britain in 1966 by
Collins
London

First Large Print Edition
published 2011
by arrangement with
HarperCollins*Publishers*
London

British Library CIP Data

Christie, Agatha, *1890 – 1976.*
  Third girl.
  1. Poirot, Hercule (Fictitious character)- -Fiction.
  2. Private investigators- -Belgium- -Fiction.
  3. Detective and mystery stories. 4. Large type books.
  I. Title
  823.9'12–dc22

  ISBN 978–1–44480–275–7

Published by
F. A. Thorpe (Publishing)
Anstey, Leicestershire

Set by Words & Graphics Ltd.
Anstey, Leicestershire
Printed and bound in Great Britain by
T. J. International Ltd., Padstow, Cornwall

This book is printed on acid-free paper

12564624

Agatha Christie is known throughout the world as the Queen of Crime. She is the most widely published author of all time and in any language, outsold only by the Bible and Shakespeare. She is the author of 80 crime novels and short story collections, 19 plays, and six novels written under the name of Mary Westmacott.

Agatha Christie's first novel, *The Mysterious Affair at Styles*, was written towards the end of the First World War, in which she served as a VAD. In it she created Hercule Poirot, the little Belgian detective who was destined to become the most popular detective in crime fiction since Sherlock Holmes.

Agatha Christie was made a Dame in 1971. She died in 1976.

# THIRD GIRL

Three young women share a London flat.
The first is a coolly efficient secretary. The
second is an artist. The third interrupts
Hercule Poirot's breakfast of *brioche* and
*chocolat* confessing that she may be a
murderer — and then promptly disap-
pears. Slowly, Poirot learns of the rumour
surrounding the mysterious third girl,
her family — and her disappearance.
Yet hard evidence is needed before the
great detective can pronounce her guilty,
innocent or insane . . .

To Norah Blackmore

# 1

Hercule Poirot was sitting at the breakfast table. At his right hand was a steaming cup of chocolate. He had always had a sweet tooth. To accompany the chocolate was a *brioche*. It went agreeably with chocolate. He nodded his approval. This was from the fourth shop he had tried. It was a Danish *pâtisserie* but infinitely superior to the so-called French one nearby. That had been nothing less than a fraud.

He was satisfied gastronomically. His stomach was at peace. His mind also was at peace, perhaps somewhat too much so. He had finished his *Magnum Opus*, an analysis of great writers of detective fiction. He had dared to speak scathingly of Edgar Allen Poe, he had complained of the lack of method or order in the romantic outpourings of Wilkie Collins, had lauded to the skies two American authors who were practically unknown, and had in various other ways given honour where honour was due and sternly withheld it where he considered it was not. He had seen the volume through the press, had looked upon the results and, apart from a really incredible number of printer's errors, pronounced that it was good. He had enjoyed this literary achievement and enjoyed the vast amount of reading he had had to do, had enjoyed snorting with disgust as he flung a book across the floor (though always remembering to rise, pick it up and dispose of it tidily in the waste-paper basket) and had enjoyed appreciatively nodding his head on the rare occasions when such approval was justified.

And now? He had had a pleasant interlude of relaxation, very necessary after his intellectual labour. But one could not relax for ever, one had to go on to the next thing. Unfortunately he had no idea what the next thing might be. Some further literary accomplishment? He thought not. Do a thing well then leave it alone. That was his maxim. The truth of the matter was, he was bored. All this strenuous mental activity in which he had been indulging — there had been too much of it. It had got him into bad habits, it had made him restless . . .

Vexatious! He shook his head and took another sip of chocolate.

The door opened and his well-trained servant, George, entered. His manner was deferential and slightly apologetic. He coughed and murmured, 'A — ' he paused, ' — a — young lady has called.'

Poirot looked at him with surprise and mild distaste.

'I do not see people at this hour,' he said reprovingly.

'No, sir,' agreed George.

Master and servant looked at each other. Communication was sometimes fraught with difficulties for them. By inflexion or innuendo or a certain choice of words George would signify that there was something that might be elicited if the right question was asked. Poirot considered what the right question in this case might be.

'She is good-looking, this young lady?' he inquired carefully.

'In my view — no, sir, but there is no accounting for tastes.'

Poirot considered his reply. He remembered the slight pause that George had made before the phrase — young lady. George was a delicate social recorder. He had been uncertain of the visitor's status but had given her the benefit of the doubt.

'You are of the opinion that she is a young lady rather than, let us say, a young person?'

'I think so, sir, though it is not always easy to tell nowadays.' George spoke with genuine regret.

'Did she give a reason for wishing to see me?'

'She said — ' George pronounced the words with some reluctance, apologising for them in advance as it were, 'that she wanted to consult you about a murder she might have committed.'

Hercule Poirot stared. His eyebrows rose. '*Might* have committed? Does she not *know*?'

'That is what she said, sir.'

'Unsatisfactory, but possibly interesting,' said Poirot.

'It might — have been a joke, sir,' said George, dubiously.

'Anything is possible, I suppose,' conceded Poirot, 'but one would hardly think — ' He lifted his cup. 'Show her in after five minutes.'

'Yes, sir.' George withdrew.

Poirot finished the last sip of chocolate. He pushed aside his cup and rose to his feet. He walked to the fireplace and adjusted his moustaches carefully in the mirror over the chimney piece. Satisfied, he returned to his chair and awaited the arrival of his visitor. He did not know exactly what to expect . . .

He had hoped perhaps for something nearer to his own estimate of female attraction. The outworn phrase 'beauty in distress' had occurred to him. He was disappointed when George returned ushering in the visitor; inwardly he shook his head and sighed. Here was no beauty — and no

4

noticeable distress either. Mild perplexity would seem nearer the mark.

'Pha!' thought Poirot disgustedly. 'These girls! Do they not even try to make something of themselves? Well made up, attractively dressed, hair that has been arranged by a good hairdresser, then perhaps she might pass. But now!'

His visitor was a girl of perhaps twenty-odd. Long straggly hair of indeterminate colour strayed over her shoulders. Her eyes, which were large, bore a vacant expression and were of a greenish blue. She wore what were presumably the chosen clothes of her generation. Black high leather boots, white open-work woollen stockings of doubtful cleanliness, a skimpy skirt, and a long and sloppy pullover of heavy wool. Anyone of Poirot's age and generation would have had only one desire. To drop the girl into a bath as soon as possible. He had often felt this same reaction walking along the streets. There were hundreds of girls looking exactly the same. They all looked dirty. And yet — a contradiction in terms — this one had the look of having been recently drowned and pulled out of a river. Such girls, he reflected, were not perhaps really dirty. They merely took enormous care and pains to look so.

He rose with his usual politeness, shook

hands, drew out a chair.

'You demanded to see me, mademoiselle? Sit down, I pray of you.'

'Oh,' said the girl. in a slightly breathless voice. She stared at him.

'*Eh bien?*' said Poirot.

She hesitated. 'I think I'd — rather stand.' The large eyes continued to stare doubtfully.

'As you please.' Poirot resumed his seat and looked at her. He waited. The girl shuffled her feet. She looked down on them then up again at Poirot.

'You — you *are* Hercule Poirot?'

'Assuredly. In what way can I be of use to you?'

'Oh, well, it's rather difficult. I mean — '

Poirot felt that she might need perhaps a little assistance. He said helpfully, 'My manservant told me that you wanted to consult me because you thought you 'might have committed a murder'. Is that correct?'

The girl nodded. 'That's right.'

'Surely that is not a matter that admits of any doubt. You must know yourself whether you have committed a murder or not.'

'Well, I don't know quite how to put it. I mean — '

'Come now,' said Poirot kindly. 'Sit down. Relax the muscles. Tell me all about it.'

'I don't think — oh dear, I don't know how

6

to — You see, it's all so difficult. I've — I've changed my mind. I don't want to be rude but — well, I think I'd better go.'

'Come now. Courage.'

'No, I can't. I thought I could come and — and ask you, ask you what I ought to do — but I can't, you see. It's all so different from — '

'From what?'

'I'm awfully sorry and I really don't want to be rude, but — '

She breathed an enormous sigh, looked at Poirot, looked away, and suddenly blurted out, '*You're too old.* Nobody told me you were so old. I really don't want to be rude but — there it is. *You're too old.* I'm really very sorry.'

She turned abruptly and blundered out of the room, rather like a desperate moth in lamplight.

Poirot, his mouth open, heard the bang of the front door.

He ejaculated: '*Nom d'un nom d'un nom . . .* '

# 2

## I

The telephone rang.

Hercule Poirot did not even seem aware of the fact.

It rang with shrill and insistent persistence.

George entered the room and stepped towards it, turning a questioning glance towards Poirot.

Poirot gestured with his hand.

'Leave it,' he said.

George obeyed, leaving the room again. The telephone continued to ring. The shrill irritating noise continued. Suddenly it stopped. After a minute or two, however, it commenced to ring again.

'Ah *Sapristi*! That must be a woman — undoubtedly a woman.'

He sighed, rose to his feet and came to the instrument.

He picked up the receiver. ''Allo,' he said.

'Are you — is that M. Poirot?'

'I, myself.'

'It's Mrs Oliver — your voice sounds different. I didn't recognise it at first.'

'*Bonjour*, Madame — you are well, I hope?'

8

'Oh, I'm all right.' Ariadne Oliver's voice came through in its usual cheerful accents. The well-known detective story writer and Hercule Poirot were on friendly terms.

'It's rather early to ring you up, but I want to ask you a favour.'

'Yes?'

'It is the annual dinner of our Detective Authors' Club; I wondered if you would come and be our Guest Speaker this year. It would be very very sweet of you if you would.'

'When is this?'

'Next month — the twenty-third.'

A deep sigh came over the telephone.

'Alas! I am too old.'

'Too old? What on earth do you mean? You're not old at all.'

'You think not?'

'Of course not. You'll be wonderful. You can tell us lots of lovely stories about real crimes.'

'And who will want to listen?'

'Everyone. They — M. Poirot, is there anything the matter? Has something happened? You sound upset.'

'Yes, I am upset. My feelings — ah, well, no matter.'

'But tell me about it.'

'Why should I make a fuss?'

'Why shouldn't you? You'd better come and

9

tell me all about it. When will you come? This afternoon. Come and have tea with me.'

'Afternoon tea, I do not drink it.'

'Then you can have coffee.'

'It is not the time of day I usually drink coffee.'

'Chocolate? With whipped cream on top? Or a tisane. You love sipping tisanes. Or lemonade. Or orangeade. Or would you like decaffeinated coffee if I can get it — '

'*Ah ça, non par example!* It is an abomination.'

'One of those sirops you like so much. I know, I've got half a bottle of Ribena in the cupboard.'

'What is Ribena?'

'Blackcurrant flavour.'

'Indeed, one has to hand it to you! You really do try, Madame. I am touched by your solicitude. I will accept with pleasure to drink a cup of chocolate this afternoon.'

'Good. And then you'll tell me all about what's upset you.'

She rang off.


## II


Poirot considered for a moment. Then he dialled a number. Presently he said: 'Mr

10

Goby? Hercule Poirot here. Are you very fully occupied at this moment?'

'Middling,' said the voice of Mr Goby. 'Middling to fair. But to oblige you, Monsieur Poirot, if you're in a hurry, as you usually are — well, I wouldn't say that my young men couldn't manage mostly what's on hand at present. Of course good boys aren't as easy to get as they used to be. Think too much of themselves nowadays. Think they know it all before they've started to learn. But there! Can't expect old heads on young shoulders. I'll be pleased to put myself at your disposal, M. Poirot. Maybe I can put one or two of the better lads on the job. I suppose it's the usual — collecting information?'

He nodded his head and listened whilst Poirot went into details of exactly what he wanted done. When he had finished with Mr Goby, Poirot rang up Scotland Yard where in due course he got through to a friend of his. When he in turn had listened to Poirot's requirements, he replied,

'Don't want much, do you? Any murder, *anywhere*. Time, place and victim unknown. Sounds a bit of a wild goose chase, if you ask me, old boy.' He added disapprovingly, 'You don't seem really to know *anything*!'

# III

At 4.15 that afternoon Poirot sat in Mrs Oliver's drawing-room sipping appreciatively at a large cup of chocolate topped with foaming whipped cream which his hostess had just placed on a small table beside him. She added a small plate full of *langue de chats* biscuits.

'*Chère* Madame, what kindness.' He looked over his cup with faint surprise at Mrs Oliver's coiffure and also at her new wallpaper. Both were new to him. The last time he had seen Mrs Oliver, her hair style had been plain and severe. It now displayed a richness of coils and twists arranged in intricate patterns all over her head. Its prolific luxury was, he suspected, largely artificial. He debated in his mind how many switches of hair might unexpectedly fall off if Mrs Oliver was to get suddenly excited, as was her wont. As for the wallpaper . . .

'These cherries — they are new?' he waved a teaspoon. It was, he felt, rather like being in a cherry orchard.

'Are there too many of them, do you think?' said Mrs Oliver. 'So hard to tell beforehand with wallpaper. Do you think my old one was better?'

Poirot cast his mind back dimly to what he

seemed to remember as large quantities of bright coloured tropical birds in a forest. He felt inclined to remark '*Plus ça change, plus c'est la même chose,*' but restrained himself.

'And now,' said Mrs Oliver, as her guest finally replaced his cup on its saucer and sat back with a sigh of satisfaction, wiping remnants of foaming cream from his moustache, 'what *is* all this about?'

'That I can tell you very simply. This morning a girl came to see me. I suggested she might make an appointment. One has one's routine, you comprehend. She sent back word that she wanted to see me at once because she thought she might have committed a murder.'

'What an odd thing to say. Didn't she *know*?'

'Precisely! *C'est inouï!* so I instructed Georges to show her in. She stood there! She refused to sit down. She just stood there staring at me. She seemed quite half-witted. I tried to encourage her. Then suddenly she said that she'd changed her mind. She said she didn't want to be rude but that — (what do you think?) — but that I was *too old* . . .'

Mrs Oliver hastened to utter soothing words. 'Oh well, girls are like that. Anyone over thirty-five they think is half dead. They've no *sense*, girls, you must realise that.'

'It wounded me,' said Hercule Poirot.

'Well, I shouldn't worry about it, if I were you. Of course it was a very rude thing to say.'

'That does not matter. And it is not only *my* feelings. I am worried. Yes, I am worried.'

'Well, I should forget all about it if I were you,' advised Mrs Oliver comfortably.

'You do not understand. I am worried about this girl. She came to me for *help*. Then she decided that I was too old. Too old to be of any use to her. She was wrong of course, that goes without saying, and then she just ran away. But I tell you that girl *needs* help.'

'I don't suppose she does really,' said Mrs Oliver soothingly. 'Girls make a fuss about things.'

'No. You are wrong. *She needs help.*'

'You don't think she really has committed a murder?'

'Why not? She said she had.'

'Yes, but — ' Mrs Oliver stopped. 'She said she *might* have,' she said slowly. 'But what can she possibly mean by that?'

'Exactly. It does not make sense.'

'Who did she murder or did she think she murdered?'

Poirot shrugged his shoulders.

'And why did she murder someone?'

Again Poirot shrugged his shoulders.

'Of course it could be all sorts of things.' Mrs Oliver began to brighten as she set her ever prolific imagination to work. 'She could have run over someone in her car and not stopped. She could have been assaulted by a man on a cliff and struggled with him and managed to push him over. She could have given someone the wrong medicine by mistake. She could have gone to one of those purple pill parties and had a fight with someone. She could have come to and found she had stabbed someone. She — '

'Assez, madame, assez!'

But Mrs Oliver was well away.

'She might have been a nurse in the operating theatre and administered the wrong anaesthetic or — ' she broke off, suddenly anxious for clearer details. 'What did she look like?'

Poirot considered for a moment.

'An Ophelia devoid of physical attraction.'

'Oh dear,' said Mrs Oliver. 'I can almost see her when you say that. How queer.'

'She is not competent,' said Poirot. 'That is how I see her. She is not one who can cope with difficulties. She is not one of those who can see beforehand the dangers that must come. She is one of whom others will look round and say 'we want a victim. That one will do'.'

15

But Mrs Oliver was no longer listening. She was clutching her rich coils of hair with both hands in a gesture with which Poirot was familiar.

'Wait,' she cried in a kind of agony. 'Wait!'

Poirot waited, his eyebrows raised.

'You didn't tell me her name,' said Mrs Oliver.

'She did not give it. Unfortunate, I agree with you.'

'Wait!' implored Mrs Oliver, again with the same agony. She relaxed her grip on her head and uttered a deep sigh. Hair detached itself from its bonds and tumbled over her shoulders, a super imperial coil of hair detached itself completely and fell on the floor. Poirot picked it up and put it discreetly on the table.

'Now then,' said Mrs Oliver, suddenly restored to calm. She pushed in a hairpin or two, and nodded her head while she thought. 'Who told this girl about you, M. Poirot?'

'No one, so far as I know. Naturally, she had heard about me, no doubt.'

Mrs Oliver thought that 'naturally' was not the word at all. What was natural was that Poirot himself was sure that everyone had always heard of him. Actually large numbers of people would only look at you blankly if the name of Hercule Poirot was mentioned, especially the younger generation. 'But how am I going to put that to him,' thought Mrs Oliver, 'in such a way that it won't hurt his feelings?'

'I think you're wrong,' she said. 'Girls — well, girls and young men — they don't know very much about detectives and things like that. They don't hear about them.'

'Everyone must have heard about Hercule Poirot,' said Poirot, superbly.

It was an article of belief for Hercule Poirot.

'But they are all so badly educated nowadays,' said Mrs Oliver. 'Really, the only people whose names they know are pop singers, or groups, or disc jockeys — that sort of thing. If you need someone special, I mean a doctor or a detective or a dentist — well, then, I mean you would *ask* someone — ask who's the right person to go to? And then the other person says — 'My dear, you must go to that absolutely wonderful man in Queen Anne's Street, twists your legs three times round your head and you're cured,' or 'All my diamonds were stolen, and Henry would have been furious, so I couldn't go to the police, but there's a simply uncanny detective, *most* discreet, and he got them back for me and Henry never knew a thing.' — That's the way it happens all the time. *Someone* sent that girl to you.'

'I doubt it very much.'

'You wouldn't know until you were told. *And you're going to be told now.* It's only just come to me. *I* sent that girl to you.'

Poirot stared. 'You? But why did you not say so at once?'

'Because it's only just come to me — when you spoke about Ophelia — long wet-looking hair, and rather plain. It seemed a description of someone I'd actually *seen.* Quite lately. And then it came to me who it was.'

'Who is she?'

'I don't actually know her name, but I can easily find out. We were talking — about private detectives and private eyes — and I spoke about you and some of the amazing things you had done.'

'And you gave her my address?'

'No, of course I didn't. I'd no idea she wanted a detective or anything like that. I thought we were just talking. But I'd mentioned the name several times, and of course it would be easy to look you up in the telephone book and just come along.'

'Were you talking about murder?'

'Not that I can remember. I don't even know how we came to be talking about detectives — unless, yes, perhaps it was *she* who started the subject . . . '

'Tell me then, tell me all you can — even if

you do not know her name, tell me all you know about her.'

'Well, it was last weekend. I was staying with the Lorrimers. They don't come into it except that they took me over to some friends of theirs for drinks. There were several people there — and I didn't enjoy myself much because, as you know, I don't really like drink, and so people have to find a soft drink for me which is rather a bore for them. And then people *say* things to me — you know — how much they like my books, and how they've been longing to meet me — and it all makes me feel hot and bothered and rather silly. But I manage to cope more or less. And they say how much they love my awful detective Sven Hjerson. If they knew how *I* hated him! But my publisher always says I'm not to say so. Anyway, I suppose the talk about detectives in real life grew out of all that, and I talked a bit about you, and this girl was standing around listening. When you said an unattractive Ophelia it clicked somehow. I thought: 'Now who does that remind me of?' And then it came to me: 'Of course. The girl at the party that day.' I rather think she belonged there unless I'm confusing her with some other girl.'

Poirot sighed. With Mrs Oliver one always needed a lot of patience.

19

'Who were these people with whom you went to have drinks?'

'Trefusis, I think, unless it was Treherne. That sort of name — he's a tycoon. Rich. Something in the City, but he's spent most of his life in South Africa — '

'He has a wife?'

'Yes. Very good-looking woman. Much younger than he is. Lots of golden hair. Second wife. The daughter was the first wife's daughter. Then there was an uncle of incredible antiquity. Rather deaf. He's frightfully distinguished — strings of letters after his name. An admiral or an air-marshal or something. He's an astronomer too, I think. Anyway, he's got a kind of big telescope sticking out of the roof. Though I suppose that might be just a hobby. There was a foreign girl there, too, who sort of trots about after the old boy. Goes up to London with him, I believe, and sees he doesn't get run over. Rather pretty, she was.'

Poirot sorted out the information Mrs Oliver had supplied him with, feeling rather like a human computer.

'There lives then in the house Mr and Mrs Trefusis — '

'It's not Trefusis — I remember now — It's Restarick.'

'That is not at all the same type of name.'

20

'Yes it is. It's a Cornish name, isn't it?'

'There lives there then, Mr and Mrs Restarick, the distinguished elderly uncle. Is his name Restarick too?'

'It's Sir Roderick something.'

'And there is the *au pair* girl, or whatever she is, and a daughter — any more children?'

'I don't think so — but I don't really know. The daughter doesn't live at home, by the way. She was only down for the weekend. Doesn't get on with the stepmother, I expect. She's got a job in London, and she's picked up with a boy friend they don't much like, so I understand.'

'You seem to know quite a lot about the family.'

'Oh well, one picks things up. The Lorrimers are great talkers. Always chattering about someone or other. One hears a lot of gossip about the people all around. Sometimes, though, one gets them mixed up. I probably have. I wish I could remember that girl's Christian name. Something connected with a song . . . Thora? *Speak to me, Thora.* Thora, Thora. Something like that, or Myra? Myra, *oh Myra my love is all for thee.* Something like that. *I dreamt I dwelt in marble halls.* Norma? Or do I mean Maritana? Norma — Norma Restarick. That's right, I'm sure.' She added inconsequently, 'She's a third girl.'

21

'I thought you said you thought she was an only child.'

'So she is — or I think so.'

'Then what do you mean by saying she is the third girl?'

'Good gracious, don't you know what a third girl is? Don't you read *The Times*?'

'I read the births, deaths, and marriages. And such articles as I find of interest.'

'No, I mean the front advertisement page. Only it isn't in the front now. So I'm thinking of taking some other paper. But I'll show you.'

She went to a side table and snatched up *The Times*, turned the pages over and brought it to him. 'Here you are — look. 'THIRD GIRL *for comfortable second floor flat, own room, central heating, Earl's Court.*' '*Third girl wanted to share flat. 5gns. week own room.*' '*4th girl wanted. Regent's Park. Own room.*' It's the way girls like living now. Better than PGs or a hostel. The main girl takes a furnished flat, and then shares out the rent. Second girl is usually a friend. Then they find a third girl by advertising if they don't know one. And, as you see, very often they manage to squeeze in a fourth girl. First girl takes the best room, second girl pays rather less, third girl less still and is stuck in a cat-hole. They fix it among themselves which one has the flat to herself which night a week

— or something like that. It works reasonably well.'

'And where does this girl whose name might just possibly be Norma live in London?'

'As I've told you I don't really know anything about her.'

'But you could find out?'

'Oh yes, I expect that would be quite easy.'

'You are sure there was no talk, no mention of an unexpected death?'

'Do you mean a death in London — or at the Restaricks' home?'

'Either.'

'I don't think so. Shall I see what I can rake up?'

Mrs Oliver's eyes sparkled with excitement. She was by now entering into the spirit of the thing.

'That would be very kind.'

'I'll ring up the Lorrimers. Actually now would be quite a good time.' She went towards the telephone. 'I shall have to think of reasons and things — perhaps invent things?'

She looked towards Poirot rather doubtfully.

'But naturally. That is understood. You are a woman of imagination — you will have no difficulty. But — not too fantastic, you understand. Moderation.'

Mrs Oliver flashed him an understanding glance.

She dialled and asked for the number she wanted. Turning her head, she hissed: 'Have you got a pencil and paper — or a notebook — something to write down names or addresses or places?'

Poirot had already his notebook arranged by his elbow and nodded his head reassuringly.

Mrs Oliver turned back to the receiver she held and launched herself into speech. Poirot listened attentively to one side of a telephone conversation.

'Hallo. Can I speak to — Oh, it's you, Naomi. Ariadne Oliver here. Oh, yes — well, it was rather a crowd . . . Oh, you mean the old boy? . . . No, you know I don't . . . Practically blind? . . . I thought he was going up to London with the little foreign girl . . . Yes, it must be rather worrying for them sometimes — but she seems to manage him quite well . . . One of the things I rang up for was to ask you what the girl's address was — No, the Restarick girl, I mean — somewhere in South Ken, isn't it? Or was it Knightsbridge? Well, I promised her a book and I wrote down the address, but of course I've lost it as usual. I can't even remember her name. Is it Thora or Norma? . . . Yes, I *thought* it was Norma: . . . Wait a minute, I'll get a pencil . . . Yes, I'm ready . . . 67 Borodene Mansions . . . I know

— that great block that looks rather like Worm-wood Scrubs prison . . . Yes, I believe the flats are very comfortable with central heating and everything . . . Who are the other two girls she lives with? . . . Friends of hers? . . . or adver-tisements? . . . Claudia Reece-Holland . . . her father's the MP, is he? Who's the other one? . . . No, I suppose you wouldn't know — she's quite nice, too, I suppose . . . What do they all do? They always seem to be secretaries, don't they? . . . Oh, the other girl's an interior deco-rator — you think — or to do with an art gallery — No, Naomi, of course I don't *really* want to know — one just wonders — what *do* all the girls do nowadays? — well, it's useful for me to know because of my books — one wants to keep up to date . . . What was it you told me about some boy friend . . . Yes, but one's so helpless, isn't one? I mean girls do just exactly as they like . . . does he look very awful? Is he the unshaven dirty kind? Oh, *that* kind — Brocade waistcoats, and long curling chestnut hair — lying on his shoulders — yes, so hard to tell whether they're girls or boys, isn't it? — Yes, they do look like Vandykes sometimes if they're good looking . . . What did you say? That Andrew Restarick simply hates him? . . . Yes, men usually do . . . Mary Restarick? . . . Well, I suppose you do usually have rows with a stepmother. I expect she was

25

quite thankful when the girl got a job in London. What do you mean about people saying things . . . Why, couldn't they find out what was the matter with her? . . . *Who* said? . . . Yes, but *what* did they hush up? . . . Oh — a nurse? — talked to the Jenners' governess? Do you mean her *husband*? Oh, I see — The doctors couldn't find out . . . No, but people are so ill-natured. I do agree with you. These things are usually *quite* untrue . . . Oh, gastric, was it? . . . But how ridiculous. Do you mean people said what's his name — Andrew — You mean it would be easy with all those weed killers about — Yes, but why? . . . I mean, it's not a case of some wife he's hated for years — she's the second wife — and much younger than he is and good looking . . . Yes, I suppose *that* could be — but why should the foreign girl want to either? . . . You mean she might have resented things that Mrs Restarick said to her . . . She's quite an attractive little thing — I suppose Andrew might have taken a fancy to her — nothing serious of course — but it might have annoyed Mary, and then she might have pitched into the girl and — '

Out of the corner of her eye, Mrs Oliver perceived Poirot signalling wildly to her.

'Just a moment, darling,' said Mrs Oliver into the telephone. 'It's the baker.' Poirot looked affronted. 'Hang on.'

She laid down the receiver, hurried across the room, and backed Poirot into a breakfast nook.

'Yes,' she demanded breathlessly.

'A baker,' said Poirot with scorn. 'Me!'

'Well, I had to think of something quickly. What were you signalling about? Did you understand what she — '

Poirot cut her short.

'You shall tell me presently. I know enough. What I want you to do is, with your rapid powers of improvisation, to arrange some plausible pretext for me to visit the Restaricks — an old friend of yours, shortly to be in the neighbourhood. Perhaps you could say — '

'Leave it to me. I'll think of something. Shall you give a false name?'

'Certainly not. Let us at least try to keep it simple.'

Mrs Oliver nodded, and hurried back to the abandoned telephone.

'Naomi? I can't remember what we were saying. Why does something always come to interrupt just when one has settled down to a nice gossip? I can't even remember now what I rang you up for to begin with — Oh yes — that child Thora's address — Norma, I mean — and you gave it to me. But there was something else I wanted to — oh, I remember. An old friend of mine. A most fascinating little man. Actually I was talking about him the other day down there. Hercule Poirot his name is. He's going to be staying quite close to the Restaricks and he is most tremendously anxious to meet old Sir Roderick. He knows a lot about him and has a terrific admiration for him, and for some wonderful discovery of his in the war — or some scientific thing he did — anyway, he is very anxious to 'call upon him and present his respects', that's how he put it. Will that be all right, do you think? Will you warn them? Yes, he'll probably just turn up out of the blue. Tell them to make him tell them some wonderful espionage stories . . . He — what? Oh! your mowers? Yes, of course you must go. Goodbye.'

She put back the receiver and sank down in an armchair. 'Goodness, how exhausting. Was that all right?'

'Not bad,' said Poirot.

'I thought I'd better pin it all to the old boy. Then you'll get to see the lot which I suppose is what you want. And one can always be vague about scientific subjects if one is a woman, and you can think up something more definite that sounds probable by the time you arrive. Now, do you want to hear what she was telling me?'

'There has been gossip, I gather. About the health of Mrs Restarick?'

'That's it. It seems she had some kind of mysterious illness — gastric in nature — and the doctors were puzzled. They sent her into hospital and she got quite all right, but there didn't seem any real cause to account for it. And she went home, and it all began to start again — and again the doctors were puzzled. And then people began to *talk*. A rather irresponsible nurse started it and her sister told a neighbour, and the neighbour went out on daily work and told someone else, and how queer it all was. And then people began saying that her husband must be trying to poison her. The sort of thing people always say — but in this case it really didn't seem to make sense. And then Naomi and I wondered about the *au pair* girl, she's a kind of secretary companion to the old boy — so really there isn't any kind of reason why she should administer weed killer to Mrs Restarick.'

'I heard you suggesting a few.'

'Well, there is usually something *possible* . . .'

'*Murder desired* . . .' said Poirot thoughtfully . . . 'But not yet committed.'

# 3

Mrs Oliver drove into the inner court of Borodene Mansions. There were six cars filling the parking space. As Mrs Oliver hesitated, one of the cars reversed out and drove away. Mrs Oliver hurried neatly into the vacant space.

She descended, banged the door and stood looking up to the sky. It was a recent block, occupying a space left by the havoc of a land mine in the last war. It might, Mrs Oliver thought, have been lifted *en bloc* from the Great West Road and, first deprived of some such legend as SKYLARK'S FEATHER RAZOR BLADES, have been deposited as a block of flats *in situ*. It looked extremely functional and whoever had built it had obviously scorned any ornamental additions.

It was a busy time. Cars and people were going in and out of the courtyard as the day's work came to a close.

Mrs Oliver glanced down at her wrist. Ten minutes to seven. About the right time, as far as she could judge. The kind of time when girls in jobs might be presumed to have returned, either to renew their make up, change their clothes to tight exotic pants or whatever their particular addiction was, and go out again, or else to settle down to home life and wash their smalls and their stockings. Anyway, quite a sensible time to try. The block was exactly the same on the east and the west, with big swing doors set in the centre. Mrs Oliver chose the left hand side but immediately found that she was wrong. All this side was numbers from 100 to 200. She crossed over to the other side.

No. 67 was on the sixth floor. Mrs Oliver pressed the button of the lift. The doors opened like a yawning mouth with a menacing clash. Mrs Oliver hurried into the yawning cavern. She was always afraid of modern lifts.

Crash. The doors came to again. The lift went up. It stopped almost immediately (that was frightening too!). Mrs Oliver scuttled out like a frightened rabbit.

She looked up at the wall and went along the right hand passage. She came to a door marked 67 in metal numbers affixed to the centre of the door. The numeral 7 detached itself and fell on her feet as she arrived.

'This place doesn't like me,' said Mrs Oliver to herself as she winced with pain and picked the number up gingerly and affixed it by its spike to the door again.

She pressed the bell. Perhaps everyone was out.

However, the door opened almost at once. A tall handsome girl stood in the doorway. She was wearing a dark well-cut suit with a very short skirt, a white silk shirt, and was very well shod. She had swept-up dark hair, good but discreet make up, and for some reason was slightly alarming to Mrs Oliver.

'Oh,' said Mrs Oliver, galvanizing herself to say the right thing. 'Is Miss Restarick in, by any chance?'

'No, I'm sorry, she's out. Can I give her a message?'

Mrs Oliver said, 'Oh' again — before proceeding. She made a play of action by producing a parcel rather untidily done up in brown paper. 'I promised her a book,' she explained. 'One of mine that she hadn't read. I hope I've remembered actually which it was. She won't be in soon, I suppose?'

'I really couldn't say. I don't know what she is doing tonight.'

'Oh. Are you Miss Reece-Holland?'

The girl looked slightly surprised.

'Yes, I am.'

'I've met your father,' said Mrs Oliver. She went on, 'I'm Mrs Oliver. I write books,' she added in the usual guilty style in which she invariably made such an announcement.

'Won't you come in?'

Mrs Oliver accepted the invitation, and Claudia Reece-Holland led her into a sitting-room. All the rooms of the flats were papered the same with an artificial raw wood pattern. Tenants could then display their modern pictures or apply any forms of decoration they fancied. There was a foundation of modern built-in furniture, cupboard, bookshelves and so on, a large settee and a pull-out type of table. Personal bits and pieces could be added by the tenants. There were also signs of individuality displayed here by a gigantic Harlequin pasted on one wall, and a stencil of a monkey swinging from branches of palm fronds on another wall.

'I'm sure Norma will be thrilled to get your book, Mrs Oliver. Won't you have a drink? Sherry? Gin?'

This girl had the brisk manner of a really good secretary. Mrs Oliver refused.

'You've got a splendid view up here,' she said, looking out of the window and blinking a little as she got the setting sun straight in her eyes.

'Yes. Not so funny when the lift goes out of order.'

'I shouldn't have thought *that* lift would dare to go out of order. It's so — so — robot-like.'

'Recently installed, but none the better for that,' said Claudia. 'It needs frequent adjusting and all that.'

Another girl came in, talking as she entered.

'Claudia, have you any idea where I put — '

She stopped, looking at Mrs Oliver.

Claudia made a quick introduction.

'Frances Cary — Mrs Oliver. Mrs *Ariadne* Oliver.'

'Oh, how exciting,' said Frances.

She was a tall willowy girl, with long black hair, a heavily made up dead white face, and eyebrows and eyelashes slightly slanted upwards — the effect heightened by mascara. She wore tight velvet pants and a heavy sweater. She was a complete contrast to the brisk and efficient Claudia.

'I brought a book I'd promised Norma Restarick,' said Mrs Oliver.

'Oh! — what a pity she's still in the country.'

'Hasn't she come back?'

There was quite definitely a pause. Mrs Oliver thought the two girls exchanged a glance.

'I thought she had a job in London,' said Mrs Oliver, endeavouring to convey innocent surprise.

'Oh yes,' said Claudia. 'She's in an interior decorating place. She's sent down with patterns occasionally to places in the country.' She smiled. 'We live rather separate lives here,' she explained. 'Come and go as we like — and don't usually bother to leave messages. But I won't forget to give her your book when she does get back.'

Nothing could have been easier than the casual explanation.

Mrs Oliver rose. 'Well, thank you very much.'

Claudia accompanied her to the door. 'I shall tell my father I've met you,' she said. 'He's a great reader of detective stories.'

Closing the door she went back into the sitting-room.

The girl Frances was leaning against the window.

'Sorry,' she said. 'Did I boob?'

'I'd just said that Norma was out.'

Frances shrugged her shoulders.

'I couldn't tell. Claudia, where *is* that girl? Why didn't she come back on Monday? Where has she gone?'

'I can't imagine.'

'She didn't stay on down with her people? That's where she went for the weekend.'

'No. I rang up, actually, to find out.'

'I suppose it doesn't really matter . . . All

the same, she is — well, there's something queer about her.'

'She's not really queerer than anyone else.' But the opinion sounded uncertain.

'Oh yes, she is,' said Frances. 'Sometimes she gives me the shivers. She's not normal, you know.'

She laughed suddenly.

'Norma isn't normal! You know she isn't, Claudia, although you won't admit it. Loyalty to your employer, I suppose.'

# 4

Hercule Poirot walked along the main street of Long Basing. That is, if you can describe as a main street a street that is to all intents and purposes the only street, which was the case in Long Basing. It was one of those villages that exhibit a tendency to length without breadth. It had an impressive church with a tall tower and a yew tree of elderly dignity in its churchyard. It had its full quota of village shops disclosing much variety. It had two antique shops, one mostly consisting of stripped pine chimney pieces, the other disclosing a full house of piled up ancient maps, a good deal of porcelain, most of it chipped, some worm-eaten old oak chests, shelves of glass, some Victorian silver, all somewhat hampered in display by lack of space. There were two cafés, both rather nasty, there was a basket shop, quite delightful, with a large variety of home-made wares, there was a post office-cum-greengrocer, there was a draper's which dealt largely in millinery and also a shoe department for children and a large miscellaneous selection of haberdashery of all kinds. There was a stationery and newspaper shop which also dealt in tobacco and sweets. There was a wool shop which was clearly the aristocrat of the place. Two white-haired severe women were in charge of shelves and shelves of knitting materials of every description. Also large quantities of dress-making patterns and knitting patterns and which branched off into a counter for art needle-work. What had lately been the local grocer's had now blossomed into calling itself 'a supermarket' complete with stacks of wire baskets and packaged materials of every cereal and cleaning material, all in dazzling paper boxes. And there was a small establishment with one small window with Lillah written across it in fancy letters, a fashion display of one French blouse, labelled 'Latest chic', and a navy skirt and a purple striped jumper labelled 'separates'. These were displayed by being flung down as by a careless hand in the window.

All of this Poirot observed with a detached interest. Also contained within the limits of the village and facing on the street were several small houses, old-fashioned in style, sometimes retaining Georgian purity, more often showing some signs of Victorian improvement, as a veranda, bow window, or a small conservatory. One or two houses had had a complete face lift and showed signs of claiming to be new and proud of it. There were also some delightful and decrepit old-world cottages, some pretending to be a hundred or so years older than they were, others completely genuine, any added comforts of plumbing or such being carefully hidden from any casual glance.

Poirot walked gently along digesting all that he saw. If his impatient friend, Mrs Oliver, had been with him, she would have immediately demanded why he was wasting time, as the house to which he was bound was a quarter of a mile beyond the village limits. Poirot would have told her that he was absorbing the local atmosphere; that these things were sometimes important. At the end of the village there came an abrupt transition. On one side, set back from the road, was a row of newly built council houses, a strip of green in front of them and a gay note set by each house having been given a different coloured front door. Beyond the council houses the sway of fields and hedges resumed its course interspersed now and then by the occasional 'desirable residences' of a house agent's list, with their own trees and gardens and a general air of reserve and of keeping themselves to themselves. Ahead of him farther down the road Poirot descried a house, the top storey of which displayed an unusual note of bulbous construction. Something had evidently been tacked on up there not so many years ago. This no doubt was the Mecca towards which his feet were bent. He arrived at a gate to which the nameplate Crosshedges was attached. He surveyed the house. It was a conventional house dating perhaps to the beginning of the century. It was neither beautiful nor ugly. Commonplace was perhaps the word to describe it. The garden was more attractive than the house and had obviously been the subject of a great deal of care and attention in its time, though it had been allowed to fall into disarray. It still had smooth green lawns, plenty of flower beds, carefully planted areas of shrubs to display a certain landscape effect. It was all in good order. A gardener was certainly employed in this garden, Poirot reflected. A personal interest was perhaps also taken, since he noted in a corner near the house a woman bending over one of the flower beds, tying up dahlias, he thought. Her head showed as a bright circle of pure gold colour. She was tall, slim but square-shouldered. He unlatched the gate, passed through and walked up towards the house. The woman turned her head and then straightened herself, turning towards him inquiringly.

She remained standing, waiting for him to speak, some garden twine hanging from her left hand. She looked, he noted, puzzled.

'Yes?' she said.

Poirot, very foreign, took off his hat with a flourish and bowed. Her eyes rested on his moustaches with a kind of fascination.

'Mrs Restarick?'

'Yes. I — '

'I hope I do not derange you, Madame.'

A faint smile touched her lips. 'Not at all. Are you — '

'I have permitted myself to pay a visit on you. A friend of mine, Mrs Ariadne Oliver — '

'Oh, of course. I know who you must be. Monsieur Poiret.'

'Monsieur Poirot,' he corrected her with an emphasis on the last syllable. 'Hercule Poirot, at your service. I was passing through this neighbourhood and I ventured to call upon you here in the hope that I might be allowed to pay my respects to Sir Roderick Horsefield.'

'Yes. Naomi Lorrimer told us you might turn up.'

'I hope it is not inconvenient?'

'Oh, it is not inconvenient at all. Ariadne Oliver was here last weekend. She came over with the Lorrimers. Her books are most amusing, aren't they? But perhaps you don't find detective stories amusing. You are a detective yourself, aren't you — a real one?'

'I am all that there is of the most real,' said Hercule Poirot.

He noticed that she repressed a smile. He studied her more closely. She was handsome in a rather artificial fashion. Her golden hair was stiffly arranged. He wondered whether she might not at heart be secretly unsure of herself, whether she were not carefully playing the part of the English lady absorbed in her garden. He wondered a little what her social background might have been.

'You have a very fine garden here,' he said.

'You like gardens?'

'Not as the English like gardens. You have for a garden a special talent in England. It means something to you that it does not to us.'

'To French people, you mean? Oh yes. I believe that Mrs Oliver mentioned that you were once with the Belgian Police Force?'

'That is so. Me, I am an old Belgian police dog.' He gave a polite little laugh and said, waving his hands, 'But your gardens, you English, I admire. I sit at your feet! The Latin races, they like the formal garden, the gardens of the château, the Château of Versailles in miniature, and also of course they invented the *potager*. Very important, the *potager*. Here in England you have the *potager*, but you got it from France and you do not love

42

your *potager* as much as you love your flowers. *Hein?* That is so?'

'Yes, I think you are right,' said Mary Restarick. 'Do come into the house. You came to see my uncle.'

'I came, as you say, to pay homage to Sir Roderick, but I pay homage to you also, Madame. Always I pay homage to beauty when I meet it.' He bowed.

She laughed with slight embarrassment. 'You mustn't pay me so many compliments.'

She led the way through an open french window and he followed her.

'I knew your uncle slightly in 1944.'

'Poor dear, he's getting quite an old man now. He's very deaf, I'm afraid.'

'It was long ago that I encountered him. He will probably have forgotten. It was a matter of espionage and of scientific developments of a certain invention. We owed that invention to the ingenuity of Sir Roderick. He will be willing, I hope, to receive me.'

'Oh, I'm sure he'll love it,' said Mrs Restarick. 'He has rather a dull life in some ways nowadays. I have to be so much in London — we are looking for a suitable house there.' She sighed and said, 'Elderly people can be very difficult sometimes.'

'I know,' said Poirot. 'Frequently I, too, am difficult.'

She laughed. 'Ah no, M. Poirot, come now, you mustn't pretend you're old.'

'Sometimes I am told so,' said Poirot. He sighed. 'By young girls,' he added mournfully.

'That's very unkind of them. It's probably the sort of thing that our daughter would do,' she added.

'Ah, you have a daughter?'

'Yes. At least, she is my stepdaughter.'

'I shall have much pleasure in meeting her,' said Poirot politely.

'Oh well, I'm afraid she is not here. She's in London. She works there.'

'The young girls, they all do jobs nowadays.'

'Everybody's supposed to do a job,' said Mrs Restarick vaguely. 'Even when they get married they're always being persuaded back into industry or back into teaching.'

'Have they persuaded you, Madame, to come back into anything?'

'No. I was brought up in South Africa. I only came here with my husband a short time ago — It's all — rather strange to me still.'

She looked round her with what Poirot judged to be an absence of enthusiasm. It was a handsomely furnished room of a conventional type — without personality. Two large portraits hung on the walls — the only personal touch. The first was that of a thin-lipped woman in a grey velvet evening dress. Facing her on the opposite wall was a man of about thirty-odd with an air of repressed energy about him.

'Your daughter, I suppose, finds it dull in the country?'

'Yes, it is much better for her to be in London. She doesn't like it here.' She paused abruptly, and then as though the last words were almost dragged out of her, she said, ' — and she doesn't like me.'

'Impossible,' said Hercule Poirot, with Gallic politeness.

'Not at all impossible! Oh well, I suppose it often happens. I suppose it's hard for girls to accept a stepmother.'

'Was your daughter very fond of her own mother?'

'I suppose she must have been. She's a difficult girl. I suppose most girls are.'

Poirot sighed and said, 'Mothers and fathers have much less control over daughters nowadays. It is not as it used to be in the old good-fashioned days.'

'No indeed.'

'One dare not say so, Madame, but I must confess I regret that they show so very little discrimination in choosing their — how do you say it? — their boy friends?'

'Norma has been a great worry to her

45

father in that way. However, I suppose it is no good complaining. People must make their own experiments. But I must take you up to Uncle Roddy — he has his own rooms upstairs.'

She led the way out of the room. Poirot looked back over his shoulder. A dull room, a room without character — except perhaps for the two portraits. By the style of the woman's dress, Poirot judged that they dated from some years back. If that was the first Mrs Restarick, Poirot did not think that he would have liked her.

He said, 'Those are fine portraits, Madame.'

'Yes. Lansberger did them.'

It was the name of a famous and exceedingly expensive fashionable portrait painter of twenty years ago. His meticulous naturalism had now gone out of fashion, and since his death, he was little spoken of. His sitters were sometimes sneeringly spoken of as 'clothes props', but Poirot thought they were a good deal more than that. He suspected that there was a carefully concealed mockery behind the smooth exteriors that Lansberger executed so effortlessly.

Mary Restarick said as she went up the stairs ahead of him:

'They have just come out of storage — and been cleaned up and — '

She stopped abruptly — coming to a dead halt, one hand on the stair-rail.

Above her, a figure had just turned the corner of the staircase on its way down. It was a figure that seemed strangely incongruous. It might have been someone in fancy dress, someone who certainly did not match with this house.

He was a figure familiar enough to Poirot in different conditions, a figure often met in the streets of London or even at parties. A representative of the youth of today. He wore a black coat, an elaborate velvet waistcoat, skin tight pants, and rich curls of chestnut hair hung down on his neck. He looked exotic and rather beautiful, and it needed a few moments to be certain of his sex.

'David!' Mary Restarick spoke sharply. 'What on earth are you doing here?'

The young man was by no means taken aback. 'Startled you?' he asked. 'So sorry.'

'What are you doing here — in this house? You — have you come down here with Norma?'

'Norma? No, I hoped to find her here.'

'Find her here — what do you mean? She's in London.'

'Oh, but my dear, she isn't. At any rate, she's not at 67 Borodene Mansions.'

'What do you mean, she isn't there?'

'Well, since she didn't come back this weekend, I thought she was probably here with you. I came down to see what she was up to.'

'She left here Sunday night as usual.' She added in an angry voice, 'Why didn't you ring the bell and let us know you were here? What are you doing roaming about the house?'

'Really, darling, you seem to be thinking I'm going to pinch the spoons or something. Surely it's natural to walk into a house in broad daylight. Why ever not?'

'Well, we're old-fashioned and we don't like it.'

'Oh dear, dear.' David sighed. 'The fuss everyone makes. Well, my dear, if I'm not going to have a welcome and you don't seem to know where your stepdaughter is, I suppose I'd better be moving along. Shall I turn out my pockets before I go?'

'Don't be absurd, David.'

'Ta-ta, then.' The young man passed them, waved an airy hand and went on down and out through the open front door.

'Horrible creature,' said Mary Restarick, with a sharpness of rancour that startled Poirot. 'I can't bear him. I simply can't stand him. Why is England absolutely full of these people nowadays?'

'Ah, Madame, do not disquiet yourself. It

48

is all a question of fashion. There have always been fashions. You see less in the country, but in London you meet plenty of them.'

'Dreadful,' said Mary. 'Absolutely dreadful. Effeminate, exotic.'

'And yet not unlike a Vandyke portrait, do you not think so, Madame? In a gold frame, wearing a lace collar, you would not then say he was effeminate or exotic.'

'Daring to come down here like that. Andrew would have been furious. It worries him dreadfully. Daughters can be very worrying. It's not even as though Andrew knew Norma well. He's been abroad since she was a child. He left her entirely to her mother to bring up, and now he finds her a complete puzzle. So do I for that matter. I can't help feeling that she is a very odd type of girl. One has no kind of authority over them these days. They seem to like the worst type of young men. She's absolutely infatuated with this David Baker. One can't do anything. Andrew forbade him the house, and look, he turns up here, walks in as cool as a cucumber. I think — I almost think I'd better not tell Andrew. I don't want him to be unduly worried. I believe she goes about with this creature in London, and not only with him. There are some much worse ones even. The kind that don't wash, completely unshaven faces and funny sprouting beards and greasy clothes.'

Poirot said cheerfully, 'Alas, Madame, you must not distress yourself. The indiscretions of youth pass.'

'I hope so, I'm sure. Norma is a very difficult girl. Sometimes I think she's not right in the head. She's so peculiar. She really looks sometimes as though she isn't all there. These extraordinary dislikes she takes — '

'Dislikes?'

'She hates me. Really hates me. I don't see why it's necessary. I suppose she was very devoted to her mother, but after all it's only reasonable that her father should marry again, isn't it?'

'Do you think she really hates you?'

'Oh, I know she does. I've had ample proof of it. I can't say how relieved I was when she went off to London. I didn't want to make trouble — ' She stopped suddenly. It was as though for the first time she realised that she was talking to a stranger.

Poirot had the capacity to attract confidences. It was as though when people were talking to him they hardly realised who it was they were talking to. She gave a short laugh now.

'Dear me,' she said, 'I don't really know why I'm saying all this to you. I expect every family has these problems. Poor stepmothers, we have a hard time of it. Ah, here we are.'

She tapped on a door.

'Come in, come in.'

It was a stentorian roar.

'Here is a visitor to see you, Uncle,' said Mary Restarick, as she walked into the room, Poirot behind her.

A broad-shouldered, square-faced, red-cheeked, irascible looking elderly man had been pacing the floor. He stumped forward towards them. At the table behind him a girl was sitting sorting letters and papers. Her head was bent over them, a sleek, dark head.

'This is Monsieur Hercule Poirot, Uncle Roddy,' said Mary Restarick.

Poirot stepped forward gracefully into action and speech. 'Ah, Sir Roderick, it is many years — many years since I have had the pleasure of meeting you. We have to go back, so far as the last war. It was, I think, in Normandy the last time. How well I remember, there was there also Colonel Race and there was General Abercromby and there was Air-Marshal Sir Edmund Collingsby. What decisions we had to take! And what difficulties we had with security. Ah, nowadays, there is no longer the need for secrecy. I recall the unmasking of that secret agent who succeeded for so long — you remember

Captain Henderson.'

'Ah. Captain Henderson indeed. Lord, that damned swine! Unmasked!'

'You may not remember me, Hercule Poirot.'

'Yes, yes, of course I remember you. Ah, it was a close shave that, a close shave. You were the French representative, weren't you? There were one or two of them, one I couldn't get on with — can't remember his name. Ah well, sit down, sit down. Nothing like having a chat over old days.'

'I feared so much that you might not remember me or my colleague, Monsieur Giraud.'

'Yes, yes, of course I remember both of you. Ah, those were the days, those were the days indeed.'

The girl at the table got up. She moved a chair politely towards Poirot.

'That's right, Sonia, that's right,' said Sir Roderick. 'Let me introduce you,' he said, 'to my charming little secretary here. Makes a great difference to me. Helps me, you know, files all my work. Don't know how I ever got on without her.'

Poirot bowed politely. '*Enchanté*, mademoiselle,' he murmured.

The girl murmured something in rejoinder. She was a small creature with black bobbed hair. She looked shy. Her dark blue eyes were usually modestly cast down, but she smiled up sweetly and shyly at her employer. He patted her on the shoulder.

'Don't know what I should do without her,' he said. 'I don't really.'

'Oh, no,' the girl protested. 'I am not much good really. I cannot type very fast.'

'You type quite fast enough, my dear. You're my memory, too. My eyes and my ears and a great many other things.'

She smiled again at him.

'One remembers,' murmured Poirot, 'some of the excellent stories that used to go the round. I don't know if they were exaggerated or not. Now, for instance, the day that someone stole your car and — ' he proceeded to follow up the tale.

Sir Roderick was delighted. 'Ha, ha, of course now. Yes, indeed, well, bit of exaggeration, I expect. But on the whole, that's how it was. Yes, yes, well, fancy your remembering *that*, after all this long time. But I could tell you a better one than that now.' He launched forth into another tale. Poirot listened, applauded. Finally he glanced at his watch and rose to his feet.

'But I must detain you no longer,' he said. 'You are engaged, I can see, in important work. It was just that being in this neighbourhood I could not help paying my respects. Years pass, but you, I see, have lost none of your vigour, of your enjoyment of life.'

'Well, well, perhaps you may say so. Anyway, you mustn't pay me too many compliments — but surely you'll stay and have tea. I'm sure Mary will give you some tea.' He looked round. 'Oh, she's gone away. Nice girl.'

'Yes, indeed, and very handsome. I expect she has been a great comfort to you for many years.'

'Oh! They've only married recently. She's my nephew's second wife. I'll be frank with you. I've never cared very much for this nephew of mine, Andrew — not a steady chap. Always restless. His elder brother Simon was my favourite. Not that I knew him well, either. As for Andrew, he behaved very badly to his first wife. Went off, you know. Left her high and dry. Went off with a thoroughly bad lot. Everybody knew about her. But he was infatuated with her. The whole thing broke up in a year or two: silly fellow. The girl he's married seems all right. Nothing wrong with her as far as I know. Now Simon was a steady chap — damned dull, though. I can't say I liked it when my sister married into that family. Marrying into trade, you know. Rich, of course, but money isn't everything — we've usually married into the Services. I never saw much of the Restarick lot.'

'They have, I believe, a daughter. A friend of mine met her last week.'

'Oh, Norma. Silly girl. Goes about in dreadful clothes and has picked up with a dreadful young man. Ah well, they're all alike nowadays. Long-haired young fellows, beatniks, Beatles, all sorts of names they've got. I can't keep up with them. Practically talk a foreign language. Still, nobody cares to hear an old man's criticisms, so there we are. Even Mary — I always thought she was a good, sensible sort, but as far as I can see she can be thoroughly hysterical in some ways — mainly about her health. Some fuss about going to hospital for observation or something. What about a drink? Whisky? No? Sure you won't stop and have a drop of tea?'

'Thank you, but I am staying with friends.'

'Well, I must say I have enjoyed this chat with you very much. Nice to remember some of the things that happened in the old days. Sonia, dear, perhaps you'll take Monsieur — sorry, what's your name, it's gone again — ah, yes, Poirot. Take him down to Mary, will you?'

'No, no,' Hercule Poirot hastily waved aside

the offer. 'I could not dream of troubling Madame any more. I am quite all right. Quite all right. I can find my way perfectly. It has been a great pleasure to meet you again.'

He left the room.

'Haven't the faintest idea who that chap was,' said Sir Roderick, after Poirot had gone.

'You do not know who he was?' Sonia asked, looking at him in a startled manner.

'Personally I don't remember who half the people are who come up and talk to me nowadays. Of course, I have to make a good shot at it. One learns to get away with that, you know. Same thing at parties. Up comes a chap and says, 'Perhaps you don't remember me. I last saw you in 1939.' I have to say 'Of course I remember,' but I don't. It's a handicap being nearly blind and deaf. We got pally with a lot of frogs like that towards the end of the war. Don't remember half of them. Oh, he'd been there all right. He knew me and I knew a good many of the chaps he talked about. That story about me and the stolen car, that was true enough. Exaggerated a bit, of course, they made a pretty good story of it at the time. Ah well, I don't think he knew I didn't remember him. Clever chap, I should say, but a thorough frog, isn't he? You know, mincing and dancing and bowing and scraping. Now then, where were we?'

Sonia picked up a letter and handed it to him. She tentatively proffered a pair of spectacles which he immediately rejected.

'Don't want those damned things — I can see all right.'

He screwed up his eyes and peered down at the letter he was holding. Then he capitulated and thrust it back into her hands.

'Well, perhaps you'd better read it to me.'

She started reading it in her clear soft voice.

# 5

## I

Hercule Poirot stood upon the landing for a
moment. His head was a little on one side
with a listening air. He could hear nothing
from downstairs. He crossed to the landing
window and looked out. Mary Restarick was
below on the terrace, resuming her gardening
work. Poirot nodded his head in satisfaction.
He walked gently along the corridor. One by
one in turn he opened the doors. A bathroom,
a linen cupboard, a double bedded spare room,
an occupied single bedroom, a woman's room
with a double bed (Mary Restarick's?). The
next door was that of an adjoining room and
was, he guessed, the room belonging to Andrew
Restarick. He turned to the other side of the
landing. The door he opened first was a single
bedroom. It was not, he judged, occupied at
the time, but it was a room which possibly
was occupied at weekends. There were toilet
brushes on the dressing-table. He listened
carefully, then tip-toed in. He opened the
wardrobe. Yes, there were some clothes hanging up there. Country clothes.

There was a writing table but there was nothing on it. He opened the desk drawers very softly. There were a few odds and ends, a letter or two, but the letters were trivial and dated some time ago. He shut the desk drawers. He walked downstairs, and going out of the house, bade farewell to his hostess. He refused her offer of tea. He had promised to get back, he said, as he had to catch a train to town very shortly afterwards.

'Don't you want a taxi? We could order you one, or I could drive you in the car.'

'No, no, Madame, you are too kind.'

Poirot walked back to the village and turned down the lane by the church. He crossed a little bridge over a stream. Presently he came to where a large car with a chauffeur was waiting discreetly under a beech tree. The chauffeur opened the door of the car, Poirot got inside, sat down and removed his patent leather shoes, uttering a gasp of relief.

'Now we return to London,' he said.

The chauffeur closed the door, returned to his seat and the car purred quietly away. The sight of a young man standing by the roadside furiously thumbing a ride was not an unusual one. Poirot's eyes rested almost indifferently on this member of the fraternity, a brightly dressed young man with long and exotic hair. There were many such but in the moment of passing him Poirot suddenly sat upright and addressed the driver.

'If you please, stop. Yes, and if you can reverse a little ... There is someone requesting a lift.'

The chauffeur turned an incredulous eye over his shoulder. It was the last remark he would have expected. However, Poirot was gently nodding his head, so he obeyed.

The young man called David advanced to the door. 'Thought you weren't going to stop for me,' he said cheerfully. 'Much obliged, I'm sure.'

He got in, removed a small pack from his shoulders and let it slide to the floor, smoothed down his copper brown locks. 'So you recognised me,' he said.

'You are perhaps somewhat conspicuously dressed.'

'Oh, do you think so? Not really. I'm just one of a band of brothers.'

'The school of Vandyke. Very dressy.'

'Oh. I've never thought of it like that. Yes, there may be something in what you say.'

'You should wear a cavalier's hat,' said Poirot, 'and a lace collar, if I might advise.'

'Oh, I don't think we go quite as far as that.' The young man laughed. 'How Mrs Restarick dislikes the mere sight of me. Actually I reciprocate her dislike. I don't care much for Restarick, either. There is something singularly unattractive about successful tycoons, don't you think?'

'It depends on the point of view. You have been paying attentions to the daughter, I understand.'

'That is such a nice phrase,' said David. 'Paying attentions to the daughter. I suppose it might be called that. But there's plenty of fifty-fifty about it, you know. She's paying attention to me, too.'

'Where is Mademoiselle now?'

David turned his head rather sharply. 'And why do you ask that?'

'I should like to meet her.' He shrugged his shoulders.

'I don't believe she'd be your type, you know, any more than I am. Norma's in London.'

'But you said to her stepmother — '

'Oh! We don't tell stepmothers everything.'

'And where is she in London?'

'She works in an interior decorator's down the King's Road somewhere in Chelsea. Can't remember the name of it for the moment. Susan Phelps, I think.'

'But that is not where she lives, I presume. You have her address?'

'Oh yes, a great block of flats. I don't really understand your interest.'

'One is interested in so many things.'

'What do you mean?'

'What brought you to that house — (what is its name? — Crosshedges) today. Brought you secretly into the house and up the stairs.'

'I came in the back door, I admit.'

'What were you looking for upstairs?'

'That's my business. I don't want to be rude — but aren't you being rather nosy?'

'Yes, I am displaying curiosity. I would like to know exactly where this young lady is.'

'I see. Dear Andrew and dear Mary — lord rot 'em — are employing you, is that it? They are trying to find her?'

'As yet,' said Poirot, 'I do not think they know that she is missing.'

'Someone must be employing you.'

'You are exceedingly perceptive,' said Poirot. He leant back.

'I wondered what you were up to,' said David. 'That's why I hailed you. I hoped you'd stop and give me a bit of dope. She's my girl. You know that, I suppose?'

'I understand that that is supposed to be the idea,' said Poirot cautiously. 'If so, you should know where she is. Is that not so, Mr — I am sorry, I do not think I know your name beyond, that is, that your Christian name is David.'

'Baker.'

'Perhaps, Mr Baker, you have had a quarrel.'

'No, we haven't had a quarrel. Why should you think we had?'

'Miss Norma Restarick left Crosshedges on Sunday evening, or was it Monday morning?'

'It depends. There is an early bus you can take. Gets you to London a little after ten. It would make her a bit late at work, but not too much. Usually she goes back on Sunday night.'

'She left there Sunday night but she has not arrived at Borodene Mansions.'

'Apparently not. So Claudia says.'

'This Miss Reece-Holland — that is her name, is it not? — was she surprised or worried?'

'Good lord, no, why should she be. They don't keep tabs on each other all the time, these girls.'

'But you thought she was going back there?'

'She didn't go back to work either. They're fed up at the shop, I can tell you.'

'Are *you* worried, Mr Baker?'

'No. Naturally — I mean, well, I'm damned if I know. I don't see any reason I should be worried, only time's getting on. What is it today — Thursday?'

'She has not quarrelled with you?'

'No. We don't quarrel.'

'But you are worried about her, Mr Baker?'

'What business is it of yours?'

'It is no business of mine but there has, I understand, been trouble at home. She does not like her stepmother.'

'Quite right too. She's a bitch, that woman. Hard as nails. She doesn't like Norma either.'

'She has been ill, has she not? She had to go to hospital.'

'Who are you talking about — Norma?'

'No, I am not talking about Miss Restarick. I am talking about Mrs Restarick.'

'I believe she did go into a nursing home. No reason she should. Strong as a horse, I'd say.'

'And Miss Restarick hates her stepmother.'

'She's a bit unbalanced sometimes, Norma. You know, goes off the deep end. I tell you, girls always hate their stepmothers.'

'Does that always make stepmothers ill? Ill enough to go to hospital?'

'What the hell are you getting at?'

'Gardening perhaps — or the use of weed killer.'

'What do you mean by talking about weed killer? Are you suggesting that Norma — that she'd dream of — that — '

'People talk,' said Poirot. 'Talk goes round the neighbourhood.'

'Do you mean that somebody has said that Norma has tried to poison her stepmother? That's ridiculous. It's absolutely absurd.'

'It is very unlikely, I agree,' said Poirot. 'Actually, people have *not* been saying that.'

'Oh. Sorry. I misunderstood. But — what *did* you mean?'

'My dear young man,' said Poirot, 'you must realise that there are rumours going about, and rumours are almost always about the same person — a husband.'

'What, poor old Andrew? Most unlikely I should say.'

'Yes. Yes, it does not seem to me very likely.'

'Well, what were you there for then? You *are* a detective, aren't you?'

'Yes.'

'Well, then?'

'We are talking at cross purposes,' said Poirot. 'I did not go down there to inquire into any doubtful or possible case of poisoning. You must forgive me if I cannot answer your question. It is all very hush-hush, you understand.'

'What on earth do you mean by that?'

'I went there,' said Poirot, 'to see Sir Roderick Horsefield.'

'What, that old boy? He's practically ga-ga, isn't he?'

'He is a man,' said Poirot, 'who is in

possession of a great many secrets. I do not mean that he takes an active part in such things nowadays, but he knows a good deal. He was connected with a great many things in the past war. He *knew* several people.'

'That's all over years ago, though.'

'Yes, yes, *his* part in things is all over years ago. But do you not realise that there are certain things that it might be useful to know?'

'What sort of things?'

'Faces,' said Poirot. 'A well known face perhaps, which Sir Roderick might recognise. A face or a mannerism, a way of talking, a way of walking, a gesture. People do remember, you know. Old people. They remember, not things that have happened last week or last month or last year, but they remember something that happened, say, nearly twenty years ago. And they may remember someone who does not want to be remembered. And they can tell you certain things about a certain man or a certain woman or something they were mixed up in — I am speaking very vaguely, you understand. I went to him for information.'

'You went to him for information, did you? *That* old boy? Ga-ga. And he gave it to you?'

'Let us say that I am quite satisfied.'

David continued to stare at him. 'I wonder

now,' he said. 'Did you go to see the old boy or did you go to see the little girl, eh? Did you want to know what *she* was doing in the house? I've wondered once or twice myself. Do you think she took that post there to get a bit of past information out of the old boy?'

'I do not think,' said Poirot, 'that it will serve any useful purpose to discuss these matters. She seems a very devoted and attentive — what shall I call her — secretary?'

'A mixture of a hospital nurse, a secretary, a companion, an *au pair* girl, an uncle's help? Yes, one could find a good many names for her, couldn't one? He's besotted about her. You noticed that?'

'It is not unnatural under the circumstances,' said Poirot primly.

'I can tell you someone who doesn't like her, and that's our Mary.'

'And she perhaps does not like Mary Restarick either.'

'So that's what you think, is it?' said David. 'That Sonia doesn't like Mary Restarick. Perhaps you go as far as thinking that she may have made a few inquiries as to where the weed killer was kept? Bah,' he added, 'the whole thing's ridiculous. All right. Thanks for the lift. I think I'll get out here.'

'Aha. This is where you want to be? We are still a good seven miles out of London.'

'I'll get out here. Goodbye, M. Poirot.'

'Goodbye.'

Poirot leant back in his seat as David slammed the door.

## II

Mrs Oliver prowled round her sitting-room. She was very restless. An hour ago she had parcelled up a typescript that she had just finished correcting. She was about to send it off to her publisher who was anxiously awaiting it and constantly prodding her about it every three or four days.

'There you are,' said Mrs Oliver, addressing the empty air and conjuring up an imaginary publisher. 'There you are, and I hope you like it! *I* don't. I think it's *lousy*! I don't believe *you* know whether anything I write is good or bad. Anyway, I warned you. I *told* you it was frightful. You said 'Oh! no, no, I don't believe that for a moment.'

'You just wait and see,' said Mrs Oliver vengefully. 'You just wait and see.'

She opened the door, called to Edith, her maid, gave her the parcel and directed that it should be taken to the post at once.

'And now,' said Mrs Oliver, 'what am I going to do with myself?'

She began strolling about again. 'Yes,' thought Mrs Oliver, 'I wish I had those tropical birds and things back on the wall instead of these idiotic cherries. I used to feel like something in a tropical wood. A lion or a tiger or a leopard or a cheetah! What could I possibly feel like in a cherry orchard except a bird scarer?'

She looked round again. 'Cheeping like a bird, that's what I ought to be doing,' she said gloomily. 'Eating cherries . . . I wish it was the right time of year for cherries. I'd like some cherries. I wonder now — ' She went to the telephone. 'I will ascertain, Madam,' said the voice of George in answer to her inquiry. Presently another voice spoke.

'Hercule Poirot, at your service, Madame,' he said.

'Where've you been?' said Mrs Oliver. 'You've been away all day. I suppose you went down to look up the Restaricks. Is that it? Did you see Sir Roderick? What did you find out?'

'Nothing,' said Hercule Poirot.

'How dreadfully dull,' said Mrs Oliver.

'No, I do not think it is really so dull. It is rather astonishing that I have *not* found out anything.'

'Why is it so astonishing? I don't under-stand.'

'Because,' said Poirot, 'it means either there

69

was nothing to find out, and that, let me tell you, does not accord with the facts; or else something was being very cleverly concealed. That, you see, would be interesting. Mrs Restarick, by the way, did not know the girl was missing.'

'You mean — she has nothing to do with the girl having disappeared?'

'So it seems. I met there the young man.'

'You mean the unsatisfactory young man that nobody likes?'

'That is right. The unsatisfactory young man.'

'Did you think he *was* unsatisfactory?'

'From whose point of view?'

'Not from the girl's point of view, I suppose.'

'The girl who came to see me I am sure would have been highly delighted with him.'

'Did he look very awful?'

'He looked very beautiful,' said Hercule Poirot.

'Beautiful?' said Mrs Oliver. 'I don't know that I *like* beautiful young men.'

'Girls do,' said Poirot.

'Yes, you're quite right. They like beautiful young men. I don't mean good-looking young men or smart-looking young men or well-dressed or well-washed looking young men. I mean they either like young men looking as though they were just going on in a Restoration comedy, or else very dirty young men looking as though they were just going to take some awful tramp's job.'

'It seemed that he also did not know where the girl is now — '

'Or else he wasn't admitting it.'

'Perhaps. He had gone down there. Why? He was actually in the house. He had taken the trouble to walk in without anyone seeing him. Again why? For what reason? Was he looking for the girl? Or was he looking for something else?'

'You think he *was* looking for something?'

'He was looking for something in the girl's room,' said Poirot.

'How do you know? Did you see him there?'

'No, I only saw him coming down the stairs, but I found a very nice little piece of damp mud in Norma's room that could have come from his shoe. It is possible that she herself may have asked him to bring her something from that room — there are a lot of possibilities. There is another girl in that house — and a pretty one — He may have come down there to meet *her*. Yes — many possibilities.'

'What are you going to do next?' demanded Mrs Oliver.

'Nothing,' said Poirot.

'That's very dull,' said Mrs Oliver disapprovingly.

'I am going to receive, perhaps, a little information from those I have employed to find it; though it is quite possible that I shall receive nothing at all.'

'But aren't you going to *do* something?'

'Not till the right moment,' said Poirot.

'Well, I shall,' said Mrs Oliver.

'Pray, pray be very careful,' he implored her.

'What nonsense! What could happen to me?'

'Where there is murder, anything can happen. I tell that to you. I, Poirot.'

# 6

## I

Mr Goby sat in a chair. He was a small shrunken little man, so nondescript as to be practically nonexistent.

He looked attentively at the claw foot of an antique table and addressed his remarks to it. He never addressed anybody direct.

'Glad you got the names for me, Mr Poirot,' he said. 'Otherwise, you know, it might have taken a lot of time. As it is, I've got the main facts — and a bit of gossip on the side . . . Always useful, that. I'll begin at Borodene Mansions, shall I?'

Poirot inclined his head graciously.

'Plenty of porters,' Mr Goby informed the clock on the chimney piece. 'I started there, used one or two different young men. Expensive, but worth it. Didn't want it thought that there was anyone making any particular inquiries! Shall I use initials, or names?'

'Within these walls you can use the names,' said Poirot.

'Miss Claudia Reece-Holland spoken of as

a very nice young lady. Father an MP. Ambitious man. Gets himself in the news a lot. She's his only daughter. She does secretarial work. Serious girl. No wild parties, no drink, no beatniks. Shares flat with two others. Number two works for the Wedderburn Gallery in Bond Street. Arty type. Whoops it up a bit with the Chelsea set. Goes around to places arranging exhibitions and art shows.

'The third one is *your* one. Not been there long. General opinion is that she's a bit 'wanting'. Not all there in the top storey. But it's all a bit vague. One of the porters is a gossipy type. Buy him a drink or two and you'll be surprised at the things he'll tell you! Who drinks, and who drugs, and who's having trouble with his income tax, and who keeps his cash behind the cistern. Of course you can't believe it all. Anyway, there was some story about a revolver being fired one night.'

'A revolver fired? Was anyone injured?'

'There seems a bit of doubt as to that. His story is he heard a shot fired one night, and he comes out and there was this girl, *your* girl, standing there with a revolver in her hand. She looked sort of dazed. And then one of the other young ladies — or both of them, in fact — they come running along. And Miss Cary (that's the arty one) says, 'Norma, what

74

on earth have you done?' and Miss Reece-Holland, she says sharp-like, 'Shut up, can't you, Frances. Don't be a fool!' and she took the revolver away from your girl and says, 'Give me that.' She slams it into her handbag and then she notices this chap Micky, and goes over to him and says, laughing-like, 'That must have startled you, didn't it?' and Micky he says it gave him quite a turn, and she says, 'You needn't worry. Matter of fact, we'd no idea this thing was loaded. We were just fooling about.' And then she says: 'Anyway, if anybody asks you questions, tell them it is quite all right,' and then she says: 'Come on, Norma,' and took her arm and led her along to the elevator, and they all went up again.

'But Micky said he was a bit doubtful still. He went and had a good look round the courtyard.'

Mr Goby lowered his eyes and quoted from his notebook:

'' 'I'll tell you, I found something, I did! I found some wet patches. Sure as anything I did. Drops of blood they were. I touched them with my finger. I tell you what *I* think. Somebody had been shot — some man as he was running away . . . I went upstairs and I asked if I could speak to Miss Holland. I says to her: 'I think there may have been someone shot, Miss,' I says. 'There are some drops of blood in the courtyard.' 'Good gracious,' she says, 'How ridiculous. I expect, you know,' she says, 'it must have been one of the pigeons.' And then she says: 'I'm sorry if it gave you a turn. Forget about it,' and she slipped me a five pound note. Five pound note, no less! Well, naturally, I didn't open my mouth after that.'

'And then, after another whisky, he comes out with some more. 'If you ask me, she took a pot shot at that low class young chap that comes to see her. I think she and he had a row and she did her best to shoot him. That's what I think. But least said soonest mended, so I'm not repeating it. If anyone asks me anything I'll say I don't know what they're talking about.'' Mr Goby paused.

'Interesting,' said Poirot.

'Yes, but it's as likely as not that it's a pack of lies. Nobody else seems to know anything about it. There's a story about a gang of young thugs who came barging into the courtyard one night, and had a bit of a fight — flick-knives out and all that.'

'I see,' said Poirot. 'Another possible source of blood in the courtyard.'

'Maybe the girl did have a row with her young man, threatened to shoot him, perhaps. And Micky overheard it and mixed the whole thing up — especially if there was a car backfiring just then.'

'Yes,' said Hercule Poirot, and sighed, 'that would account for things quite well.'

Mr Goby turned over another leaf of his notebook and selected his confidant. He chose an electric radiator.

'Joshua Restarick Ltd. Family firm. Been going over a hundred years. Well thought of in the City. Always very sound. Nothing spectacular. Founded by Joshua Restarick in 1850. Launched out after the first war, with greatly increased investments abroad, mostly South Africa, West Africa and Australia. Simon and Andrew Restarick — the last of the Restaricks. Simon, the elder brother, died about a year ago, no children. His wife had died some years previously. Andrew Restarick seems to have been a restless chap. His heart was never really in the business though everyone says he had plenty of ability. Finally ran off with some woman, leaving his wife and a daughter of five years old. Went to South Africa, Kenya, and various other places. No divorce. His wife died two years ago. Had been an invalid for some time. He travelled about a lot, and wherever he went he seems to have made money. Concessions for minerals mostly. Everything he touched prospered.

'After his brother's death, he seems to have decided it was time to settle down. He'd married again and he thought the right thing to do was to come back and make a home for his daughter. They're living at the moment with his uncle Sir Roderick Horsefield — uncle by marriage that is. That's only temporary. His wife's looking at houses all over London. Expense no object. They're rolling in money.'

Poirot sighed. 'I know,' he said. 'What you outline to me is a success story! Everyone makes money! Everybody is of good family and highly respected. Their relations are distinguished. They are well thought of in business circles.

'There is only one cloud in the sky. A girl who is said to be 'a bit wanting', a girl who is mixed up with a dubious boy friend who has been on probation more than once. A girl who may quite possibly have tried to poison her stepmother, and who either suffers from hallucinations, or else has committed a crime! I tell you, none of that accords well with the success story you have brought me.'

Mr Goby shook his head sadly and said rather obscurely:

'There's one in every family.'

'This Mrs Restarick is quite a young woman. I presume she is *not* the woman he

78

originally ran away with?'

'Oh no, that bust up quite soon. She was a pretty bad lot by all accounts, and a tartar as well. He was a fool ever to be taken in by her.' Mr Goby shut his notebook and looked inquiringly at Poirot. 'Anything more you want me to do?'

'Yes. I want to know a little more about the late Mrs Andrew Restarick. She was an invalid, she was frequently in nursing homes. What *kind* of nursing homes? Mental homes?'

'I take your point, Mr Poirot.'

'And any history of insanity in the family — on either side?'

'I'll see to it, Mr Poirot.'

Mr Goby rose to his feet. 'Then I'll take leave of you, sir. Good night.'

Poirot remained thoughtful after Mr Goby had left. He raised and lowered his eyebrows. He wondered, he wondered very much.

Then he rang Mrs Oliver:

'I told you before,' he said, 'to be careful. I repeat that — Be very careful.'

'Careful of what?' said Mrs Oliver.

'Of yourself. I think there might be danger. Danger to anyone who goes poking about where they are not wanted. There is murder in the air — I do not want it to be yours.'

'Have you had the information you said you might have?'

'Yes,' said Poirot, 'I have had a little information. Mostly rumour and gossip, but it seems something happened at Borodene Mansions.'

'What sort of thing?'

'Blood in the courtyard,' said Poirot.

'Really!' said Mrs Oliver. 'That's just like the title of an old-fashioned detective story. *The Stain on the Staircase*. I mean nowadays you say something more like *She Asked for Death*.'

'Perhaps there may not have been blood in the courtyard. Perhaps it is only what an imaginative, Irish porter imagined.'

'Probably an upset milk bottle,' said Mrs Oliver. 'He couldn't see it at night. What happened?'

Poirot did not answer directly.

'The girl thought she 'might have committed a murder'. Was that the murder she meant?'

'You mean she *did* shoot someone?'

'One might presume that she did shoot *at* someone, but for all intents and purposes missed them. A few drops of blood . . . That was all. No body.'

'Oh dear,' said Mrs Oliver, 'it's all very confused. Surely if anyone could still run out of a courtyard, you wouldn't think you'd killed him, would you?'

'*C'est difficile*,' said Poirot, and rang off.

80

'I'm worried,' said Claudia Reece-Holland.

She refilled her cup from the coffee percolator. Frances Cary gave an enormous yawn. Both girls were breakfasting in the small kitchen of the flat. Claudia was dressed and ready to start for her day's work. Frances was still in dressing-gown and pyjamas. Her black hair fell over one eye.

'I'm worried about Norma,' continued Claudia. Frances yawned.

'I shouldn't worry if I were you. She'll ring up or turn up sooner or later, I suppose.'

'Will she? You know, Fran, I can't help wondering — '

'I don't see why,' said Frances, pouring herself out more coffee. She sipped it doubtfully. 'I mean — Norma's not really our business, is she? I mean, we're not looking after her or spoon-feeding her or anything. She just shares the flat. Why all this motherly solicitude? I certainly wouldn't worry.'

'I daresay *you* wouldn't. You never worry over anything. But it's not the same for you as it is for me.'

'Why isn't it the same? You mean because you're the tenant of the flat or something?'

'Well, I'm in rather a special position, as you might say.'

Frances gave another enormous yawn.

'I was up too late last night,' she said. 'At Basil's party. I feel dreadful. Oh well, I suppose black coffee will be helpful. Have some more before I've drunk it all? Basil *would* make us try some new pills — Emerald Dreams. I don't think it's really worth trying all these silly things.'

'You'll be late at your gallery,' said Claudia.

'Oh well, I don't suppose it matters much. Nobody notices or cares.

'I saw David last night,' she added. 'He was all dressed up and really looked rather wonderful.'

'Now don't say *you're* falling for him, too, Fran. He really is too *awful*.'

'Oh, I know *you* think so. You're such a conventional type, Claudia.'

'Not at all. But I cannot say I care for all your arty set. Trying out all these drugs and passing out or getting fighting mad.'

Frances looked amused.

'I'm not a drug fiend, dear — I just like to see what these things are like. And some of the gang are all right. David can paint, you know, if he wants to.'

'David doesn't very often want to, though, does he?'

'You've always got your knife into him, Claudia . . . You hate him coming here to see

Norma. And talking of knives . . . '

'Well? Talking of knives?'

'I've been worrying,' said Frances slowly, 'whether to tell you something or not.'

Claudia glanced at her wrist-watch.

'I haven't got time now,' she said. 'You can tell me this evening if you want to tell me something. Anyway, I'm not in the mood. Oh dear,' she sighed, 'I wish I knew what to do.'

'About Norma?'

'Yes. I'm wondering if her parents ought to know that *we* don't know where she is . . . '

'That would be *very* unsporting. Poor Norma, why shouldn't she slope off on her own if she wants to?'

'Well, Norma isn't exactly — ' Claudia stopped.

'No, she isn't, is she? *Non compos mentis.* That's what you meant. Have you rung up that terrible place where she works? 'Homebirds', or whatever it's called? Oh yes, of course you did. I remember.'

'So where *is* she?' demanded Claudia. 'Did David say anything last night?'

'David didn't seem to know. Really, Claudia, I *can't* see that it matters.'

'It matters for me,' said Claudia, 'because my boss happens to be her father. Sooner or later, if anything peculiar *has* happened to her, they'll ask me why I didn't mention the fact that she hadn't come home.'

'Yes, I suppose they might pitch on you. But there's no real reason, is there, why Norma should have to report to us every time she's going to be away from here for a day or two. Or even a few nights. I mean, she's not a paying guest or anything. You're not in charge of the girl.'

'No, but Mr Restarick did mention he felt glad to know that she had got a room here with us.'

'So that entitles *you* to go and tittle-tattle about her every time she's absent without leave? She's probably got a crush on some new man.'

'She's got a crush on David,' said Claudia. 'Are you sure she isn't holed up at his place?'

'Oh, I shouldn't think so. He doesn't really care for her, you know.'

'You'd like to think he doesn't,' said Claudia. 'You are rather sweet on David yourself.'

'Certainly not,' said Frances sharply. 'Nothing of the kind.'

'David's really keen on her,' said Claudia. 'If not, why did he come round looking for her here the other day?'

'*You* soon marched him out again,' said Frances. 'I think,' she added, getting up and looking at her face in a rather unflattering small kitchen mirror, 'I think it *might* have been me he really came to see.'

'You're too idiotic! He came here looking for Norma.'

'That girl's mental,' said Frances.

'Sometimes I really think she is!'

'Well, I *know* she is. Look here, Claudia, I'm going to tell you that something *now*. You ought to know. I broke the string of my bra the other day and I was in a hurry. I know you don't like anyone fiddling with *your* things — '

'I certainly don't,' said Claudia.

' — but Norma never minds, or doesn't notice. Anyway, I went into her room and I rootled in her drawer and I — well, I found something. A knife.'

'A knife!' said Claudia, surprised. 'What sort of a knife?'

'You know we had that sort of shindy thing in the courtyard? A group of beats, teenagers who'd come in here and were having a fight with flick-knives and all that? And Norma came in just after.'

'Yes, yes, I remember.'

'One of the boys got stabbed, so a reporter told me, and he ran away. Well, the knife in Norma's drawer was a flick-knife. It had got a stain on it — looked like dried blood.'

'Frances! You're being absurdly dramatic.'

'Perhaps. But I'm sure that's what it was. And what on earth was that doing hidden away in Norma's drawer, I should like to know?'

'I suppose — she might have picked it up.'

'What — a souvenir? And hidden it away and never told us?'

'What did you do with it?'

'I put it back,' said Frances slowly. 'I — I didn't know what else to do . . . I couldn't decide whether to tell you or not. Then yesterday I looked again and *it was gone, Claudia*. Not a trace of it.'

'You think she sent David here to get it?'

'Well, she might have done . . . I tell you, Claudia, in future I'm going to keep my door locked at night.'

# 7

Mrs Oliver woke up dissatisfied. She saw stretching before her a day with nothing to do. Having packed off her completed manuscript with a highly virtuous feeling, work was over. She had now only, as many times before, to relax, to enjoy herself; to lie fallow until the creative urge became active once more. She walked about her flat in a rather aimless fashion, touching things, picking them up, putting them down, looking in the drawers of her desk, realising that there were plenty of letters there to be dealt with but feeling also that in her present state of virtuous accomplishment, she was certainly not going to deal with anything so tiresome as that now. She wanted something *interesting* to do. She wanted — what did she want?

She thought about the conversation she had had with Hercule Poirot, the warning he had given her. Ridiculous! After all, why shouldn't she participate in this problem which she was sharing with Poirot? Poirot might choose to sit in a chair, put the tips of his fingers together, and set his grey cells whirring to work while his body reclined comfortably within four walls. That was not the procedure that appealed to Ariadne Oliver. She had said, very forcibly, that she at least was going to do something. She was going to find out more about this mysterious girl. Where was Norma Restarick? What was she doing? What more could she, Ariadne Oliver, find out about her?

Mrs Oliver prowled about, more and more disconsolate. What *could* one do? It wasn't very easy to decide. Go somewhere and ask questions? Should she go down to Long Basing? But Poirot had already been there — and found out presumably what there was to be found out. And what excuse could she offer for barging into Sir Roderick Horsefield's house?

She considered another visit to Borodene Mansions. Something still to be found out there, perhaps? She would have to think of another excuse for going there. She wasn't quite sure *what* excuse she would use but anyway, that seemed the only possible place where more information could be obtained. What was the time? Ten a.m. There were certain possibilities . . .

On the way there she concocted an excuse. Not a very original excuse. In fact, Mrs Oliver would have liked to have found something more intriguing, but perhaps, she reflected prudently, it was just as well to keep to something completely everyday and plausible. She arrived at the stately if grim elevation of Borodene Mansions and walked slowly round the courtyard considering it.

A porter was conversing with a furniture van — A milkman, pushing his milk-float, came to join Mrs Oliver near the service lift.

He rattled bottles, cheerfully whistling, whilst Mrs Oliver continued to stare abstractedly at the furniture van.

'Number 76 moving out,' explained the milkman to Mrs Oliver, mistaking her interest. He transferred a clutch of bottles from his float to the lift.

'Not that she hasn't moved already in a manner of speaking,' he added, emerging again. He seemed a cheery kind of milkman.

He pointed a thumb upwards.

'Pitched herself out of a window — seventh floor — only a week ago, it was. Five o'clock in the morning. Funny time to choose.'

Mrs Oliver didn't think it so funny.

'Why?'

'Why did she do it? Nobody knows. Balance of mind disturbed, they said.'

'Was she — young?'

'Nah! Just an old trout. Fifty if she was a day.'

Two men struggled in the van with a chest

of drawers. It resisted them and two mahogany drawers crashed to the ground — a loose piece of paper floated toward Mrs Oliver who caught it.

'Don't smash everything, Charlie,' said the cheerful milkman reprovingly, and went up in the lift with his cargo of bottles.

An altercation broke out between the furniture movers. Mrs Oliver offered them the piece of paper, but they waved it away.

Making up her mind, Mrs Oliver entered the building and went up to No. 67. A clank came from inside and presently the door was opened by a middle-aged woman with a mop who was clearly engaged in household labours.

'Oh,' said Mrs Oliver, using her favourite monosyllable. 'Good morning. Is — I wonder — is anyone in?'

'No, I'm afraid not, Madam. They're all out. They've gone to work.'

'Yes, of course . . . As a matter of fact when I was here last I left a little diary behind. *So* annoying. It must be in the sitting-room somewhere.'

'Well, I haven't picked up anything of the kind, Madam, as far as I know. Of course I mightn't have known it was yours. Would you like to come in?' She opened the door hospitably, set aside the mop with which she had been treating the kitchen floor, and accompanied Mrs Oliver into the sitting-room.

'Yes,' said Mrs Oliver, determined to establish friendly relations, 'yes, I see here — that's the book I left for Miss Restarick, Miss Norma. Is she back from the country yet?'

'I don't think she's living here at the moment. Her bed wasn't slept in. Perhaps she's still down with her people in the country. I know she was going there last weekend.'

'Yes, I expect that's it,' said Mrs Oliver. 'This was a book I brought her. One of *my* books.'

One of Mrs Oliver's books did not seem to strike any chord of interest in the cleaning woman.

'I was sitting here,' went on Mrs Oliver, patting an armchair, 'at least I *think* so. And then I moved to the window and perhaps to the sofa.'

She dug down vehemently behind the cushions of the chair. The cleaning woman obliged by doing the same thing to the sofa cushions.

'You've no idea how maddening it is when one loses something like that,' went on Mrs Oliver, chattily. 'One has all one's engagements written down there. I'm quite sure I'm

91

lunching with someone very important today, and I can't remember who it was or where the luncheon was to be. Only, of course, it may be *tomorrow*. If so, I'm lunching with someone else *quite* different. Oh dear.'

'Very trying for you, ma'am, I'm sure,' said the cleaning woman with sympathy.

'They're such nice flats, these,' said Mrs Oliver, looking round.

'A long way up.'

'Well, that gives you a very good view, doesn't it?'

'Yes, but if they face east you get a lot of cold wind in winter. Comes right through these metal window frames. Some people have had double windows put in. Oh yes, I wouldn't care for a flat facing this way in winter. No, give me a nice ground floor flat every time. Much more convenient too if you've got children. For prams and all that, you know. Oh yes, I'm all for the ground floor, I am. Think if there was to be a fire.'

'Yes, of course, that would be terrible,' said Mrs Oliver. 'I suppose there are fire escapes?'

'You can't always get to a fire door. Terrified of fire, I am. Always have been. And they're ever so expensive, these flats. You wouldn't believe the rents they ask! That's why Miss Holland, she gets two other girls to go in with her.'

'Oh yes, I think I met them both. Miss Cary's an artist, isn't she?'

'Works for an art gallery, she does. Don't work at it very hard, though. She paints a bit — cows and trees that you'd never recognise as being what they're meant to be. An untidy young lady. The state her room is in — you wouldn't believe it! Now Miss Holland, everything is always as neat as a new pin. She was a secretary in the Coal Board at one time but she's a private secretary in the City now. She likes it better, she says. She's secretary to a very rich gentleman just come back from South America or somewhere like that. He's Miss Norma's father, and it was he who asked Miss Holland to take her as a boarder when the last young lady went off to get married — and she mentioned as she was looking for another girl. Well, she couldn't very well refuse, could she? Not since he was her employer.'

'Did she want to refuse?'

The woman sniffed.

'I think she would have — if she'd known.'

'Known what?' The question was too direct.

'It's not for me to say anything, I'm sure. It's not my business — '

Mrs Oliver continued to look mildly inquiring. Mrs Mop fell.

'It's not that she isn't a nice young lady. Scatty but then they're nearly all scatty. But I think as a doctor ought to see her. There are times when she doesn't seem to know rightly what she's doing, or where she is. It gives you quite a turn, sometimes — Looks just how my husband's nephew does after he's had a fit. (Terrible fits he has — you wouldn't believe!) Only I've never known her have fits. Maybe she takes things — a lot do.'

'I believe there is a young man her family doesn't approve of.'

'Yes, so I've heard. He's come here to call for her once or twice — though I've never seen him. One of these Mods by all accounts. Miss Holland doesn't like it — but what can you do nowadays? Girls go their own way.'

'Sometimes one feels very upset about girls nowadays,' said Mrs Oliver, and tried to look serious and responsible.

'Not brought up right, that's what *I* says.'

'I'm afraid not. No, I'm afraid not. One feels really a girl like Norma Restarick would be better at home than coming all alone to London and earning her living as an interior decorator.'

'She don't like it at home.'

'Really?'

'Got a stepmother. Girls don't like stepmothers. From what I've heard the stepmother's done her best, tried to pull her up, tried to keep flashy young men out of the house, that sort of thing. She knows girls pick up with the wrong young man and a lot of harm may come of it. Sometimes — ' the cleaning woman spoke impressively, ' — I'm thankful I've never had any daughters.'

'Have you got sons?'

'Two boys, we've got. One's doing very well at school, and the other one, he's in a printer's, doing well there too. Yes, very nice boys they are. Mind you, boys can cause you trouble, too. But girls is more worrying, I think. You feel you ought to be able to do something about them.'

'Yes,' said Mrs Oliver, thoughtfully, 'one does feel that.'

She saw signs of the cleaning woman wishing to return to her cleaning.

'It's too bad about my diary,' she said. 'Well, thank you very much and I hope I haven't wasted your time.'

'Well, I hope you'll find it, I'm sure,' said the other woman obligingly.

Mrs Oliver went out of the flat and considered what she should do next. She couldn't think of anything she could do further that day, but a plan for tomorrow began to form in her mind.

When she got home, Mrs Oliver, in an

important way, got out a notebook and jotted down in it various things under the heading 'Facts I have learned.' On the whole the facts did not amount to very much but Mrs Oliver, true to her calling, managed to make the most of them that could be made. Possibly the fact that Claudia Reece-Holland was employed by Norma's father was the most salient fact of any. She had not known that before, she rather doubted if Hercule Poirot had known it either. She thought of ringing him up on the telephone and acquainting him with it but decided to keep it to herself for the moment because of her plan for the morrow. In fact, Mrs Oliver felt at this moment less like a detective novelist than like an ardent bloodhound. She was on the trail, nose down on the scent, and tomorrow morning — well, tomorrow morning we would see.

True to her plan, Mrs Oliver rose early, partook of two cups of tea and a boiled egg and started out on her quest. Once more she arrived in the vicinity of Borodene Mansions. She wondered whether she might be getting a bit well known there, so this time she did not enter the courtyard, but skulked around either one entrance to it or the other, scanning the various people who were turning out into the morning drizzle to trot off on their way to work. They were mostly girls, and looked deceptively alike. How extraordinary human beings were when you considered them like this, emerging purposefully from these large tall buildings — just like anthills, thought Mrs Oliver. One had never considered an anthill properly, she decided. It always looked so aimless, as one disturbed it with the toe of a shoe. All those little things rushing about with bits of grass in their mouths, streaming along industriously, worried, anxious, looking as though they were running to and fro and going nowhere, but presumably they were just as well organised as these human beings here. That man, for instance, who had just passed her. Scurrying along, muttering to himself. 'I wonder what's upsetting *you*,' thought Mrs Oliver. She walked up and down a little more, then she drew back suddenly.

Claudia Reece-Holland came out of the entranceway walking at a brisk businesslike pace. As before, she looked very well turned out. Mrs Oliver turned away so that she should not be recognised. Once she had allowed Claudia to get a sufficient distance ahead of her, she wheeled round again and followed in her tracks. Claudia Reece-Holland came to the end of the street and turned right into a main thoroughfare. She came to a bus stop and joined the queue. Mrs

Oliver, still following her, felt a momentary uneasiness. Supposing Claudia should turn round, look at her, recognise her? All Mrs Oliver could think of was to do several protracted but noiseless blows of the nose. But Claudia Reece-Holland seemed totally absorbed in her own thoughts. She looked at none of her fellow waiters for buses. Mrs Oliver was about third in the queue behind her. Finally the right bus came and there was a surge forward. Claudia got on the bus and went straight up to the top. Mrs Oliver got inside and was able to get a seat close to the door as the uncomfortable third person. When the conductor came round for fares Mrs Oliver pressed a reckless one and sixpence into his hand. After all, she had no idea by what route the bus went or indeed how far the distance was to what the cleaning woman had described vaguely as 'one of those new buildings by St Paul's'. She was on the alert and ready when the venerable dome was at last sighted. Any time now, she thought to herself, and fixed a steady eye on those who descended from the platform above. Ah yes, there came Claudia, neat and chic in her smart suit. She got off the bus. Mrs Oliver followed her in due course and kept at a nicely calculated distance.

'Very interesting,' thought Mrs Oliver.

'Here I am actually *trailing* someone! Just like in my books. And, what's more, I must be doing it very well because she hasn't the least idea.'

Claudia Reece-Holland, indeed, looked very much absorbed in her own thoughts. 'That's a very capable looking girl,' thought Mrs Oliver, as indeed she had thought before. 'If I was thinking of having a go at guessing a murderer, a good capable murderer, I'd choose someone very like her.'

Unfortunately, nobody had been murdered yet, that is to say, unless the girl Norma had been entirely right in her assumption that she herself had committed a murder.

This part of London seemed to have suffered or profited from a large amount of building in the recent years. Enormous skyscrapers, most of which Mrs Oliver thought very hideous, mounted to the sky with a square matchbox-like air.

Claudia turned into a building. 'Now I shall find out exactly,' thought Mrs Oliver and turned into it after her. Four lifts appeared to be all going up and down with frantic haste. This, Mrs Oliver thought, was going to be more difficult. However, they were of a very large size and by getting into Claudia's one at the last minute Mrs Oliver was able to interpose large masses of tall men between herself and the figure she was following. Claudia's destination turned out to be the fourth floor. She went along a corridor and Mrs Oliver, lingering behind two of her tall men, noted the door where she went in. Three doors from the end of the corridor. Mrs Oliver arrived at the same door in due course and was able to read the legend on it. 'Joshua Restarick Ltd.' was the legend it bore.

Having got as far as that Mrs Oliver felt as though she did not quite know what to do next. She had found Norma's father's place of business and the place where Claudia worked, but now, slightly disabused, she felt that this was not as much of a discovery as it might have been. Frankly, did it help? Probably it didn't.

She waited around a few moments, walking from one end to the other of the corridor looking to see if anybody else interesting went in at the door of Restarick Enterprises. Two or three girls did but they did not look particularly interesting. Mrs Oliver went down again in the lift and walked rather disconsolately out of the building. She couldn't quite think what to do next. She took a walk round the adjacent streets, she meditated a visit to St Paul's.

'I might go up in the Whispering Gallery and whisper,' thought Mrs Oliver. 'I wonder now how the Whispering Gallery would do for the scene of a murder?

'No,' she decided, 'too profane, I'm afraid. No, I don't think that would be quite nice.' She walked thoughtfully towards the Mermaid Theatre. That, she thought, had far more possibilities.

She walked back in the direction of the various new buildings. Then, feeling the lack of a more substantial breakfast than she had had, she turned into a local café. It was moderately well filled with people having extra late breakfast or else early 'elevenses'. Mrs Oliver, looking round vaguely for a suitable table, gave a gasp. At a table near the wall the girl Norma was sitting, and opposite her was sitting a young man with lavish chestnut hair curled on his shoulders, wearing a red velvet waistcoat and a very fancy jacket.

'David,' said Mrs Oliver under her breath. 'It must be David.' He and the girl Norma were talking excitedly together.

Mrs Oliver considered a plan of campaign, made up her mind, and nodding her head in satisfaction, crossed the floor of the café to a discreet door marked 'Ladies'.

Mrs Oliver was not quite sure whether Norma was likely to recognise her or not. It was not always the vaguest looking people who proved the vaguest in fact. At the moment Norma did not look as though she was likely to look at anybody but David, but who knows?

'I expect I can *do* something to myself anyway,' thought Mrs Oliver. She looked at herself in a small fly-blown mirror provided by the café's management, studying particularly what she considered to be the focal point of a woman's appearance, her hair. No-one knew this better than Mrs Oliver, owing to the innumerable times that she had changed her mode of hairdressing, and had failed to be recognised by her friends in consequence. Giving her head an appraising eye she started work. Out came the pins, she took off several coils of hair, wrapped them up in her handkerchief and stuffed them into her handbag, parted her hair in the middle, combed it sternly back from her face and rolled it up into a modest bun at the back of her neck. She also took out a pair of spectacles and put them on her nose. There was a really earnest look about her now! 'Almost intellectual,' Mrs Oliver thought approvingly. She altered the shape of her mouth by an application of lipstick, and emerged once more into the café; moving carefully since the spectacles were only for reading and in consequence the landscape was blurred. She crossed the café, and made her way to an empty table next to that occupied by Norma and David. She sat down so that she was facing David. Norma, on the near side, sat with her back to her. Norma, therefore, would not see her unless she turned her head right round. The waitress drifted up. Mrs Oliver ordered a cup of coffee and a Bath bun and settled down to be inconspicuous.

Norma and David did not even notice her. They were deeply in the middle of a passionate discussion. It took Mrs Oliver just a minute or two to tune in to them.

' . . . But you only fancy these things,' David was saying. 'You *imagine* them. They're all utter, utter nonsense, my dear girl.'

'I don't know. I can't tell.' Norma's voice had a queer lack of resonance in it.

Mrs Oliver could not hear her as well as she heard David, since Norma's back was turned to her, but the dullness of the girl's tone struck her disagreeably. There was something wrong here, she thought. Very wrong. She remembered the story as Poirot had first told it to her. '*She thinks she may have committed a murder.*' What *was* the matter with the girl? Hallucinations? Was her mind really slightly affected, or was it no more and no less than truth, and in consequence the girl had suffered a bad shock?

'If you ask me, it's all fuss on Mary's part! She's a thoroughly stupid woman anyway, and she imagines she has illnesses and all that sort of thing.'

'She *was* ill.'

'All right then, she *was* ill. Any sensible woman would get the doctor to give her some antibiotic or other, and not get het up.'

'She thought *I* did it to her. My father thinks so too.'

'I tell you, Norma, you imagine all these things.'

'You just say that to me, David. You say it to me to cheer me up. Supposing I *did* give her the stuff?'

'What do you mean, suppose? You must *know* whether you did or you didn't. You can't be so idiotic, Norma.'

'I *don't* know.'

'You keep saying that. You keep coming back to that, and saying it again and again. 'I don't know.' 'I don't know.''

'You don't understand. You don't understand in the least what hate is. I hated her from the first moment I saw her.'

'I know. You told me that.'

'That's the queer part of it. I told you that, and yet I don't even *remember* telling you

104

that. D'you see? Every now and then I — I tell people things. I tell people things that I want to do, or that I have done, or that I'm going to do. But I don't even remember telling them the things. It's as though I was *thinking* all these things in my mind, and sometimes they come out in the open and I say them to people. I did say them to you, didn't I?'

'Well — I mean — look here, don't let's harp back to that.'

'But I did say it to you? Didn't I?'

'All right, all right! One says things like that. 'I hate her and I'd like to kill her. I think I'll poison her!' But that's only kid stuff, if you know what I mean, as though you weren't quite grown up. It's a very natural thing. Children say it a lot. 'I hate so and so. I'll cut off his head!' Kids say it at school. About some master they particularly dislike.'

'You think it was just that? But — that sounds as though *I* wasn't grown up.'

'Well, you're not in some ways. If you'd just pull yourself together, realise how silly it all is. What can it matter if you do hate her? You've got away from home and don't have to live with her.'

'Why shouldn't I live in my own home — with my own father?' said Norma. 'It's not fair. It's not fair. First he went away and left

105

my mother, and now, just when he's coming back to me, he goes and marries Mary. Of course I hate her and she hates me too. I used to think about killing her, used to think of ways of doing it. I used to enjoy thinking like that. But then — when she *really* got ill . . . '

David said uneasily:

'You don't think you're a witch or anything, do you? You don't make figures in wax and stick pins into them or do that sort of thing?'

'Oh no. That would be silly. What I did was real. Quite real.'

'Look here, Norma, what do you mean when you say it was real?'

'The bottle was there, in my drawer. Yes, I opened the drawer and found it.'

'What bottle?'

'*The Dragon Exterminator. Selective weed killer.* That's what it was labelled. Stuff in a dark green bottle and you were supposed to spray it on things. And it had labels with *Caution* and *Poison*, too.'

'Did you buy it? Or did you just find it?'

'I don't know where I got it, but it was there, in my drawer, and it was half empty.'

'And then you — you — remembered — '

'Yes,' said Norma. 'Yes . . . ' Her voice was vague, almost dreamy. 'Yes . . . I think it was then it all came back to me. You think so too, don't you, David?'

'I don't know what to make of you, Norma. I really don't. I think in a way, you're making it all up, you're telling it to *yourself*.'

'But she went to hospital, for observation. They said they were puzzled. Then they said they couldn't find anything wrong so she came home — and then she got ill again, and I began to be frightened. My father began looking at me in a queer sort of way, and then the doctor came and they talked together, shut up in Father's study. I went round outside, and crept up to the window and I tried to listen. I wanted to hear what they were saying. They were planning together — to send me away to a place where I'd be shut up! A place where I'd have a 'course of treatment' — or something. They thought, you see, that I was crazy, and I was frightened ... Because — because I wasn't sure what I'd done or what I hadn't done.'

'Is that when you ran away?'

'No — that was later — '

'Tell me.'

'I don't want to talk about it any more.'

'You'll have to let them know sooner or later where you are — '

'I won't! I hate them. I hate my father as much as I hate Mary. I wish they were dead. I wish they were both dead. Then — then I think I'd be happy again.'

'Don't get all het up! Look here, Norma — ' He paused in an embarrassed manner — 'I'm not very set on marriage and all that rubbish . . . I mean I didn't think I'd ever do anything of that kind . . . oh well, not for years. One doesn't want to tie oneself up — but I think it's the best thing we could do, you know. Get married. At a registry office or something. You'll have to say you're over twenty-one. Roll up your hair, put on some spectacles or something. Make you look a bit older. Once we're married, your father can't do a thing! He can't send you away to what you call a 'place'. He'll be powerless.'

'I hate him.'

'You seem to hate everybody.'

'Only my father and Mary.'

'Well, after all, it's quite natural for a man to marry again.'

'Look what he did to my mother.'

'All that must have been a long time ago.'

'Yes. I was only a child, but I remember. He went away and left us. He sent me presents at Christmas — but he never came himself. I wouldn't even have known him if I'd met him in the street by the time he did come back. He didn't mean anything to me by then. I think he got my mother shut up, too. She used to go away when she was ill. I don't know where. I don't know what was the matter with her. Sometimes I wonder . . . I wonder, David. I think, you know, there's something wrong in my head, and some day it will make me do something really bad. Like the knife.'

'What knife?'

'It doesn't matter. Just a knife.'

'Well, can't you tell me what you're talking about?'

'I think it had bloodstains on it — it was hidden there . . . under my stockings.'

'Do you remember hiding a knife there?'

'I think so. But I can't remember what I'd done with it *before* that. I can't remember where I'd *been* . . . There is a whole hour gone out of that evening. A whole hour I didn't know where I'd been. I'd been somewhere and done something.'

'Hush!' He hissed it quickly as the waitress approached their table. 'You'll be all right. I'll look after you. Let's have something more,' he said to the waitress in a loud voice, picking up the menu — 'Two baked beans on toast.'

# 8

## I

Hercule Poirot was dictating to his secretary, Miss Lemon.

'*And while I much appreciate the honour you have done me, I must regretfully inform you that* . . . '

The telephone rang. Miss Lemon stretched out a hand for it. 'Yes? Who did you say?' She put her hand over the receiver and said to Poirot, 'Mrs Oliver.'

'Ah . . . Mrs Oliver,' said Poirot. He did not particularly want to be interrupted at this moment, but he took the receiver from Miss Lemon. ' 'Allo,' he said, 'Hercule Poirot speaks.'

'Oh, M. Poirot, I'm so glad I got you! I've found her for you!'

'I beg your pardon?'

'*I've found her for you.* Your girl! You know, the one who's committed a murder or thinks she has. She's talking about it too, a great deal. I think she is off her head. But never mind that now. Do you want to come and get her?'

'Where are you, *chère* Madame?'

'Somewhere between St Paul's and the Mermaid Theatre and all that. Calthorpe Street,' said Mrs Oliver, suddenly looking out of the telephone box in which she was standing. 'Do you think you can get here quickly? They're in a restaurant.'

'They?'

'Oh, she and what I suppose is the unsuitable boy friend. He is rather nice really, and he seems very fond of her. I can't think why. People are odd. Well, I don't want to talk because I want to get back again. I followed them, you see. I came into the restaurant and saw them there.'

'Aha? You have been very clever, Madame.'

'No, I haven't really. It was a pure accident. I mean, I walked into a small café place and there the girl was, just sitting there.'

'Ah. You had the good fortune then. That is just as important.'

'And I've been sitting at the next table to them, only she's got her back to me. And anyway I don't suppose she'd recognise me. I've done things to my hair. Anyway, they've been talking as though they were alone in the world, and when they ordered another course — baked beans — (I can't bear baked beans, it always seems to me so funny that people should) — '

'Never mind the baked beans. Go on. You left them and came out to telephone. Is that right?'

'Yes. Because the baked beans gave me time. And I shall go back now. Or I might hang about outside. Anway, try and get here quickly.'

'What is the name of this café?'

'The Merry Shamrock — but it doesn't look very merry. In fact, it looks rather sordid, but the coffee is quite good.'

'Say no more. Go back. In due course, I will arrive.'

'Splendid,' said Mrs Oliver, and rang off.

## II

Miss Lemon, always efficient, had preceded him to the street, and was waiting by a taxi. She asked no questions and displayed no curiosity. She did not tell Poirot how she would occupy her time whilst he was away. She did not need to tell him. She always knew what she was going to do and she was always right in what she did.

Poirot duly arrived at the corner of Calthorpe Street. He descended, paid the taxi, and looked around him. He saw The Merry Shamrock but he saw no one in its vicinity who looked at all like Mrs Oliver, however well disguised. He walked to the end of the street and back. No Mrs Oliver. So either the couple in which they were interested had left the café and Mrs Oliver had gone on a shadowing expedition, or else — To answer 'or else' he went to the café door. One could not see the inside very well from the outside, on account of steam, so he pushed the door gently open and entered. His eyes swept round it.

He saw at once the girl who had come to visit him at the breakfast table. She was sitting by herself at a table against the wall. She was smoking a cigarette and staring in front of her. She seemed to be lost in thought. No, Poirot thought, hardly that. There did not seem to be any thought there. She was lost in a kind of oblivion. She was somewhere else.

He crossed the room quietly and sat down in the chair opposite her. She looked up then, and he was at least gratified to see that he was recognised.

'So we meet again, Mademoiselle,' he said pleasantly. 'I see you recognise me.'

'Yes. Yes, I do.'

'It is always gratifying to be recognised by a young lady one has only met once and for a very short time.'

She continued to look at him without speaking.

'And how did you know me, may I ask? What made you recognise me?'

'Your moustache,' said Norma immediately. 'It couldn't be anyone else.'

He was gratified by that observation and stroked it with the pride and vanity that he was apt to display on these occasions.

'Ah yes, very true. Yes, there are not many moustaches such as mine. It is a fine one, hein?'

'Yes — well, yes — I suppose it is.'

'Ah, you are perhaps not a connoisseur of moustaches, but I can tell you, Miss Restarick — Miss Norma Restarick, is it not? — that it is a very fine moustache.'

He had dwelt deliberately upon her name. She had at first looked so oblivious to everything around her, so far away, that he wondered if she would notice. She did. It startled her.

'How did you know my name?' she said.

'True, you did not give your name to my servant when you came to see me that morning.'

'How did you know it? How did you get to know it? Who told you?'

He saw the alarm, the fear.

'A friend told me,' he said. 'One's friends

114

can be very useful.'

'Who was it?'

'Mademoiselle, you like keeping your little secrets from me. I, too, have a preference for keeping my little secrets from you.'

'I don't see *how* you could know who I was.'

'I am Hercule Poirot,' said Poirot, with his usual magnificence. Then he left the initiative to her, merely sitting there smiling gently at her.

'I — ' she began, then stopped. ' — Would — ' Again she stopped.

'We did not get very far that morning, I know,' said Hercule Poirot. 'Only so far as your telling me that you had committed a murder.'

'Oh *that!*'

'Yes, Mademoiselle, *that*.'

'But — I didn't mean it of course. I didn't mean anything like that. I mean, it was just a joke.'

'*Vraiment?* You came to see me rather early in the morning, at breakfast time. You said it was urgent. The urgency was because you might have committed a murder. That is your idea of a joke, eh?'

A waitress who had been hovering, looking at Poirot with a fixed attention, suddenly came up to him and proffered him what appeared to be a paper boat such as is made for children to sail in a bath.

'This for you?' she said. 'Mr Porritt? A lady left it.'

'Ah yes,' said Poirot. 'And how did you know who I was?'

'The lady said I'd know by your moustache. Said I wouldn't have seen a moustache like that before. And it's true enough,' she added, gazing at it.

'Well, thank you very much.'

Poirot took the boat from her, untwisted it and smoothed it out; he read some hastily pencilled words: 'He's just going. She's staying behind, so I'm going to leave her for you, and follow him.' It was signed Ariadne.

'Ah yes,' said Hercule Poirot, folding it and slipping it into his pocket. 'What were we talking about? Your sense of humour, I think, Miss Restarick.'

'Do you know just my name or — or do you know everything about me?'

'I know a few things about you. You are Miss Norma Restarick, your address in London is 67 Borodene Mansions. Your home address is Crosshedges, Long Basing. You live there with a father, a stepmother, a great-uncle and — ah yes, an *au pair* girl. You see, I am quite well informed.'

'You've been having me followed.'

'No, no,' said Poirot. 'Not at all. As to that,

I give you my word of honour.'

'But you are not police, are you? You didn't say you were.'

'I am not police, no.'

Her suspicion and defiance broke down.

'I don't know what to do,' she said.

'I am not urging you to employ me,' said Poirot. 'For that you have said already that I am too old. Possibly you are right. But since I know who you are and something about you, there is no reason we should not discuss together in a friendly fashion the troubles that afflict you. The old, you must remember, though considered incapable of action, have nevertheless a good fund of experience on which to draw.'

Norma continued to look at him doubtfully, that wide-eyed stare that had disquieted Poirot before. But she was in a sense trapped, and she had at this particular moment, or so Poirot judged, a wish to talk about things. For some reason, Poirot had always been a person it was easy to talk to.

'They think I'm crazy,' she said bluntly. 'And — and I rather think I'm crazy, too. Mad.'

'That is most interesting,' said Hercule Poirot, cheerfully. 'There are many different names for these things. Very grand names. Names rolled out happily by psychiatrists, psychologists and others. But when you say crazy, that describes very well what the general appearance may be to ordinary, everyday people. *Eh bien*, then, you are crazy, or you appear crazy or you think you are crazy, and possibly you *may* be crazy. But all the same that is not to say the condition is serious. It is a thing that people suffer from a good deal, and it is usually easily cured with the proper treatment. It comes about because people have had too much mental strain, too much worry, have studied too much for examinations, have dwelled too much per-haps on their emotions, have too much religion or have a lamentable lack of religion, or have good reasons for hating their fathers or their mothers! Or, of course, it can be as simple as having an unfortunate love affair.'

'I've got a stepmother. I hate her and I rather think I hate my father too. That seems rather a lot, doesn't it?'

'It is more usual to hate one or the other,' said Poirot. 'You were, I suppose, very fond of your own mother. Is she divorced or dead?'

'Dead. She died two or three years ago.'

'And you cared for her very much?'

'Yes. I suppose I did. I mean of course I did. She was an invalid, you know, and she had to go to nursing homes a good deal.'

'And your father?'

'Father had gone abroad a long time before that. He went to South Africa when I was about five or six. I think he wanted Mother to divorce him but she wouldn't. He went to South Africa and was mixed up with mines or something like that. Anyway, he used to write to me at Christmas, and send me a Christmas present or arrange for one to come to me. That was about all. So he didn't really seem very real to me. He came home about a year ago because he had to wind up my uncle's affairs and all that sort of financial thing. And when he came home he — he brought this new wife with him.'

'And you resented the fact?'

'Yes, I did.'

'But your mother was dead by then. It is not unusual, you know, for a man to marry again. Especially when he and his wife have been estranged for many years. This wife he brought, was she the same lady he had wished to marry previously, when he asked your mother for a divorce?'

'Oh, no, this one is quite young. And she's very good-looking and she acts as though she just owns my father!'

She went on after a pause — in a different, rather childish voice. 'I thought perhaps when he came home this time he would be fond of *me* and take notice of *me* and — but she

119

won't let him. She's *against* me. She's crowded me out.'

'But that does not matter at all at the age you are. It is a good thing. You do not need anyone to look after you now. You can stand on your own feet, you can enjoy life, you can choose your own friends — '

'You wouldn't think so, the way they go on at home! Well, I mean to choose my own friends.'

'Most girls nowadays have to endure criticism about their friends,' said Poirot.

'It was all so different,' said Norma. 'My father isn't at all like I remember him when I was five years old. He used to play with me, all the time, and be so gay. He's not gay now. He's worried and rather fierce and — oh quite different.'

'That must be nearly fifteen years ago, I presume. People change.'

'But ought people to change so much?'

'Has he changed in appearance?'

'Oh no, no, not that. Oh no! If you look at his picture just over his chair, although it's of him when he was much younger, it's exactly like him now. But it isn't at all the way I remember him.'

'But you know, my dear,' said Poirot gently, 'people are never like what you remember them. You make them, as the years go by, more and more the way you *wish* them to be, and as you *think* you remember them. If you want to remember them as agreeable and gay and handsome, you make them far more so than they actually were.'

'Do you think so? Do you really think so?' She paused and then said abruptly, 'But why do you think I want to kill people?' The question came out quite naturally. It was there between them. They had, Poirot felt, got at last to a crucial moment.

'That may be quite an interesting question,' said Poirot, 'and there may be quite an interesting reason. The person who can probably tell you the answer to that will be a doctor. The kind of doctor who *knows*.'

She reacted quickly.

'I won't go to a doctor. I won't go *near* a doctor! They wanted to send me to a doctor, and then I'll be shut up in one of those loony places and they won't let me out again. I'm not going to do anything like that.' She was struggling now to rise to her feet.

'It is not I who can send you to one! You need not be alarmed. You could go to a doctor entirely on your own behalf if you liked. You can go and say to him the things you have been saying to me, and you may ask him *why*, and he will perhaps tell you the cause.'

'That's what David says. That's what David says I should do but I don't think — I don't think he *understands*. I'd have to tell a doctor that I — I might have tried to do things . . . '

'What makes you think you have?'

'Because I don't always remember what I've done — or where I've been. I lose an hour of time — two hours — and I can't *remember*. I was in a corridor once — a corridor outside a door, her door. I'd something in my hand — I don't know how I got it. She came walking along towards me — But when she got near me, her face changed. It wasn't her at all. She'd changed into somebody else.'

'You are remembering, perhaps, a nightmare. There people do change into somebody else.'

'It wasn't a nightmare. I picked up the revolver — It was lying there at my feet — '

'In a corridor?'

'No, in the courtyard. She came and took it away from me.'

'Who did?'

'Claudia. She took me upstairs and gave me some bitter stuff to drink.'

'Where was your stepmother then?'

'She was there, too — No, she wasn't. She was at Crosshedges. Or in hospital. That's where they found out she was being poisoned

— and that it was me.'

'It need not have been you — It could have been someone else.'

'Who else could it have been?'

'Perhaps — her husband.'

'Father? Why on earth should Father want to poison *Mary*. He's devoted to her. He's silly about her!'

'There are others in the house, are there not?'

'Old Uncle Roderick? Nonsense!'

'One does not know,' said Poirot, 'he might be mentally afflicted. He might think it was his duty to poison a woman who might be a beautiful spy. Something like that.'

'That would be very interesting,' said Norma, momentarily diverted, and speaking in a perfectly natural manner. 'Uncle Roderick *was* mixed up a good deal with spies and things in the last war. Who else is there? Sonia? I suppose *she* might be a beautiful spy, but she's not quite my idea of one.'

'No, and there does not seem very much reason why she should wish to poison your stepmother. I suppose there might be servants, gardeners?'

'No, they just come in for the days. I don't think — well, they wouldn't be the kind of people to have any *reason*.'

'She might have done it herself.'

'Committed *suicide*, do you mean? Like the other one?'

'It is a possibility.'

'I can't imagine *Mary* committing suicide. She's far too sensible. And why should she want to?'

'Yes, you feel that if she did, she would put her head in the gas oven, or she would lie on a bed nicely arranged and take an overdose of sleeping draughts. Is that right?'

'Well, it would have been more natural. So you see,' said Norma earnestly, '*it must have been me.*'

'Aha,' said Poirot, 'that interests me. You would almost, it would seem, *prefer* that it should be you. You are attracted to the idea that it was your hand who slipped the fatal dose of this, that or the other. Yes, you *like* the idea.'

'How dare you say such a thing! How can you?'

'*Because I think it is true,*' said Poirot. 'Why does the thought that you may have committed murder excite you, please you?'

'It's not true.'

'I wonder,' said Poirot.

She scooped up her bag and began feeling in it with shaking fingers.

'I'm not going to stop here and have you

say these horrible things to me.' She signalled to the waitress who came, scribbled on a pad of paper, detached it and laid it down by Norma's plate.

'Permit me,' said Hercule Poirot.

He removed the slip of paper deftly, and prepared to draw his notecase from his pocket. The girl snatched it back again.

'No, I won't let you pay for me.'

'As you please,' said Poirot.

He had seen what he wanted to see. The bill was for two. It would seem therefore that David of the fine feathers had no objection to having his bills paid by an infatuated girl.

'So it is you who entertain a friend to elevenses, I see.'

'How did you know that I was with anyone?'

'I tell you, I know a good deal.'

She placed coins on the table and rose. 'I'm going now,' she said, 'and I forbid you to follow me.'

'I doubt if I could,' said Poirot. 'You must remember my advanced age. If you were to run down the street I should certainly not be able to follow you.'

She got up and went towards the door.

'Do you hear? You are *not* to follow me.'

'You permit me at least to open the door for you.' He did so with something of a flourish. '*Au revoir*, Mademoiselle.'

She threw a suspicious glance at him and walked away down the street with a rapid step, turning her head back over her shoulder from time to time. Poirot remained by the door watching her, but made no attempt to gain the pavement or to catch her up. When she was out of sight, he turned back into the café.

'And what the devil does all that mean?' said Poirot to himself.

The waitress was advancing upon him, displeasure on her face. Poirot regained his seat at the table and placated her by ordering a cup of coffee. 'There is something here very curious,' he murmured to himself. 'Yes, something very curious indeed.'

A cup of pale beige fluid was placed in front of him. He took a sip of it and made a grimace.

He wondered where Mrs Oliver was at this moment.

# 9

Mrs Oliver was seated in a bus. She was slightly out of breath though full of the zest of the chase. What she called in her own mind the Peacock, had led a somewhat brisk pace. Mrs Oliver was not a rapid walker. Going along the Embankment she followed him at a distance of some twenty yards or so. At Charing Cross he got into the underground. Mrs Oliver also got into the underground. At Sloane Square he got out, so did Mrs Oliver. She waited in a bus queue some three or four people behind him. He got on a bus and so did she. He got out at World's End, so did Mrs Oliver. He plunged into a bewildering maze of streets between King's Road and the river. He turned into what seemed a builder's yard. Mrs Oliver stood in the shadow of a doorway and watched. He turned into an alleyway, Mrs Oliver gave him a moment or two and then followed — he was nowhere to be seen. Mrs Oliver reconnoitred her general surroundings. The whole place appeared somewhat decrepit. She wandered farther down the alleyway. Other alleyways led off from it — some of them cul-de-sacs. She had completely lost her sense of direction when she once more came to the builder's yard and a voice spoke behind her, startling her considerably. It said, politely, 'I hope I didn't walk too fast for you.'

She turned sharply. Suddenly what had recently been almost fun, a chase undertaken light-heartedly and in the best of spirits, now was that no longer. What she felt now was a sudden unexpected throb of fear. Yes, she was afraid. The atmosphere had suddenly become tinged with menace. Yet the voice was pleasant, polite; but behind it she knew there was anger. The sudden kind of anger that recalled to her in a confused fashion all the things one read in newspapers. Elderly women attacked by gangs of young men. Young men who were ruthless, cruel, who were driven by hate and the desire to do harm. This was the young man whom she had been following. He had known she was there, had given her the slip and had then followed her into this alleyway, and he stood there now barring her way out. As is the precarious fashion of London, one moment you are amongst people all round you and the next moment there is nobody in sight. There must be people in the next street, someone in the houses near, but nearer than that is a masterful figure, a figure with strong cruel hands. She felt that in this moment he was thinking of using those hands ... The Peacock. A proud peacock. In his velvets, his tight, elegant black trousers, speaking in that quiet ironical amused voice that held behind it anger ... Mrs Oliver took three big gasps. Then, in a lightning moment of decision she put up a quickly imagined defence. Firmly and immediately she sat down on a dustbin which was against the wall quite close to her.

'Goodness, how you startled me,' she said. 'I'd no idea you were there. I hope you're not annoyed.'

'So you *were* following me?'

'Yes, I'm afraid I was. I expect it must have been rather annoying to you. You see I thought it would be such an excellent opportunity. I'm sure you're frightfully angry but you needn't be, you know. Not really. You see — ' Mrs Oliver settled herself more firmly on the dustbin, 'you see I write books. I write detective stories and I've really been very worried this morning. In fact I went into a café to have a cup of coffee just to try and think things out. I'd just got to the point in my book where I was following somebody. I mean my hero was following someone and I thought to myself, 'Really I know very little about following people.' I mean, I'm always using the phrase in a book and I've read a lot of books where people do follow other people, and I wondered if it was as easy as it seems to be in some people's books or if it was as almost entirely impossible as it seemed in other people's books. So I thought 'Well, really, the only thing was to try it out *myself* — because until you try things out yourself you can't really tell what it's like. I mean you don't know what you feel like, or whether you get worried at losing a person. As it happened, I just looked up and you were sitting at the next table to me in the café and I thought you'd be — I hope you won't be annoyed again — but I thought you'd be an especially good person to follow.'

He was still staring at her with those strange, cold blue eyes, yet she felt somehow that the tension had left them.

'Why was I an especially good person to follow?'

'Well, you were so decorative,' explained Mrs Oliver. 'They are really very attractive clothes — almost Regency, you know, and I thought, well, I might take advantage of your being fairly easy to distinguish from other people. So you see, when you went out of the café I went out too. And it's not really easy at all.' She looked up at him. 'Do you mind telling me if you knew I was there all the time?'

'Not at once, no.'

'I see,' said Mrs Oliver thoughtfully. 'But of course I'm not as distinctive as you are. I mean you wouldn't be able to tell me very easily from a lot of other elderly women. I don't stand out very much, do I?'

'Do you write books that are published? Have I ever come across them?'

'Well, I don't know. You may have. I've written forty-three by now. My name's Oliver.'

'Ariadne Oliver?'

'So you do know my name,' said Mrs Oliver. 'Well, that's rather gratifying, of course, though I daresay you wouldn't like my books very much. You probably would find them rather old-fashioned — not violent enough.'

'You didn't know me personally beforehand?'

Mrs Oliver shook her head. 'No, I'm sure I don't — didn't, I mean.'

'What about the girl I was with?'

'You mean the one you were having — baked beans, was it — with in the café? No, I don't think so. Of course I only saw the back of her head. She looked to me — well, I mean girls do look rather alike, don't they?'

'She knew you,' said the boy suddenly. His tone in a moment had a sudden acid sharpness. 'She mentioned once that she'd

131

met you not long ago. About a week ago, I believe.'

'Where? Was it at a party? I suppose I might have met her. What's her name? Perhaps I'd know that.'

She thought he was in two moods whether to mention the name or not, but he decided to and he watched her face very keenly as he did so.

'Her name's Norma Restarick.'

'Norma Restarick. Oh, of course, yes, it was at a party in the country. A place called — wait a minute — Long Norton was it? — I don't remember the name of the house. I went there with some friends. I don't think I would have recognised her anyway, though I believe she did say something about my books. I even promised I'd give her one. It's very odd, isn't it, that I should make up my mind and actually choose to follow a person who was sitting with somebody I more or less knew. Very odd. I don't think I could put anything like that in my book. It would look rather too much of a coincidence, don't you think?'

Mrs Oliver rose from her seat.

'Good gracious, what have I been sitting on? A dustbin! Really! Not a very nice dustbin either.' She sniffed. 'What *is* this place I've got to?'

David was looking at her. She felt suddenly that she was completely mistaken in everything she had previously thought. 'Absurd of me,' thought Mrs Oliver, 'absurd of me. Thinking that he was dangerous, that he might do something to me.' He was smiling at her with an extraordinary charm. He moved his head slightly and his chestnut ringlets moved on his shoulders. What fantastic creatures there were in the way of young men nowadays!

'The least I can do,' he said, 'is to show you, I think, where you've been brought to, just by following me. Come on, up these stairs.' He indicated a ramshackle outside staircase running up to what seemed to be a loft.

'Up those stairs?' Mrs Oliver was not so certain about this. Perhaps he was trying to lure her up there with his charm, and he would then knock her on the head. 'It's no good, Ariadne,' said Mrs Oliver to herself, 'you've got yourself into this spot, and now you've got to go on with it and find out what you can find out.'

'Do you think they'll stand my weight?' she said, 'they look frightfully rickety.'

'They're quite all right. I'll go up first,' he said, 'and show you the way.'

Mrs Oliver mounted the ladder-like stairs

behind him. It was no good. She was, deep down, still frightened. Frightened, not so much of the Peacock, as frightened of where the Peacock might be taking her. Well, she'd know very soon. He pushed open the door at the top and went into a room. It was a large, bare room and it was an artist's studio, an improvised kind of one. A few mattresses lay here and there on the floor, there were canvasses stacked against the wall, a couple of easels. There was a pervading smell of paint. There were two people in the room. A bearded young man was standing at an easel, painting. He turned his head as they entered.

'Hallo, David,' he said, 'bringing us company?'

He was, Mrs Oliver thought, quite the dirtiest-looking young man she'd ever seen. Oily black hair hung in a kind of circular bob down the back of his neck and over his eyes in front. His face apart from the beard was unshaven, and his clothes seemed mainly composed of greasy black leather and high boots. Mrs Oliver's glance went beyond him to a girl who was acting as a model. She was on a wooden chair on a dais, half flung across it, her head back and her dark hair drooping down from it. Mrs Oliver recognised her at once. It was the second one of the three girls in Borodene Mansions. Mrs Oliver couldn't remember her last name, but she remembered her first one. It was the highly decorative and languid-looking girl called Frances.

'Meet Peter,' said David, indicating the somewhat revolting looking artist. 'One of our budding geniuses. And Frances who is posing as a desperate girl demanding abortion.'

'Shut up, you ape,' said Peter.

'I believe I know you, don't I?' said Mrs Oliver, cheerfully, without any air of conscious certainty. 'I'm sure I've met you somewhere! Somewhere quite lately, too.'

'You're Mrs Oliver, aren't you?' said Frances.

'That's what she said she was,' said David. 'True, too, is it?'

'Now, where *did* I meet you,' continued Mrs Oliver. 'Some party, was it? No. Let me think. I know. It was Borodene Mansions.'

Frances was sitting up now in her chair and speaking in weary but elegant tones. Peter uttered a loud and miserable groan.

'Now you've ruined the pose! Do you have to have all this wriggling about? Can't you keep still?'

'No, I couldn't any longer. It was an awful pose. I've got the most frightful crick in my shoulder.'

'I've been making experiments in following people,' said Mrs Oliver. 'It's much more difficult than I thought. Is this an artist's studio?' she added, looking round her brightly.

'That's what they're like nowadays, a kind of loft — and lucky if you don't fall through the floor,' said Peter.

'It's got all you need,' said David. 'It's got a north light and plenty of room and a pad to sleep on, and a fourth share in the loo downstairs — and what they call cooking facilities. And it's got a bottle or two,' he added. Turning to Mrs Oliver, but in an entirely different tone, one of utter politeness, he said, 'And can we offer you a drink?'

'I don't drink,' said Mrs Oliver.

'The lady doesn't drink,' said David. 'Who would have thought it!'

'That's rather rude but you're quite right,' said Mrs Oliver. 'Most people come up to me and say, 'I always thought you drank like a fish'.'

She opened her handbag — and immediately three coils of grey hair fell on the floor. David picked them up and handed them to her.

'Oh! thank you.' Mrs Oliver took them. 'I hadn't time this morning. I wonder if I've got any more hairpins.' She delved in her bag and started attaching the coils to her head.

Peter roared with laughter — 'Bully for you,' he said.

'How extraordinary,' Mrs Oliver thought to herself, 'that I should ever have had this silly idea that I was in danger. *Danger* — from *these* people? No matter what they look like, they're really very nice and friendly. It's quite true what people always say to me. I've far too much imagination.'

Presently she said she must be going, and David, with Regency gallantry, helped her down the rickety steps, and gave her definite directions as to how to rejoin the King's Road in the quickest way.

'And then,' he said, 'you can get a bus — or a taxi if you want it.'

'A taxi,' said Mrs Oliver. 'My feet are absolutely dead. The sooner I fall into a taxi the better. Thank you,' she added, 'for being so very nice about my following you in what must have seemed a very peculiar way. Though after all I don't suppose private detectives, or private eyes or whatever they call them, would look anything at all like me.'

'Perhaps not,' said David gravely. 'Left here — and then right, and then left again until you see the river and go towards it, and then sharp right and straight on.'

Curiously enough, as she walked across the

shabby yard the same feeling of unease and suspense came over her. 'I mustn't let my imagination go again.' She looked back at the steps and the window of the studio. The figure of David still stood looking after her. 'Three perfectly nice young people,' said Mrs Oliver to herself. 'Perfectly nice and very kind. Left here, and then right. Just because they *look* rather peculiar, one goes and has silly ideas about their being dangerous. Was it right again? or left? Left, I think — Oh goodness, my feet. It's going to rain, too.' The walk seemed endless and the King's Road incredibly far away. She could hardly hear the traffic now — And where on earth was the river? She began to suspect that she had followed the directions wrongly.

'Oh! well,' thought Mrs Oliver, 'I'm bound to get *somewhere* soon — the river, or Putney or Wandsworth or somewhere.' She asked her way to the King's Road from a passing man who said he was a foreigner and didn't speak English.

Mrs Oliver turned another corner wearily and there ahead of her was the gleam of the water. She hurried towards it down a narrow passageway, heard a footstep behind her, half turned, when she was struck from behind and the world went up in sparks.

# 10

## I

A voice said:

'Drink this.'

Norma was shivering. Her eyes had a dazed look. She shrank back a little in the chair. The command was repeated. 'Drink this.' This time she drank obediently, then choked a little.

'It's — it's very strong,' she gasped.

'It'll put you right. You'll feel better in a minute. Just sit still and wait.'

The sickness and the giddiness which had been confusing her passed off. A little colour came into her cheeks, and the shivering diminished. For the first time she looked round her, noting her surroundings. She had been obsessed by a feeling of fear and horror but now things seemed to be returning to normal. It was a medium-sized room and it was furnished in a way that seemed faintly familiar. A desk, a couch, an armchair and an ordinary chair, a stethoscope on a side table and some machine that she thought had to do with eyes. Then her attention went from the

139

general to the particular. The man who had told her to drink.

She saw a man of perhaps thirty-odd with red hair and a rather attractive ugly face, the kind of face that is craggy but interesting. He nodded at her in a reassuring fashion.

'Beginning to get your bearings?'

'I — I think so. I — did you — what happened?'

'Don't you remember?'

'The traffic. I — it came at me — it — ' She looked at him. 'I was run over.'

'Oh no, you weren't run over.' He shook his head. 'I saw to that.'

'You?'

'Well, there you were in the middle of the road, a car bearing down on you and I just managed to snatch you out of its way. What were you thinking of to go running into the traffic like that?'

'I can't remember. I — yes, I suppose I must have been thinking of something else.'

'A Jaguar was coming pretty fast, and there was a bus bearing down on the other side of the road. The car wasn't trying to run you down or anything like that, was it?'

'I — no, no, I'm sure it wasn't. I mean I — '

'Well, I wondered — It just might have been something else, mightn't it?'

'What do you mean?'

'Well, it could have been deliberate, you know.'

'What do you mean by deliberate?'

'Actually I just wondered whether you were trying to get yourself killed?' He added casually, 'Were you?'

'I — no — well — no, of course not.'

'Damn' silly way to do it, if so.' His tone changed slightly. 'Come now, you must remember *something* about it.'

She began shivering again. 'I thought — I thought it would be all over. I thought — '

'So you were trying to kill yourself, weren't you? What's the matter? You can tell me. Boy friend? That can make one feel pretty bad. Besides, there's always the hopeful thought that if you kill yourself you make him sorry — but one should never trust to that. People don't like feeling sorry or feeling anything is their fault. All the boy friend will probably say is, 'I always thought she was unbalanced. It's really all for the best.' Just remember that next time you have an urge to charge Jaguars. Even Jaguars have feelings to be considered. *Was* that the trouble? Boy friend walk out on you?'

'No,' said Norma. 'Oh no. It was quite the opposite.' She added suddenly, 'He wanted to marry me.'

'That's no reason for throwing yourself down in front of a Jaguar.'

'Yes it is. I did it because — ' She stopped.

'You'd better tell me about it, hadn't you?'

'How did I get here?' asked Norma.

'I brought you here in a taxi. You didn't seem injured — a few bruises, I expect. You merely looked shaken to death, and in a state of shock. I asked you your address, but you looked at me as though you didn't know what I was talking about. A crowd was about to collect. So I hailed a taxi and brought you here.'

'Is this a — a doctor's surgery?'

'This is a doctor's consulting room and I'm the doctor. Stillingfleet, my name is.'

'I don't want to see a doctor! I don't want to talk to a doctor! I don't — '

'Calm down, calm down. You've been talking to a doctor for the last ten minutes. What's the matter with doctors, anyway?'

'I'm afraid. I'm afraid a doctor would say — '

'Come, now, my dear girl, you're not consulting me professionally. Regard me as a mere outsider who's been enough of a busybody to save you from being killed or, what is far more likely, having a broken arm or a fractured leg or a head injury or something extremely unpleasant which might

142

incapacitate you for life. There are other disadvantages. Formerly, if you deliberately tried to commit suicide you could be had up in Court. You still can if it's a suicide pact. There now, you can't say I haven't been frank. You could oblige now by being frank with me, and telling me why on earth you're afraid of doctors. What's a doctor ever done to you?'

'Nothing. Nothing has been *done* to me. But I'm afraid that they might — '

'Might what?'

'Shut me up.'

Dr Stillingfleet raised his sandy eyebrows and looked at her.

'Well, well,' he said. 'You seem to have some very curious ideas about doctors. Why should I want to shut you up? Would you like a cup of tea,' he added, 'or would you prefer a purple heart or a tranquilliser? That's the kind of thing people of your age go in for. Done a bit yourself in that line, haven't you?'

She shook her head. 'Not — not *really*.'

'I don't believe you. Anyway, why the alarm and despondency? You're not really mental, are you? I shouldn't have said so. Doctors aren't at all anxious to have people shut up. Mental homes are far too full already. Difficult to squeeze in another body. In fact lately they've been letting a good many

143

people out — in desperation — pushing them out, you might say — who jolly well ought to have been kept in. Everything's so over-crowded in this country.

'Well,' he went on, 'what are your tastes? Something out of my drug cupboard or a good solid old-fashioned English cup of tea?'

'I — I'd like some tea,' said Norma.

'Indian or China? That's the thing to ask, isn't it? Mind you, I'm not sure if I've got any China.'

'I like Indian better.'

'Good.'

He went to the door, opened it and shouted, 'Annie. Pot of tea for two.'

He came back and sat down and said, 'Now you get this quite clear, young lady. What's your name, by the way?'

'Norma Res — ' she stopped.

'Yes?'

'Norma West.'

'Well, Miss West, let's get this clear. I'm not treating you, you're not consulting me. You are the victim of a street accident — that is the way we'll put it and that is the way I suppose you meant it to appear, which would have been pretty hard on the fellow in the Jaguar.'

'I thought of throwing myself off a bridge first.'

144

'Did you? You wouldn't have found that so easy. People who build bridges are rather careful nowadays. I mean you'd have had to climb up on to the parapet and it's not so easy. Somebody stops you. Well, to continue with my dissertation, I brought you home as you were in too much of a state of shock to tell me your address. What is it, by the way?'

'I haven't got an address. I — I don't live anywhere.'

'Interesting,' said Dr Stillingfleet. 'What the police call "of no fixed abode". What do you do — sit out on the Embankment all night?'

She looked at him suspiciously.

'I could have reported the accident to the police but there was no obligation upon me to do so. I preferred to take the view that in a state of maiden meditation you were crossing the street before looking left first.'

'You're not at all like my idea of a doctor,' said Norma.

'Really? Well, I've been getting gradually disillusioned in my profession in this country. In fact, I'm giving up my practice here and I'm going to Australia in about a fortnight. So you're quite safe from me, and you can if you like tell me how you see pink elephants walking out of the wall, how you think the trees are leaning out their branches to wrap round and strangle you, how you think you

145

know just when the devil looks out of people's eyes, or any other cheerful fantasy, and I shan't do a thing about it! You *look* sane enough, if I may say so.'

'I don't think I am.'

'Well, you may be right,' said Dr Stillingfleet handsomely. 'Let's hear what your reasons are.'

'I do things and don't remember about them . . . I tell people things about what I've done but I don't *remember* telling them . . . '

'It sounds as though you have a bad memory.'

'You don't understand. They're all — wicked things.'

'Religious mania? Now that would be very interesting.'

'It's not religious. It's just — just *hate*.'

There was a tap at the door and an elderly woman came in with a tea tray. She put it down on the desk and went out again.

'Sugar?' said Dr Stillingfleet.

'Yes, please.'

'Sensible girl. Sugar is very good for you when you've had a shock.' He poured out two cups of tea, set hers at her side and placed the sugar basin beside it. 'Now then,' he sat down. 'What were we talking about? Oh yes, hate.'

'It is possible, isn't it, that you could hate

146

someone so much that you really want to kill them?'

'Oh, yes,' said Stillingfleet, cheerfully still. 'Perfectly possible. In fact, most natural. But even if you really want to do it you can't always screw yourself up to the point, you know. The human being is equipped with a natural braking system and it applies the brakes for you just at the right moment.'

'You make it sound so ordinary,' said Norma. There was a distinct overtone of annoyance in her voice.

'Oh, well, it is quite natural. Children feel like it almost every day. Lose their tempers, say to their mothers or their fathers: 'You're wicked, I hate you, I wish you were dead.' Mothers, being sometimes sensible people, don't usually pay any attention. When you grow up, you still hate people, but you can't take quite so much trouble wanting to kill them by then. Or if you still do — well, then you go to prison. That is, if you actually brought yourself to do such a messy and difficult job. You aren't putting all this on, are you, by the way?' he asked casually.

'Of course not.' Norma sat up straight. Her eyes flashed with anger. 'Of course not. Do you think I would say such awful things if they weren't true?'

'Well, again,' said Dr Stillingfleet, 'people

do. They say all sorts of awful things about themselves and enjoy saying them.' He took her empty cup from her. 'Now then,' he said, 'you'd better tell me all about everything. Who you hate, why you hate them, what you'd like to do to them.'

'Love can turn to hate.'

'Sounds like a melodramatic ballad. But remember hate can turn to love, too. It works both ways. And you say it's not a boy friend. *He was your man and he did you wrong.* None of that stuff, eh?'

'No, no. Nothing like that. It's — it's my stepmother.'

'The cruel stepmother *motif*. But that's nonsense. At your age you can get away from a stepmother. What has she done to you besides marrying your father? Do you hate him too, or are you so devoted to him that you don't want to share him?'

'It's not like that at all. Not at all. I used to love him once. I loved him dearly. He was — he was — I thought he was wonderful.'

'Now then,' said Dr Stillingfleet, 'listen to me. I'm going to suggest something. You see that door?'

Norma turned her head and looked in a puzzled fashion at the door.

'Perfectly ordinary door, isn't it? Not locked. Opens and shuts in the ordinary way.

148

Go on, try it for yourself. You saw my housekeeper come in and go out through it, didn't you? No illusions. Come on. Get up. Do what I tell you.'

Norma rose from her chair and rather hesitatingly went to the door and opened it. She stood in the aperture, her head turned towards him inquiringly.

'Right. What do you see? A perfectly ordinary hallway, wants redecorating but it's not worth having it done when I'm just off to Australia. Now go to the front door, open it, also no tricks about it. Go outside and down to the pavement and that will show you that you are perfectly free with no attempts to shut you up in any way. After that, when you have satisfied yourself that you could walk out of this place at any minute you like, come back, sit in that comfortable chair over there and tell me all about yourself. After which I will give you my valuable advice. You needn't take it,' he added consolingly. 'People seldom do take advice, but you might as well have it. See? Agreed?'

Norma got up slowly, she went a little shakily out of the room, out into — as the doctor had described — the perfectly ordinary hallway, opened the front door with a simple catch, down four steps and stood on the pavement in a street of decorous but rather uninteresting houses. She stood there a moment, unaware that she was being watched through a lace blind by Dr Stillingfleet himself. She stood there for about two minutes, then with a slightly more resolute bearing she turned, went up the steps again, shut the front door and came back into the room.

'All right?' said Dr Stillingfleet. 'Satisfied you there's nothing up my sleeve? All clear and above board.'

The girl nodded.

'Right. Sit down there. Make yourself comfortable. Do you smoke?'

'Well, I — '

'Only reefers — something of that kind? Never mind, you needn't tell me.'

'Of course I don't take anything of that kind.'

'I shouldn't have said there was any 'of course' about it, but one must believe what the patient tells one. All right. Now tell me about yourself.'

'I — I don't know. There's nothing to tell really. Don't you want me to lie down on a couch?'

'Oh, you mean your memory of dreams and all that stuff? No, not particularly. I just like to get a background. You know. You were born, you lived in the country or the town, you have brothers and sisters or you're an only child and so on. When your own mother died, were you very upset by her death?'

'Of course I was.' Norma sounded indignant.

'You're much too fond of saying of course, Miss West. By the way, West isn't really your name, is it? Oh, never mind, I don't want to know any other one. Call yourself West or East or North or anything you like. Anyway, what went on after your mother died?'

'She was an invalid for a long time before she died. In nursing homes a good deal. I stayed with an aunt, rather an old aunt, down in Devonshire. She wasn't really an aunt, she was Mother's first cousin. And then my father came home just about six months ago. It — it was wonderful.' Her face lighted up suddenly. She was unaware of the quick, shrewd glance the apparently casual young man shot at her. 'I could hardly remember him, you know. He must have gone away when I was about five. I didn't really think I'd ever see him again. Mother didn't very often talk about him. I think at first she hoped that he'd give up this other woman and come back.'

'Other woman?'

'Yes. He went away with someone. She was a very bad woman, Mother said. Mother talked about her very bitterly and very bitterly

151

about Father too, but I used to think that perhaps — perhaps Father wasn't as bad as she thought, that it was all this woman's fault.'

'Did they marry?'

'No. Mother said she would never divorce Father. She was a — is it an Anglican? — very High Church, you know. Rather like a Roman Catholic. She didn't believe in divorce.'

'Did they go on living together? What was the woman's name or is that a secret too?'

'I don't remember her last name.' Norma shook her head. 'No, I don't think they lived together long, but I don't know much about it all, you see. They went to South Africa but I think they quarrelled and parted quite soon because that's when Mother said she hoped Father might come back again. But he didn't. He didn't write even. Not even to me. But he sent me things at Christmas. Presents always.'

'He was fond of you?'

'I don't know. How could I tell? Nobody ever spoke about him. Only Uncle Simon — his brother, you know. He was in business in the City and he was very angry that Father had chucked up everything. He said he had always been the same, could never settle to anything, but he said he wasn't a bad chap really. He said he was just weak. I didn't often see Uncle Simon. It was always Mother's friends. Most of them were dreadfully dull. My whole life has been very dull . . .

'Oh, it seemed so wonderful that Father was really coming home. I tried to remember him better. You know, things he had said, games he had played with me. He used to make me laugh a lot. I tried to see if I couldn't find some old snapshots or photographs of him. They seem all to have been thrown away. I think Mother must have torn them all up.'

'She had remained vindictive then.'

'I think it was really Louise she was vindictive against.'

'Louise?'

He saw a slight stiffening on the girl's part.

'I don't remember — I told you — I don't remember any names.'

'Never mind. You're talking about the woman your father ran away with. Is that it?'

'Yes. Mother said she drank too much and took drugs and would come to a bad end.'

'But you don't know whether she did?'

'I don't know anything.' . . . Her emotion was rising. 'I wish you wouldn't ask me questions! I don't know anything about her! I never heard of her again! I'd forgotten her until you spoke about her. I tell you I don't know *anything*.'

'Well, well,' said Dr Stillingfleet. 'Don't get

153

so agitated. You don't need to bother about past history. Let's think about the future. What are you going to do next?'

Norma gave a deep sigh.

'I don't know. I've nowhere to go. I can't — it's much better — I'm sure it's much better to — to end it all — only — '

'Only you can't make the attempt a second time, is that it? It would be very foolish if you did, I can tell you that, my girl. All right, you've nowhere to go, no one to trust; got any money?'

'Yes, I've got a banking account, and Father pays so much into it every quarter but I'm not sure . . . I think perhaps, by now, they might be looking for me. *I don't want to be found.*'

'You needn't be. I'll fix that up for you all right. Place called Kenway Court. Not as fine as it sounds. It's a kind of convalescent nursing home where people go for a rest cure. It's got no doctors or couches, and you won't be shut up there, I can promise you. You can walk out any time you like. You can have breakfast in bed, stay in bed all day if you like. Have a good rest and I'll come down one day and talk to you and we'll solve a few problems together. Will that suit you? Are you willing?'

Norma looked at him. She sat, without

expression, staring at him; slowly she nodded her head.

## II

Later that evening Dr Stillingfleet made a telephone call.

'Quite a good operation kidnap,' he said. 'She's down at Kenway Court. Came like a lamb. Can't tell you much yet. The girl's full of drugs. I'd say she'd been taking purple hearts, and dream bombs, and probably LSD . . . She's been all hopped up for some time. She says no, but I wouldn't trust much to what she says.'

He listened for a moment. 'Don't ask me! One will have to go carefully there. She gets the wind up easy . . . Yes, she's scared of something, or she's pretending to be scared of something . . .

'I don't know yet, I can't tell. Remember people who take drugs are tricky. You can't believe what they say always. We haven't rushed things and I don't want to startle her . . .

'A father complex as a child. I'd say didn't care much for her mother who sounds a grim woman by all accounts — the self-righteous martyr type. I'd say Father was a gay one, and

155

couldn't quite stand the grimness of married life — Know of anyone called Louise? . . . The name seemed to frighten her — She was the girl's first hate, I should say. She took Father away at the time the child was five. Children don't understand very much at that age, but they're very quick to feel resentment of the person they feel was responsible. She didn't see Father again until apparently a few months ago. I'd say she'd had sentimental dreams of being her father's companion and the apple of his eye. She got disillusioned apparently. Father came back with a wife, a new young attractive wife. *She's* not called Louise, is she? . . . Oh well, I only asked. I'm giving you roughly the picture, the general picture, that is.'

The voice at the other end of the wire said sharply, 'What is that you say? Say it again.'

'I said I'm giving you roughly the picture.'

There was a pause.

'By the way, here's one little fact might interest you. The girl made a rather ham-handed attempt to commit suicide. Does that startle you? . . .

'Oh, it doesn't . . . No, she didn't swallow the aspirin bottle, or put her head in the gas oven. She rushed into the traffic in the path of a Jaguar going faster than it should have done . . . I can tell you I only got to her just in time ... Yes, I'd say it was a genuine impulse ... She admitted it. Usual classic phrase — she 'wanted to get out of it all'.'

He listened to a rapid flow of words, then he said: 'I don't know. At this stage, I can't be sure — The picture presented is clear. A nervy girl, neurotic and in an overwrought state from taking drugs of too many kinds. No, I couldn't tell you definitely what kind. There are dozens of these things going about all producing slightly different effects. There can be confusion, loss of memory, aggression, bewilderment, or sheer fuzzleheadedness! The difficulty is to tell what the real reactions are as opposed to the reactions produced by drugs. There are two choices, you see. Either this is a girl who is playing herself up, depicting herself as neurotic and nervy and claiming suicidal tendencies. It could be actually so. Or it could be a whole pack of lies. I wouldn't put it past her to be putting up this story for some obscure reason of her own — wanting to give an entirely false impression of herself. If so, she's doing it very cleverly. Every now and then, there seems something not quite right in the picture she's giving. Is she a very clever little actress acting a part? Or is she a genuine semi-moronic suicidal victim? She could be either ... What did you say? ... Oh, the Jaguar! ... Yes, it was being driven far too fast. You think it mightn't have been an attempt at suicide? That the Jaguar was deliberately meaning to run her down?'

He thought for a minute or two. 'I *can't* say,' he said slowly. 'It just *could* be so. Yes, it could be so, but I hadn't thought of it that way. The trouble is, everything's possible, isn't it? Anyway, I'm going to get more out of her shortly. I've got her in a position where she's semi-willing to trust me, so long as I don't go too far too quickly, and make her suspicious. She'll become more trusting soon, and tell me more, and if she's a genuine case, she'll pour out her whole story to me — force it on me in the end. At the moment she's frightened of something . . .

'If, of course, she's leading me up the garden path we'll have to find out the reason why. She's at Kenway Court and I *think* she'll stay there. I'd suggest that you keep someone with an eye on it for a day or so and if she does attempt to leave, someone she doesn't know by sight had better follow her.'

# 11

## I

Andrew Restarick was writing a cheque — he made a slight grimace as he did so.

His office was large and handsomely furnished in typical conventional tycoon fashion — the furnishing and fittings had been Simon Restarick's and Andrew Restarick had accepted them without interest and had made few changes except for removing a couple of pictures and replacing them by his own portrait which he had brought up from the country, and a water colour of Table Mountain.

Andrew Restarick was a man of middle age, beginning to put on flesh, yet strangely little changed from the man some fifteen years younger in the picture hanging above him. There was the same jutting out chin, the lips firmly pressed together, and the slightly raised quizzical eyebrows. Not a very noticeable man — an ordinary type and at the moment not a very happy man. His secretary entered the room — she advanced towards his desk, as he looked up.

'A Monsieur Hercule Poirot is here. He insists that he has an appointment with you — but I can find no trace of one.'

'A Monsieur Hercule Poirot?' The name seemed vaguely familiar, but he could not remember in what context. He shook his head — 'I can't remember anything about him — though I seem to have heard the name. What does he look like?'

'A very small man — foreign — French I should say — with an enormous moustache — '

'Of course! I remember Mary describing him. He came to see old Roddy. But what's all this about an appointment with me?'

'He says you wrote him a letter.'

'Can't remember it — even if I did. Perhaps Mary — Oh well, never mind — bring him in. I suppose I'd better see what this is all about.'

A moment or two later Claudia Reece-Holland returned ushering with her a small man with an egg-shaped head, large moustaches, pointed patent leather shoes and a general air of complacency which accorded very well with the description he had had from his wife.

'Monsieur Hercule Poirot,' said Claudia Reece-Holland.

She went out again as Hercule Poirot

advanced towards the desk. Restarick rose.

'Monsieur Restarick? I am Hercule Poirot, at your service.'

'Oh yes. My wife mentioned that you'd called upon us or rather called upon my uncle. What can I do for you?'

'I have presented myself in answer to your letter.'

'What letter? I did not write to you, M. Poirot.'

Poirot stared at him. Then he drew from his pocket a letter, unfolded it, glanced at it and handed it across the desk with a bow.

'See for yourself, Monsieur.'

Restarick stared at it. It was typewritten on his own office stationery. His signature was written in ink at the bottom.

*Dear Monsieur Poirot,*

*I should be very glad if you could call upon me at the above address at your earliest convenience. I understand from what my wife tells me and also from what I have learned by making various inquiries in London, that you are a man to be trusted when you agree to accept a mission that demands discretion.*

*Yours truly,*
*Andrew Restarick*

He said sharply:

'When did you receive this?'

'This morning. I had no matters of moment on my hands so I came along here.'

'This is an extraordinary thing, M. Poirot. That letter was not written by me.'

'Not written by you?'

'No. My signature is quite different — look for yourself.' He cast out a hand as though looking for some example of his handwriting and without conscious thought turned the cheque book on which he had just written his signature, so that Poirot could see it. 'You see? The signature on the letter is not in the least like mine.'

'But that is extraordinary,' said Poirot. 'Absolutely extraordinary. Who could have written this letter?'

'That's just what I'm asking myself.'

'It could not — excuse me — have been your wife?'

'No, no. Mary would never do a thing like that. And anyway why should she sign it with my name? Oh no, she would have told me if she'd done such a thing, prepared me for your visit.'

'Then you have no idea why anyone might have sent this letter?'

'No, indeed.'

'Have you no knowledge, Mr Restarick, as

to what the matter might be on which in this letter you apparently want to engage me?'

'How could I have an idea?'

'Excuse me,' said Poirot, 'you have not yet completely read this letter. You will notice at the bottom of the first page after the signature, there is a small p.t.o.'

Restarick turned the letter over. At the top of the next page the typewriting continued.

*The matter on which I wish to consult you concerns my daughter, Norma.*

Restarick's manner changed. His face darkened.

'So, that's it! But who could know — who could possibly meddle in this matter? Who knows about it?'

'Could it be a way of urging you to consult me? Some well-meaning friend? You have really *no* idea who the writer may have been?'

'I've no idea whatever.'

'And you are not in trouble over a daughter of yours — a daughter named Norma?'

Restarick said slowly:

'I have a daughter named Norma. My only daughter.' His voice changed slightly as he said the last words.

'And she is in trouble, difficulty of some kind?'

'Not that I know of.' But he hesitated slightly as he spoke the words.

Poirot leaned forward.

'I don't think that is exactly right, Mr Restarick. I think there *is* some trouble or difficulty concerning your daughter.'

'Why should you think that? Has someone spoken to you on the subject?'

'I was going entirely by your intonation, Monsieur. Many people,' added Hercule Poirot, 'are in trouble over daughters at the present date. They have a genius, young ladies, for getting into various kinds of trouble and difficulty. It is possible that the same obtains here.'

Restarick was silent for some few moments, drumming with his fingers on the desk.

'Yes, I am worried about Norma,' he said at last. 'She is a difficult girl. Neurotic, inclined to be hysterical. I — unfortunately I don't know her very well.'

'Trouble, no doubt, over a young man?'

'In a way, yes, but that is not entirely what is worrying me. I think — ' he looked appraisingly at Poirot. 'Am I to take it that you are a man of discretion?'

'I should be very little good in my profession if I were not.'

'It is a case, you see, of wanting my daughter *found*.'

'Ah?'

'She came home last weekend as she usually does to our house in the country. She went back on Sunday night ostensibly to the flat which she occupies in common with two other girls, but I now find that she did *not* go there. She must have gone — somewhere else.'

'In fact, she has disappeared?'

'It sounds too much of a melodramatic statement, but it does amount to that. I expect there's a perfectly natural explanation, but — well, I suppose any father would be worried. She hasn't rung up, you see, or given any explanation to the girls with whom she shares her flat.'

'They too are worried?'

'No, I should not say so. I think — well, I think they take such things easily enough. Girls are very independent. More so than when I left England fifteen years ago.'

'What about the young man of whom you say you do not approve? Can she have gone away with him?'

'I devoutly hope not. It's possible, but I don't — my wife doesn't think so. You saw him, I believe, the day you came to our house to call on my uncle — '

'Ah yes, I think I know the young man of whom you speak. A very handsome young man but not, if I may say so, a man of whom a father would approve. I noticed that your wife was not pleased, either.'

'My wife is quite certain that he came to the house that day hoping to escape observation.'

'He knows, perhaps, that he is not welcome there?'

'He knows all right,' said Restarick grimly.

'Do you not then think that it is only too likely your daughter may have joined him?'

'I don't know what to think. I didn't — at first.'

'You have been to the police.'

'No.'

'In the case of anyone who is missing, it is usually much better to go to the police. They too are discreet and they have many means at their disposal which persons like myself have not.'

'I don't want to go to the police. It's my *daughter*, man, you understand? *My* daughter. If she's chosen to — to go away for a short time and not let us know, well, that's up to her. There's no reason to believe that she's in any danger or anything like that. I — I just want to know for my own satisfaction where she is.'

'Is it possible, Mr Restarick — I hope I am not unduly presuming, that that is not the only thing that is worrying you about your daughter?'

'Why should you think there was anything else?'

'Because the mere fact that a girl is absent for a few days without telling her parents, or the friends with whom she is living, where she is going, is not particularly unusual nowadays. It is that, taken in conjunction with *something else*, I think, which has caused you this alarm.'

'Well, perhaps you're right. It's — ' he looked doubtfully at Poirot. 'It is very hard to speak of these things to strangers.'

'Not really,' said Poirot. 'It is infinitely easier to speak to strangers of such things than it would be to speak of them to friends or acquaintances. Surely you must agree to that?'

'Perhaps. Perhaps. I can see what you mean. Well, I will admit I am upset about my girl. You see she — she's not quite like other girls and there's been something already that has definitely worried me ... worried us both.'

Poirot said: 'Your daughter, perhaps, is at that difficult age of young girlhood, an emotional adolescence when, quite frankly, they are capable of performing actions for which they are hardly to be held responsible.

167

Do not take it amiss if I venture to make a surmise. Your daughter perhaps resents having a stepmother?'

'That is unfortunately true. And yet she has no reason to do so, M. Poirot. It is not as though my first wife and I had recently parted. The parting took place many years ago.' He paused and then said, 'I might as well speak frankly to you. After all, there has been no concealment about the matter. My first wife and I drifted apart. I need not mince matters. I had met someone else, someone with whom I was quite infatuated. I left England and went to South Africa with the other woman. My wife did not approve of divorce and I did not ask her for one. I made suitable financial provision for my wife and for the child — she was only five years old at the time — '

He paused and then went on:

'Looking back, I can see that I had been dissatisfied with life for some time. I'd been yearning to travel. At that period of my life I hated being tied down to an office desk. My brother reproached me several times with not taking more interest in the family business, now that I had come in with him. He said that I was not pulling my weight. But I didn't want that sort of life. I was restless. I wanted an adventurous life. I wanted to see the world and wild places . . . '

He broke off abruptly.

'Anyway — you don't want to hear the story of my life. I went to South Africa and Louise went with me. It wasn't a success. I'll admit that straight away. I was in love with her but we quarrelled incessantly. She hated life in South Africa. She wanted to get back to London and Paris — all the sophisticated places. We parted only about a year after we arrived there.'

He sighed.

'Perhaps I ought to have gone back then, back to the tame life that I disliked the idea of so much. But I didn't. I don't know whether my wife would have had me back or not. Probably she would have considered it her duty to do so. She was a great woman for doing her duty.'

Poirot noted the slight bitterness that ran through that sentence.

'But I ought to have thought more about Norma, I suppose. Well, there it was. The child was safely with her mother. Financial arrangements had been made. I wrote to her occasionally and sent her presents, but I never once thought of going back to England and seeing her. That was not entirely blameworthy on my part. I had adopted a different way of life and I thought it would be merely unsettling for the child to have a father who came and went, and perhaps disturbed her own peace of mind. Anyway, let's say I thought I was acting for the best.'

Restarick's words came fast now. It was as though he was feeling a definite solace in being able to pour out his story to a sympathetic listener. It was a reaction that Poirot had often noticed before and he encouraged it.

'You never wished to come home on your own account?'

Restarick shook his head very definitely. 'No. You see, I was living the kind of life I liked, the kind of life I was meant for. I went from South Africa to East Africa. I was doing very well financially, everything I touched seemed to prosper; projects with which I was associated, occasionally with other people, sometimes on my own, all went well. I used to go off into the bush and trek. That was the life I'd always wanted. I am by nature an out-of-door man. Perhaps that's why when I was married to my first wife I felt trapped, held down. No, I enjoyed my freedom and I'd no wish to go back to the conventional type of life that I'd led here.'

'But you did come back in the end?'

Restarick sighed. 'Yes. I did come back. Ah well, one grows old, I suppose. Also, another man and I had made a very good strike. We'd secured a concession which might have very important consequences. It would need negotiation in London. There I could have depended on my brother to act, but my brother died. I was still a partner in the firm. I could return if I chose and see to things myself. It was the first time I had thought of doing so. Of returning, I mean, to City life.'

'Perhaps your wife — your second wife — '

'Yes, you may have something there. I had been married to Mary just a month or two when my brother died. Mary was born in South Africa but she had been to England several times and she liked the life there. She liked particularly the idea of having an English garden!

'And I? Well, for the first time perhaps I felt I would like life in England, too. And I thought of Norma as well. Her mother had died two years earlier. I talked to Mary about it all, and she was quite willing to help me make a home for my daughter. The prospects all seemed good and so — ' he smiled, ' — and so I came home.'

Poirot looked at the portrait that hung behind Restarick's head. It was in a better light here than it had been at the house in the country. It showed very plainly the man who was sitting at the desk; there were the distinctive features, the obstinancy of the chin, the quizzical eyebrows, the poise of the head, but the portrait had one thing that the man sitting in the chair beneath it lacked. Youth!

Another thought occurred to Poirot. Why had Andrew Restarick moved the portrait from the country to his London office? The two portraits of him and his wife had been companion portraits done at the same time and by that particular fashionable artist of the day whose speciality was portrait painting. It would have been more natural, Poirot thought, to have left them together, as they had been meant to be originally. But Restarick had moved one portrait, his own, to his office. Was it a kind of vanity on his part — a wish to display himself as a City man, as someone important to the City? Yet he was a man who had spent his time in wild places, who professed to prefer wild places. Or did he perhaps do it in order to keep before his mind himself in his City personality? Did he feel the need of reinforcement?

'Or, of course,' thought Poirot, 'it could be simple vanity!

'Even I myself,' said Poirot to himself, in an unusual fit of modesty, 'even I myself am capable of vanity on occasions.'

The short silence, of which both men had

seemed unaware, was broken. Restarick spoke apologetically.

'You must forgive me, M. Poirot. I seem to have been boring you with the story of my life.'

'There is nothing to excuse, Mr Restarick. You have been talking really only of your life as it may have affected that of your daughter. You are much disquieted about your daughter. But I do not think that you have yet told me the real reason. You want her found, you say?'

'Yes, I want her found.'

'You want her found, yes, but do you want her found by *me*? Ah, do not hesitate. *La politesse* — it is very necessary in life, but it is not necessary here. Listen. I tell you, if you want your daughter found I advise you, I — Hercule Poirot — to go to the police for they have the facilities. And from my own knowledge they can be discreet.'

'I won't go to the police unless — well, unless I get very desperate.'

'You would rather go to a private agent?'

'Yes. But you see, I don't know anything about private agents. I don't know who — who can be trusted. I don't know who — '

'And what do you know about me?'

'I do know something about you. I know, for instance, that you held a responsible

173

position in Intelligence during the war, since, in fact, my own uncle vouches for you. That is an admitted fact.'

The faintly cynical expression on Poirot's face was not perceived by Restarick. The admitted fact was, as Poirot was well aware, a complete illusion — although Restarick must have known how undependable Sir Roderick was in the matter of memory and eyesight — he had swallowed Poirot's own account of himself, hook, line and sinker. Poirot did not disillusion him. It merely confirmed him in his long-held belief that you should never believe anything anyone said without first checking it. *Suspect everybody*, had been for many years, if not his whole life, one of his first axioms.

'Let me reassure you,' said Poirot. 'I have been throughout my career exceptionally successful. I have been indeed in many ways unequalled.'

Restarick looked less reassured by this than he might have been! Indeed, to an Englishman, a man who praised himself in such terms aroused some misgivings.

He said: 'What do you feel yourself, M. Poirot? Have you confidence that you can find my daughter?'

'Probably not as quickly as the police could do, but yes. I shall find her.'

'And — and if you do — '

'But if you wish me to find her, Mr Restarick, you must tell me all the circumstances.'

'But I have told them to you. The time, the place, where she ought to be. I can give you a list of her friends . . . '

Poirot was making some violent shakings of his head. 'No, no, I suggest you tell me the truth.'

'Do you suggest I haven't told you the truth?'

'You have not told me all of it. Of that I am assured. What are you afraid of? What are the unknown facts — the facts that I have to know if I am to have success? Your daughter dislikes her stepmother. That is plain. There is nothing strange about that. It is a very natural reaction. You must remember that she may have secretly idealised you for many many years. That is quite possible in the case of a broken marriage where a child has had a severe blow in her affections. Yes, yes, I know what I am talking about. You say a child forgets. That is true. Your daughter could have forgotten you in the sense that when she saw you again she might not remember your face or your voice. She would make her own image of you. You went away. She wanted you to come back. Her mother, no doubt,

175

discouraged her from talking about you, and therefore she thought about you perhaps all the more. You *mattered* to her all the more. And because she could not talk about you to her own mother she had what is a very natural reaction with a child — the blaming of the parent who remains for the absence of the parent who has gone. She said to herself something in the nature of 'Father was fond of me. It's Mother he didn't like,' and from that was born a kind of idealisation, a kind of secret liaison between you and her. What had happened was not her father's fault. She will not believe it!

'Oh yes, that often happens, I assure you. I know something of the psychology. So when she learns that you are coming home, that you and she will be reunited, many memories that she has pushed aside and not thought of for years return. Her father is coming back! He and she will be happy together! She hardly realises the stepmother, perhaps, until she sees her. And then she is violently jealous. It is most natural, I assure you. She is violently jealous partly because your wife is a good-looking woman, sophisticated, and well poised, which is a thing girls often resent because they frequently lack confidence in themselves. She herself is possibly gauche with perhaps an inferiority complex. So when

176

she sees her competent and good-looking stepmother, quite possibly she hates her; but hates her as an adolescent girl who is still half a child might do.'

'Well — ' Restarick hesitated. 'That *is* more or less what the doctor said when we consulted him — I mean — '

'Aha,' said Poirot, 'so you consulted a doctor? You must have had some reason, is it not so, for calling in a doctor?'

'Nothing really.'

'Ah no, you cannot say that to Hercule Poirot. It was not *nothing*. It was something serious and you had better tell me, because if I know just what has been in this girl's mind, I shall make more progress. Things will go quicker.'

Restarick was silent for several moments, then he made up his mind.

'This is in absolute confidence, M. Poirot? I can rely on you — I have your assurance as to that?'

'By all means. What was the trouble?'

'I cannot be — be sure.'

'Your daughter entered into some action against your wife? Something more than being merely childishly rude or saying unpleasant things. It was something worse than that — something more serious. Did she perhaps attack her *physically*?'

'No, it was not an attack — not a physical attack but — nothing was proved.'

'No, no. We will admit that.'

'My wife became far from well — ' He hesitated.

'Ah,' said Poirot. 'Yes, I see . . . And what was the nature of her illness? Digestive, possibly? A form of enteritis?'

'You're quick, M. Poirot. You're very quick. Yes, it *was* digestive. This complaint of my wife's was puzzling, because she had always had excellent health. Finally they sent her to hospital for 'observation', as they call it. A check-up.'

'And the result?'

'I don't think they were completely satisfied . . . She appeared to regain her health completely and was sent home in due course. But the trouble recurred. We went carefully over the meals she had, the cooking. She seemed to be suffering from a form of intestinal poisoning for which there appeared to be no cause. A further step was taken, tests were made of the dishes she ate. By taking samples of everything, it was definitely proved that a certain substance had been administered in various dishes. In each case it was a dish of which only my wife had partaken.'

'In plain language somebody was giving her arsenic. Is that right?'

'Quite right. In small doses which would in the end have a cumulative effect.'

'You suspected your daughter?'

'No.'

'I think you did. Who else could have done it? You suspected your daughter.'

Restarick gave a deep sigh.

'Frankly, yes.'

## II

When Poirot arrived home, George was awaiting him:

'A woman named Edith rang up, sir — '

'Edith?' Poirot frowned.

'She is, I gather, in the service of Mrs Oliver. She asked me to inform you that Mrs Oliver is in St Giles's Hospital.'

'What has happened to her?'

'I understand she has been — er — coshed.' George did not add the latter part of the message, which had been — ' — and you tell him it's been all his fault.'

Poirot clicked his tongue. 'I warned her — I was uneasy last night when I rang her up, and there was no answer. *Les Femmes*!'

# 12

'Let's buy a peacock,' said Mrs Oliver suddenly and unexpectedly. She did not open her eyes as she made this remark, and her voice was weak though full of indignation.

Three people brought startled eyes to bear upon her. She made a further statement.

'Hit on the head.'

She opened badly focused eyes and endeavoured to make out where she was.

The first thing she saw was a face entirely strange to her. A young man who was writing in a notebook. He held the pencil poised in his hand.

'Policeman,' said Mrs Oliver decisively.

'I beg your pardon, Madam?'

'I said you were a policeman,' said Mrs Oliver. 'Am I right?'

'Yes, Madam.'

'Criminal assault,' said Mrs Oliver and closed her eyes in a satisfied manner. When she opened them again, she took in her surroundings more fully. She was in a bed, one of those rather high hygienic-looking hospital beds, she decided. The kind that you shoot up and down and round and about.

She was not in her own house. She looked round and decided on her environment.

'Hospital, or could be nursing home,' she said.

A sister was standing with an air of authority at the door, and a nurse was standing by her bed. She identified a fourth figure. 'Nobody,' said Mrs Oliver, 'could mistake those moustaches. What are you doing here, M. Poirot?'

Hercule Poirot advanced towards the bed. 'I told you to be careful, Madame,' he said.

'Anyone might lose their way,' said Mrs Oliver, somewhat obscurely, and added, 'My head aches.'

'With good cause. As you surmise, you were hit on the head.'

'Yes. By the Peacock.'

The policeman stirred uneasily then said, 'Excuse me, Madam, you say you were assaulted by a peacock?'

'Of course. I'd had an uneasy feeling for some time — you know, atmosphere.' Mrs Oliver tried to wave her hand in an appropriate gesture to describe atmosphere, and winced. 'Ouch,' she said, 'I'd better not try that again.'

'My patient must not get over-excited,' said the sister with disapproval.

'Can you tell me where this assault occurred?'

181

'I haven't the faintest idea. I'd lost my way. I was coming from a kind of studio. Very badly kept. Dirty. The other young man hadn't shaved for days. A greasy leather jacket.'

'Is this the man who assaulted you?'

'No, it's another one.'

'If you could just tell me — '

'I am telling you, aren't I? I'd followed him, you see, all the way from the café — only I'm not very good at following people. No practice. It's much more difficult than you'd think.'

Her eyes focused on the policeman. 'But I suppose you know all about that. You have courses — in following people, I mean? Oh, never mind, it doesn't matter. You see,' she said, speaking with sudden rapidity, 'it's quite simple. I had got off at The World's End, I think it was, and naturally I thought he had stayed with the others — or gone the other way. But instead, he came up behind me.'

'Who was this?'

'The Peacock,' said Mrs Oliver, 'and he startled me, you see. It does startle you when you find things are the wrong way round. I mean he following you instead of you following him — only it was earlier — and I had a sort of uneasy feeling. In fact, you know, I was *afraid*. I don't know why. He spoke quite politely but I was *afraid*. Anyway there it was and he said 'Come up and see the studio' and so I came up rather a rickety staircase. A kind of ladder staircase and there was this other young man — the dirty young man — and he was painting a picture, and the girl was acting as model. She was quite clean. Rather pretty really. And so there we were and they were quite nice and polite, and then I said I must be getting home, and they told me the right way to get back to the King's Road. But they can't really have told me the right way. Of course I *might* have made a mistake. You know, when people tell you second left and third right, well, you sometimes do it the wrong way round. At least I do. Anyway, I got into a rather peculiar slummy part quite close to the river. The afraid feeling had gone away by then. I must have been quite off my guard when the Peacock hit me.'

'I think she's delirous,' said the nurse in an explanatory voice.

'No, I'm not,' said Mrs Oliver. 'I know what I'm talking about.'

The nurse opened her mouth, caught the sister's admonitory eye and shut it again quickly.

'Velvets and satins and long curly hair,' said Mrs Oliver.

'A peacock in satin? A real peacock,

183

Madam. You thought you saw a peacock near the river in Chelsea?'

'A real peacock?' said Mrs Oliver. 'Of course not. How silly. What would a real peacock be doing down on Chelsea Embankment?'

Nobody appeared to have an answer to this question.

'He struts,' said Mrs Oliver, 'that's why I nicknamed him a peacock. Shows off, you know. Vain, I should think. Proud of his looks. Perhaps a lot of other things as well.' She looked at Poirot. 'David something. You know who I mean.'

'You say this young man of the name of David assaulted you by striking you on the head?'

'Yes I do.'

Hercule Poirot spoke. 'You *saw* him?'

'I didn't see him,' said Mrs Oliver, 'I didn't know anything about it. I just thought I heard something behind me, and before I could turn my head to look — it all happened! Just as if a ton of bricks or something fell on me. I think I'll go to sleep now,' she added.

She moved her head slightly, made a grimace of pain, and relapsed into what appeared to be a perfectly satisfactory unconsciousness.

# 13

Poirot seldom used the key to his flat. Instead, in an old-fashioned manner, he pressed the bell and waited for that admirable factotum, George, to open the door. On this occasion, however, after his visit to the hospital, the door was opened to him by Miss Lemon.

'You've got two visitors,' said Miss Lemon, pitching her voice in an admirable tone, not as carrying as a whisper but a good many notes lower than her usual pitch. 'One's Mr Goby and the other is an old gentleman called Sir Roderick Horsefield. I don't know which you want to see first.'

'Sir Roderick Horsefield,' mused Poirot. He considered this with his head on one side, looking rather like a robin while he decided how this latest development was likely to affect the general picture. Mr Goby, however, materialised with his usual suddenness from the small room which was sacred to Miss Lemon's typewriting and where she had evidently kept him in storage.

Poirot removed his overcoat. Miss Lemon hung it up on the hall-stand, and Mr Goby, as was his fashion, addressed the back of Miss Lemon's head.

'I'll have a cup of tea in the kitchen with George,' said Mr Goby. 'My time is my own. I'll keep.'

He disappeared obligingly into the kitchen. Poirot went into his sitting-room where Sir Roderick was pacing up and down full of vitality.

'Run you down, my boy,' he said genially. 'Wonderful thing the telephone.'

'You remembered my name? I am gratified.'

'Well, I didn't exactly remember your name,' said Sir Roderick. 'Names, you know, have never been my strong point. Never forget a face,' he ended proudly. 'No. I rang up Scotland Yard.'

'Oh!' Poirot looked faintly startled, though reflecting that that was the sort of thing that Sir Roderick *would* do.

'Asked me who I wanted to speak to. I said, put me on to the top. That's the thing to do in life, my boy. Never accept second in charge. No good. Go to the top, that's what I say. I said who I was, mind you. Said I wanted to speak to the top brass and I got on to it in the end. Very civil fellow. Told him I wanted the address of a chap in Allied Intelligence who was out with me at a certain place in France at a certain date. The chap seemed a bit at sea, so I said: 'You know who I mean.' A Frenchman, I said, or a Belgian. Belgian, weren't you? I said: 'He's got a Christian name something like Achilles. It's not Achilles,' I said, 'but it's *like* Achilles. Little chap,' I said, 'big moustaches.' And then he seemed to catch on, and he said you'd be in the telephone book, he thought. I said that's all right, but I said: 'He won't be listed under Achilles or Hercules (as he said it was), will he? and I can't remember his second name.' So then he gave it me. Very civil sort of fellow. Very civil, I must say.'

'I am delighted to see you,' said Poirot, sparing a hurried thought for what might be said to him later by Sir Roderick's telephone acquaintance. Fortunately it was not likely to have been quite the top brass. It was presumably someone with whom he was already acquainted, and whose job it was to produce civility on tap for distinguished persons of a bygone day.

'Anyway,' said Sir Roderick, 'I got here.'

'I am delighted. Let me offer you some refreshment. Tea, a grenadine, a whisky and soda, some *sirop de cassis* — '

'Good lord, no,' said Sir Roderick, alarmed at the mention of *sirop de cassis*. 'I'll take whisky for choice. Not that I'm allowed it,' he added, 'but doctors are all fools, as we know. All they care for is stopping you having anything you've a fancy for.'

Poirot rang for George and gave him the proper instructions. The whisky and the siphon were placed at Sir Roderick's elbow and George withdrew.

'Now,' said Poirot, 'what can I do for you?'

'Got a job for you, old boy.'

After the lapse of time, he seemed even more convinced of the close liaison between him and Poirot in the past, which was as well, thought Poirot, since it would produce an even greater dependence on his, Poirot's, capabilities by Sir Roderick's nephew.

'Papers,' said Sir Roderick, dropping his voice. 'Lost some papers and I've got to find 'em, see? So I thought what with my eyes not being as good as they were, and the memory being a trifle off key sometimes, I'd better go to someone in the know. See? You came along in the nick of time the other day, just in time to be useful, because I've got to cough 'em up, you understand.'

'It sounds most interesting,' said Poirot. 'What are these papers, if I may ask?'

'Well, I suppose if you're going to find them, you'll have to ask, won't you? Mind you, they're very secret and confidential. Top secret — or they were once. And it seems as though they are going to be again. An interchange of letters, it was. Not of any particular importance at the time — or it was thought they were of no importance; but then of course politics change. You know the way it is. They go round and face the other way. You know how it was when the war broke out. None of us knew whether we were on our head or on our heels. One war we're pals with the Italians, next war we're enemies. I don't know which of them all was the worst. First war the Japanese were our dear allies, and the next war there they are blowing up Pearl Harbor! Never knew where you were! Start one way with the Russians, and finish the opposite way. I tell you, Poirot, nothing's more difficult nowadays than the question of allies. They can change overnight.'

'And you have lost some papers,' said Poirot, recalling the old man to the subject of his visit.

'Yes. I've got a lot of papers, you know, and I've dug 'em out lately. I had 'em put away safely. In a bank, as a matter of fact, but I got 'em all out and I began sorting through them because I thought why not write my memoirs. All the chaps are doing it nowadays. We've had Montgomery and Alanbrooke and Auchinleck all shooting their mouths off in print, mostly saying what they thought of the other generals. We've even had old Moran, a respectable physician, blabbing about his important patient. Don't know what things will come to next! Anyway, there it is, and I thought I'd be quite interested myself in telling a few facts about some people I knew! Why shouldn't I have a go as well as everyone else? I was in it all.'

'I am sure it could be a matter of much interest to people,' said Poirot.

'Ah-ha, yes! One knew a lot of people in the news. Everyone looked at them with awe. They didn't know they were complete fools, but I knew. My goodness, the mistakes some of those brass-hats made — you'd be surprised. So I got out my papers, and I had the little girl help me sort 'em out. Nice little girl, that, and quite bright. Doesn't know English very well, but apart from that, she's very bright and helpful. I'd salted away a lot of stuff, but everything was in a bit of a muddle. The point of the whole thing is, *the papers I wanted weren't there.*'

'Weren't there?'

'No. We thought we'd given it a miss by mistake to begin with, but we went over it again and I can tell you, Poirot, a lot of stuff seemed to me to have been pinched. Some of it wasn't important. Actually, the stuff I was looking for wasn't particularly important — I mean, nobody had thought it was, otherwise I suppose I shouldn't have been allowed to keep it. But anyway, these particular letters weren't there.'

'I wish of course to be discreet,' said Poirot, 'but can you tell me at all the nature of these letters you refer to?'

'Don't know that I can, old boy. The nearest I can go is of somebody who's shooting off his mouth nowadays about what he did and what he said in the past. But he's not speaking the truth, and these letters just show exactly how much of a liar he is! Mind you, I don't suppose they'd be published now. We'll just send him nice copies of them, and tell him this is exactly what he did say at the time, and that we've got it in writing. I shouldn't be surprised if — well, things went a bit differently after that. See? I hardly need ask that, need I? You're familiar with all that kind of talky-talky.'

'You're quite right, Sir Roderick. I know exactly the kind of thing you mean, but you see also that it is not easy to help you recover something if one does not know what that something is, and where it is likely to be now.'

'First things first: I want to know who pinched 'em, because you see that's the important point. There may be more top secret stuff in my little collection, and I want to know who's tampering with it.'

'Have you any ideas yourself?'

'You think I ought to have, heh?'

'Well, it would seem that the principal possibility — '

'I know. You want me to say it's the little girl. Well, I don't think it *is* the little girl. She says she didn't, and I believe her. Understand?'

'Yes,' said Poirot with a slight sigh, 'I understand.'

'For one thing she's too young. She wouldn't know these things were important. It's before her time.'

'Someone else might have instructed her as to that,' Poirot pointed out.

'Yes, yes, that's true enough. But it's too obvious as well.'

Poirot sighed. He doubted if it was any use insisting in view of Sir Roderick's obvious partiality. 'Who else had access?'

'Andrew and Mary, of course, but I doubt if Andrew would even be interested in such things. Anyway, he's always been a very decent boy. Always was. Not that I've ever known him very well. Used to come for the holidays once or twice with his brother and that's about all. Of course, he ditched his wife, and went off with an attractive bit of goods to South Africa, but that might happen to any man, especially with a wife like Grace. Not that I ever saw much of her, either. Kind of woman who looked down her nose and was full of good works. Anyway you can't imagine a chap like Andrew being a spy. As for Mary, she seems all right. Never looks at anything but a rose bush as far as I can make out. There's a gardener but he's eighty-three and has lived in the village all his life, and there are a couple of women always dodging about the house making a noise with Hoovers, but I can't see them in the role of spies either. So you see it's got to be an outsider. Of course Mary wears a wig,' went on Sir Roderick rather inconsequently. 'I mean it might make you think she was a spy because she wore a wig, but that's not the case. She lost her hair in a fever when she was eighteen. Pretty bad luck for a young woman. I'd no idea she wore a wig to begin with but a rose bush caught in her hair one day and whisked it sideways. Yes, very bad luck.'

'I thought there was something a little odd about the way she had arranged her hair,' said Poirot.

'Anyway, the best secret agents never wear wigs,' Sir Roderick informed him. 'Poor devils have to go to plastic surgeons and get their faces altered. But someone's been mucking about with my private papers.'

'You don't think that you may perhaps have placed them in some different container — in a drawer or a different file. When did you see them last?'

'I handled these things about a year ago. I remember I thought then, they'd make rather good copy, and I noted those particular letters. Now they're gone. Somebody's taken them.'

'You do not suspect your nephew Andrew, his wife or the domestic staff. What about the daughter?'

'Norma? Well Norma's a bit off her onion, I'd say. I mean she *might* be one of those kleptomaniacs who take people's things without knowing they're taking them but I don't see her fumbling about among my papers.'

'Then what *do* you think?'

'Well, you've been in the house. You saw what the house is like. Anyone can walk in and out any time they like. We don't lock our doors. We never have.'

'Do you lock the door of your own room — if you go up to London, for instance?'

'I never thought of it as necessary. I do now of course, but what's the use of that? Too late. Anyway, I've only an ordinary key, fits any of the doors. Someone must have come in from outside. Why nowadays that's how all the burglaries take place. People walk in in the middle of the day, stump up the stairs, go into any room they like, rifle the jewel box, go out again, and nobody sees them or cares who they are. They probably look like mods or rockers or beatniks or whatever they call these chaps nowadays with the long hair and the dirty nails. I've seen more than one of them prowling about. One doesn't like to say 'Who the devil are you?' You never know which sex they are, which is embarrassing. The place crawls with them. I suppose they're Norma's friends. Wouldn't have been allowed in the old days. But you turn them out of the house, and then you find out it's Viscount Endersleigh or Lady Charlotte Marjoribanks. Don't know where you are nowadays.' He paused. 'If anyone can get to the bottom of it, you can, Poirot.' He swallowed the last mouthful of whisky and got up.

'Well, that's that. It's up to you. You'll take it on, won't you?'

'I will do my best,' said Poirot.

The front-door bell rang.

'That's the little girl,' said Sir Roderick. 'Punctual to the minute. Wonderful, isn't it? Couldn't go about London without her, you know. Blind as a bat. Can't see to cross the road.'

'Can you not have glasses?'

'I've got some somewhere, but they're always falling off my nose or else I lose them. Besides, I don't like glasses. I've never had glasses. When I was sixty-five I could see to read without glasses and that's pretty good.'

'Nothing,' said Hercule Poirot, 'lasts for ever.'

George ushered in Sonia. She was looking extremely pretty. Her slightly shy manner became her very well, Poirot thought. He moved forward with Gallic *empressement*.

'*Enchanté*, Mademoiselle,' he said, bowing over her hand.

'I'm not late, am I, Sir Roderick,' she said, looking past him. 'I have not kept you waiting. Please I hope not.'

'Exactly to the minute, little girl,' said Sir Roderick. 'All ship-shape and Bristol fashion,' he added.

Sonia looked slightly perplexed.

'Made a good tea, I hope,' Sir Roderick went on. 'I told you, you know, to have a good tea, buy yourself some buns or éclairs or whatever it is young ladies like nowadays, eh? You obeyed orders, I hope.'

'No, not exactly. I took the time to buy a pair of shoes. Look, they are pretty, are they not?' She stuck out a foot.

It was certainly a very pretty foot. Sir Roderick beamed at it.

'Well, we must go and catch our train,' he said. 'I may be old-fashioned but I'm all for trains. Start to time and get there on time, or they should do. But these cars, they get in a queue in the rush hour and you may idle the time away for about an hour and a half more than you need. Cars! Pah!'

'Shall I ask Georges to get you a taxi?' asked Hercule Poirot. 'It will be no trouble, I assure you.'

'I have a taxi already waiting,' said Sonia.

'There you are,' said Sir Roderick, 'you see, she thinks of everything.' He patted her on the shoulder. She looked at him in a way that Hercule Poirot fully appreciated.

Poirot accompanied them to the hall door and took a polite leave of them. Mr Goby had come out of the kitchen and was standing in the hall giving, it could be said, an excellent performance of a man who had come to see about the gas.

George shut the hall door as soon as they had disappeared into the lift, and turned to meet Poirot's gaze.

'And what is your opinion of that young lady, Georges, may I ask?' said Poirot. On certain points he always said George was infallible.

'Well, sir,' said George, 'if I might put it that way, if you'll allow me, I would say he'd got it badly, sir. All over her as you might say.'

'I think you are right,' said Hercule Poirot.
'It's not unusual of course with gentlemen
of that age. I remember Lord Mountbryan.
He'd had a lot of experience in his life and
you'd say he was as fly as anyone. But you'd
be surprised. A young woman as came to give
him massage. You'd be surprised at what he
gave her. An evening frock, and a pretty
bracelet. Forget-me-nots, it was. Turquoise
and diamonds. Not *too* expensive but costing
quite a pretty penny all the same. Then a fur
wrap — not mink, Russian ermine, and a
petty point evening bag. After that her
brother got into trouble, debt or something,
though whether she ever *had* a brother I
sometimes wondered. Lord Mountbryan gave
her the money to square it — she was so
upset about it! All platonic, mind you, too.
Gentlemen seem to lose their sense that way
when they get to that age. It's the clinging
ones they go for, not the bold type.'

'I have no doubt that you are quite right,
Georges,' said Poirot. 'It is all the same not a
complete answer to my question. I asked
what you thought of the *young lady*.'

'Oh, the young lady . . . Well, sir, I wouldn't
like to say definitely, but she's quite a definite
type. There's never anything that you could
put your finger on. But they know what
they're doing, I'd say.'

Poirot entered his sitting-room and Mr Goby followed him, obeying Poirot's gesture. Mr Goby sat down on an upright chair in his usual attitude. Knees together, toes turned in. He took a rather dog-eared little notebook from his pocket, opened it carefully and then proceeded to survey the soda water siphon severely.

'Re the backgrounds you asked me to look up.

'Restarick family, perfectly respectable and of good standing. No scandal. The father, James Patrick Restarick, said to be a sharp man over a bargain. Business has been in the family three generations. Grandfather founded it, father enlarged it, Simon Restarick kept it going. Simon Restarick had coronary trouble two years ago, health declined. Died of coronary thrombosis, about a year ago.

'Young brother Andrew Restarick came into the business soon after he came down from Oxford, married Miss Grace Baldwin. One daughter, Norma. Left his wife and went out to South Africa. A Miss Birell went with him. No divorce proceedings. Mrs Andrew Restarick died two and a half years ago. Had been an invalid for some time. Miss Norma Restarick was a boarder at Meadowfield Girls' School. Nothing against her.'

Allowing his eyes to sweep across Hercule

Poirot's face, Mr Goby observed, 'In fact everything about the family seems quite OK and according to Cocker.'

'No black sheep, no mental instability?'

'It doesn't appear so.'

'Disappointing,' said Poirot.

Mr Goby let this pass. He cleared his throat, licked his finger, and turned over a leaf of his little book.

'David Baker. Unsatisfactory record. Been on probation twice. Police are inclined to be interested in him. He's been on the fringe of several rather dubious affairs, thought to have been concerned in an important art robbery but no proof. He's one of the arty lot. No particular means of subsistence but he does quite well. Prefers girls with money. Not above living on some of the girls who are keen on him. Not above being paid off by their fathers either. Thorough bad lot if you ask me but enough brains to keep himself out of trouble.'

Mr Goby shot a sudden glance at Poirot.

'You met him?'

'Yes,' said Poirot.

'What conclusions did you form, if I may ask?'

'The same as you,' said Poirot. 'A gaudy creature,' he added thoughtfully.

'Appeals to women,' said Mr Goby.

'Trouble is nowadays they won't look twice at a nice hard-working lad. They prefer the bad lots — the scroungers. They usually say 'he hasn't had a *chance*, poor boy'.'

'Strutting about like peacocks,' said Poirot.

'Well, you might put it like that,' said Mr Goby, rather doubtfully.

'Do you think he'd use a cosh on anyone?'

Mr Goby thought, then very slowly shook his head at the electric fire.

'Nobody's accused him of anything like that. I don't say he'd be past it, but I wouldn't say it was his line. He is a smooth-spoken type, not one for the rough stuff.'

'No,' said Poirot, 'no, I should not have thought so. He could be bought off? That was your opinion?'

'He'd drop any girl like a hot coal if it was made worth his while.'

Poirot nodded. He was remembering something. Andrew Restarick turning a cheque towards him so that he could read the signature on it. It was not only the signature that Poirot had read, it was the person to whom the cheque was made out. It had been made out to David Baker and it was for a large sum. Would David Baker demur at taking such a cheque, Poirot wondered. He thought not on the whole. Mr Goby clearly was of that opinion. Undesirable young men had been bought off in any time or age, so had undesirable young women. Sons had sworn and daughters had wept but money was money. To Norma, David had been urging marriage. Was he sincere? Could it be that he really cared for Norma? If so, he would not be so easily paid off. He had sounded genuine enough. Norma no doubt believed him genuine. Andrew Restarick and Mr Goby and Hercule Poirot thought differently. They were very much more likely to be right.

Mr Goby cleared his throat and went on.

'Miss Claudia Reece-Holland? She's all right. Nothing against her. Nothing dubious, that is. Father a Member of Parliament, well off. No scandals. Not like some MPs we've heard about. Educated Roedean, Lady Margaret Hall, came down and did a secretarial course. First secretary to a doctor in Harley Street, then went to the Coal Board. First-class secretary. Has been secretary to Mr Restarick for the last two months. No special attachments, just what you'd call minor boy friends. Eligible and useful if she wants a date. Nothing to show there's anything between her and Restarick. I shouldn't say there is, myself. Has had a flat in Borodene Mansions for the last three years. Quite a high rent there. She usually has two other girls sharing it, no special friends. They come and go. Young lady, Frances Cary, the second girl, has been there some time. Was at RADA for a time, then went to the Slade. Works for the Wedderburn Gallery — well-known place in Bond Street. Specialises in arranging art shows in Manchester, Birmingham, sometimes abroad. Goes to Switzerland and Portugal. Arty type and has a lot of friends amongst artists and actors.'

He paused, cleared his throat and gave a brief look at the little notebook.

'Haven't been able to get much from South Africa yet. Don't suppose I shall. Restarick moved about a lot. Kenya, Uganda, Gold Coast, South America for a while. He just moved about. Restless chap. Nobody seems to have known him particularly well. He'd got plenty of money of his own to go where he liked. He made money, too, quite a lot of it. Liked going to out of the way places. Everyone who came across him seems to have liked him. Just seems as though he was a born wanderer. He never kept in touch with anyone. Three times I believe he was reported dead — gone off into the bush and not turned up again — but he always did in the end. Five or six months and he'd pop up in some entirely different place or country.

'Then last year his brother in London died suddenly. They had a bit of trouble in tracing him. His brother's death seemed to give him a shock. Perhaps he'd had enough, and perhaps he'd met the right woman at last. Good bit younger than him, she was, and a teacher, they say. The steady kind. Anyway he seems to have made up his mind then and there to chuck wandering about, and come home to England. Besides being a very rich man himself, he's his brother's heir.'

'A success story and an unhappy girl,' said Poirot. 'I wish I knew more about her. You have ascertained for me all that you could, the facts I needed. The people who surrounded that girl, who might have influenced her, who perhaps *did* influence her. I wanted to know something about her father, her stepmother, the boy she is in love with, the people she lived with, and worked for in London. You are sure that in connection with this girl there have been no deaths? That is important — '

'Not a smell of one,' said Mr Goby. 'She worked for a firm called Homebirds — on the verge of bankruptcy, and they didn't pay her much. Stepmother was in hospital for observation recently — in the country, that was. A lot of rumours flying about, but they didn't seem to come to anything.'

'She did not die,' said Poirot. 'What I need,' he added in a bloodthirsty manner, 'is a *death*.'

Mr Goby said he was sorry about that and rose to his feet. 'Will there be anything more you are wanting at present?'

'Not in the nature of information.'

'Very good, sir.' As he replaced his notebook in his pocket, Mr Goby said: 'You'll excuse me, sir, if I'm speaking out of turn, but that young lady you had here just now — '

'Yes, what about her?'

'Well, of course it's — I don't suppose it's anything to do with this, but I thought I might just mention it to you, sir — '

'Please do. You have seen her before, I gather?'

'Yes. Couple of months ago.'

'Where did you see her?'

'Kew Gardens.'

'Kew Gardens?' Poirot looked slightly surprised.

'I wasn't following *her*. I was following someone else, the person who met her.'

'And who was that?'

'I don't suppose as it matters mentioning it to you, sir. It was one of the junior attachés of the Hertzogovinian Embassy.'

Poirot raised his eyebrows. 'That is interesting. Yes, very interesting. Kew Gardens,' he mused. 'A pleasant place for a rendezvous. Very pleasant.'

'I thought so at the time.'

'They talked together?'

'No, sir, you wouldn't have said they knew each other. The young lady had a book with her. She sat down on a seat. She read the book for a little then she laid it down beside her. Then my bloke came and sat there on the seat also. They didn't speak — only the young lady got up and wandered away. He just sat there and presently he gets up and walks off. He takes with him the book that the young lady has left behind. That's all, sir.'

'Yes,' said Poirot. 'It is very interesting.'

Mr Goby looked at the bookcase and said good night to it. He went.

Poirot gave an exasperated sigh.

'*Enfin*,' he said, 'it is too much! There is far too much. Now we have espionage and counter espionage. All I am seeking is one perfectly simple murder. I begin to suspect that that murder only occurred in a drug addict's brain!'

# 14

'*Chère* Madame,' Poirot bowed and presented Mrs Oliver with a bouquet, very
stylised, a posy in the Victorian manner.

'M. Poirot! Well, really, that is very nice of
you, and it's very like you somehow. All
my flowers are always so untidy.' She looked
towards a vase of rather temperamental-
looking chrysanthemums, then back to the
prim circle of rosebuds. 'And how nice of you
to come and see me.'

'I come, Madame, to offer you my
felicitations on your recovery.'

'Yes,' said Mrs Oliver, 'I suppose I am all
right again.' She shook her head to and fro
rather gingerly. 'I get headaches, though,' she
said. 'Quite bad headaches.'

'You remember, Madame, that I warned
you not to do anything dangerous.'

'Not to stick my neck out, in fact. That I
suppose is just what I did do.' She added,
'I felt something evil was about. I was
frightened, too, and I told myself I was a fool
to be frightened, because what was I
frightened of? I mean, it was London. Right
in the middle of London. People all about. I

mean — how *could* I be frightened? It wasn't like a lonely wood or anything.'

Poirot looked at her thoughtfully. He wondered, had Mrs Oliver really felt this nervous fear, had she really suspected the presence of evil, the sinister feeling that something or someone wished her ill, or had she read it into the whole thing afterwards? He knew only too well how easily that could be done. Countless clients had spoken in much the same words that Mrs Oliver had just used. 'I knew something was wrong. I could feel evil. I knew something was going to happen,' and actually they had not felt anything of the kind. What kind of a person was Mrs Oliver?

He looked at her consideringly. Mrs Oliver in her own opinion was famous for her intuition. One intuition succeeded another with remarkable rapidity and Mrs Oliver always claimed the right to justify the particular intuition which turned out to be right!

And yet one shared very often with animals the uneasiness of a dog or a cat before a thunderstorm, the knowledge that there is *something* wrong, although one does not know what it is that is wrong.

'When did it come upon you, this fear?'

'When I left the main road,' said Mrs

Oliver. 'Up till then it was all ordinary and quite exciting and — yes, I was enjoying myself, though vexed at finding how difficult it was to trail anybody.'

She paused, considering. 'Just like a *game*. Then suddenly it didn't seem so much like a game, because there were queer little streets and rather sort of broken-down places, and sheds and open spaces being cleared for building — oh, I don't know, I can't explain it. But it was all *different*. Like a dream really. You know how dreams are. They start with one thing, a party or something, and then suddenly you find you're in a jungle or somewhere quite different — and it's all sinister.'

'A jungle?' said Poirot. 'Yet, it is interesting you should put it like that. So it felt to you as though you were in a jungle and you were afraid of a peacock?'

'I don't know that I was especially afraid of him. After all, a peacock isn't a dangerous sort of animal. It's — well I mean I thought of him as a peacock because I thought of him as a *decorative* creature. A peacock is very decorative, isn't it? And this awful boy is decorative too.'

'You didn't have any idea anyone was following you before you were hit?'

'No. No, I'd no idea — but I think he

directed me wrong all the same.'

Poirot nodded thoughtfully.

'But of course it must have been the Peacock who hit me,' said Mrs Oliver. 'Who else? The dirty boy in the greasy clothes? He smelt nasty but he wasn't sinister. And it could hardly be that limp Frances something — she was draped over a packing case with long black hair streaming all over the place. She reminded me of some actress or other.'

'You say she was acting as a model?'

'Yes. Not for the Peacock. For the dirty boy. I can't remember if you've seen her or not.'

'I have not yet had that pleasure — if it is a pleasure.'

'Well, she's quite nice looking in an untidy, arty sort of way. Very much made up. Dead white and lots of mascara and the usual kind of limp hair hanging over her face. Works in an art gallery so I suppose it's quite natural that she should be all among the beatniks, acting as a model. How these girls *can*! I suppose she *might* have fallen for the Peacock. But it's probably the dirty one. All the same I don't see her coshing me on the head somehow.'

'I had another possibility in mind, Madame. Someone may have noticed you following David — and in turn followed you.'

'Someone saw *me* trailing David, and then they trailed *me*?'

'Or someone may have been already in the mews or the yard, keeping perhaps an eye on the same people that you were observing.'

'That's an idea, of course,' said Mrs Oliver. 'I wonder who they could be?'

Poirot gave an exasperated sigh. 'Ah, it is there. It is difficult — too difficult. Too many people, too many things. I cannot see anything clearly. I see only a girl who said that she may have committed a murder! That is all that I have to go on and you see even there there are difficulties.'

'What do you mean by difficulties?'

'Reflect,' said Poirot.

Reflection had never been Mrs Oliver's strong point.

'You always mix me up,' she complained.

'I am talking about a murder, but what murder?'

'The murder of the stepmother, I suppose.'

'But the stepmother is not murdered. She is alive.'

'You really are the most maddening man,' said Mrs Oliver.

Poirot sat up in his chair. He brought the tips of his fingers together and prepared — or so Mrs Oliver suspected — to enjoy himself.

'You refuse to reflect,' he said. 'But to get

anywhere we *must* reflect.'

'I don't want to reflect. What I want to know is what you've been doing about everything while I've been in hospital. You must have done *something*. What *have* you done?'

Poirot ignored this question.

'We must begin at the beginning. One day you ring me up. I was in distress. Yes, I admit it, I was in distress. Something extremely painful had been said to me. You, Madame, were kindness itself. You cheered me, you encouraged me. You gave me a delicious *tasse de chocolat*. And what is more you not only offered to help me, but you *did* help me. You helped me to find a girl who had come to me and said that she thought she might have committed a murder! Let us ask ourselves, Madame, what about this murder? Who has been murdered? Where have they been murdered? Why have they been murdered?'

'Oh do stop,' said Mrs Oliver. 'You're making my head ache again, and that's bad for me.'

Poirot paid no attention to this plea. 'Have we got a murder at all? You say — the stepmother — but I reply that the stepmother is not dead — so as yet we *have* no murder. But there *ought* to have been a murder. So me, I inquire first of all, *who* is dead?

212

Somebody comes to me and mentions a murder. A murder that has been committed somewhere and somehow. But I cannot *find* that murder, and what you are about to say once again, that the attempted murder of Mary Restarick will do very well, does not satisfy Hercule Poirot.'

'I really can't think what more you want,' said Mrs Oliver.

'*I want a murder*,' said Hercule Poirot.

'It sounds very bloodthirsty when you say it like that!'

'I look for a murder and I cannot find a murder. It is exasperating — so I ask you to reflect with me.'

'I've got a splendid idea,' said Mrs Oliver. 'Suppose Andrew Restarick murdered his first wife before he went off in a hurry to South Africa. Had you thought of that possibility?'

'I certainly did not think of any such thing,' said Poirot indignantly.

'Well, *I've* thought of it,' said Mrs Oliver. 'It's very interesting. He was in love with this other woman, and he wanted like Crippen to go off with her, and so he murdered the first one and nobody ever suspected.'

Poirot drew a long, exasperated sigh. '*But his wife did not die until eleven or twelve years after he'd left this country for South*

213

Africa, and his child could not have been concerned in the murder of her own mother at the age of five years old.'

'She could have given her mother the wrong medicine or perhaps Restarick just said that she died. After all, we don't *know* that she's dead.'

'I do,' said Hercule Poirot. 'I have made inquiries. The first Mrs Restarick died on the 14th April, 1963.'

'How can you know these things?'

'Because I have employed someone to check the facts. I beg of you, Madame, do not jump to impossible conclusions in this rash way.'

'I thought I was being rather clever,' said Mrs Oliver obstinately. 'If I was making it happen in a book that's how *I* would arrange it. And I'd make the child have done it. Not meaning to, but just by her father telling her to give her mother a drink made of pounded up box hedge.'

'*Non d'un nom d'un nom!*' said Poirot.

'All right,' said Mrs Oliver. 'You tell it your way.'

'Alas, I have nothing to tell. I look for a murder and I do not find one.'

'Not after Mary Restarick is ill and goes to hospital and gets better and comes back and is ill again, and if they looked they'd probably find arsenic or something hidden away by Norma somewhere.'

'That is exactly what they did find.'

'Well, really, M. Poirot, what *more* do you want?'

'I want you to pay some attention to the meaning of language. That girl said to me the same thing as she had said to my manservant, Georges. She did not say on either occasion 'I have tried to kill someone' or 'I have tried to kill my stepmother.' She spoke each time of a deed that *had* been *done*, something that had already *happened*. Definitely *happened*. In the *past* tense.'

'I give up,' said Mrs Oliver. 'You just won't believe that Norma tried to kill her stepmother.'

'Yes, I believe it is perfectly possible that Norma may have tried to kill her stepmother. I think it is probably what happened — it is in accord psychologically. With her distraught frame of mind. But it is not *proved*. Anyone, remember, could have hidden a preparation of arsenic amongst Norma's things. It could even have been put there by the husband.'

'You always seem to think that husbands are the ones who kill their wives,' said Mrs Oliver.

'A husband is usually the most likely person,' said Hercule Poirot, 'so one considers him first. It could have been the girl,

Norma, or it could have been one of the servants, or it could have been the *au pair* girl, or it could have been old Sir Roderick. Or it could have been *Mrs Restarick herself.*'

'Nonsense. Why?'

'There *could* be reasons. Rather far-fetched reasons, but not beyond the bounds of belief.'

'Really, Monsieur Poirot, you can't suspect *everybody.*'

'*Mais oui*, that is just what I can do. I suspect everybody. First I suspect, then I look for reasons.'

'And what reason would that poor foreign child have?'

'It might depend on what she is doing in that house, and what her reasons are for coming to England and a good deal more beside.'

'You're really crazy.'

'Or it could have been the boy David. Your Peacock.'

'Much too far-fetched. David wasn't there. He's never been near the house.'

'Oh yes he has. He was wandering about its corridors the day I went there.'

'But not putting poison in Norma's room.'

'How do you know?'

'But she and that awful boy are in love with each other.'

'They appear to be so, I admit.'

'You always want to make everything difficult,' complained Mrs Oliver.

'Not at all. Things have been made difficult for *me*. I need information and there is only one person who can give me information. And she has disappeared.'

'You mean Norma.'

'Yes, I mean Norma.'

'But she hasn't disappeared. We found her, you and I.'

'She walked out of that café and once more she has disappeared.'

'And you let her go?' Mrs Oliver's voice quivered with reproach.

'Alas!'

'*You let her go?* You didn't even try to find her again?'

'I did not say I had not tried to find her.'

'But so far you have not succeeded. M. Poirot, I really am disappointed with you.'

'There is a pattern,' said Hercule Poirot almost dreamily. 'Yes, there is a pattern. But because there is one factor missing, the pattern does not make sense. You see that, don't you?'

'No,' said Mrs Oliver, whose head was aching.

Poirot continued to talk more to himself than his listener. If Mrs Oliver could be said to be listening. She was highly indignant with

Poirot and she thought to herself that the Restarick girl had been quite right and that Poirot *was* too old! There, she herself had found the girl for him, had telephoned him so that he might arrive in time, had gone off herself to shadow the other half of the couple. She had left the girl to Poirot, and what had Poirot done — lost her! In fact she could not really see that Poirot had done anything at all of any use at any time whatever. She was disappointed in him. When he stopped talking she would tell him so again.

Poirot was quietly and methodically outlining what he called 'the pattern'.

'It interlocks. Yes, it interlocks and that is why it is difficult. One thing relates to another and then you find that it relates to something else that seems outside the pattern. But it is not outside the pattern. And so it brings more people again into a ring of suspicion. Suspicion of what? There again one does not know. We have first the girl and through all the maze of conflicting patterns I have to search the answer to the most poignant of questions. Is the girl a victim, is she in danger? Or is the girl very astute? Is the girl creating the impression she wants to create for her own purposes? It can be taken either way. I need something still. Some one sure pointer, and it is *there* somewhere. I am sure

218

it is there somewhere.'

Mrs Oliver was rummaging in her handbag.

'I can't think why I can never find my aspirin when I want it,' she said in a vexed voice.

'We have one set of relationships that hook up. The father, the daughter, the stepmother. Their lives are interrelated. We have the elderly uncle, somewhat gaga, with whom they live. We have the girl Sonia. She is linked with the uncle. She works for him. She has pretty manners, pretty ways. He is delighted with her. He is, shall we say, a little soft about her. But what is her role in the household?'

'Wants to learn English, I suppose,' said Mrs Oliver.

'She meets one of the members of the Herzogovinian Embassy — in Kew Gardens. She meets him there, but she does not speak to him. She leaves behind her a book and he takes it away — '

'What is all this?' said Mrs Oliver.

'Has this anything to do with the other pattern? We do not as yet know. It seems unlikely but it may not be unlikely. Had Mary Restarick unwittingly stumbled upon something which might be dangerous to the girl?'

'Don't tell me all this has something to do

with *espionage* or something.'

'I am not telling you. I am wondering.'

'You said yourself that old Sir Roderick was gaga.'

'It is not a question of whether he is gaga or not. He was a person of some importance during the war. Important papers passed through his hands. Important letters can have been written to him. Letters which he was at perfect liberty to have kept once they had lost their importance.'

'You're talking of the war and that was ages ago.'

'Quite so. But the past is not always done with, because it is ages ago. New alliances are made. Public speeches are made repudiating this, denying that, telling various lies about something else. And suppose there exist still certain letters or documents that will change the picture of a certain personality. I am not telling you anything, you understand. I am only making assumptions. Assumptions such as I have known to be true in the past. It might be of the utmost importance that some letters or papers should be destroyed, or else passed to some foreign government. Who better to undertake that task than a charming young lady who assists and aids an elderly notability to collect material for his memoirs. Everyone is writing their memoirs nowadays.

One cannot stop them from doing so! Suppose that the stepmother gets a little something in her food on the day that the helpful secretary plus *au pair* girl is doing the cooking? And suppose it is she who arranges that suspicion should fall on Norma?'

'What a mind you have,' said Mrs Oliver. 'Tortuous, that's what I call it. I mean, *all* these things can't have happened.'

'That is just it. There are too many patterns. Which is the right one? The girl Norma leaves home, goes to London. She is, as you have instructed me, a third girl sharing a flat with two other girls. There again you may have a pattern. The two girls are strangers to her. But then what do I learn? Claudia Reece-Holland is private secretary to Norma Restarick's father. Here again we have a *link*. Is that mere chance? Or could there be a pattern of some kind behind it? The other girl, you tell me, acts as a model, and is acquainted with the boy you call 'the Peacock' with whom Norma is in love. Again a link. More links. And what is David — the Peacock — doing in all this? Is he in love with Norma? It would seem so. Her parents dislike it as is only probable and natural.'

'It's odd about Claudia Reece-Holland being Restarick's secretary,' said Mrs Oliver thoughtfully. 'I should judge she was unusually efficient at anything she undertook. Perhaps it was she who pushed the woman out of the window on the seventh floor.'

Poirot turned slowly towards her.

'What are you saying?' he demanded. 'What are you saying?'

'Just someone in the flats — I don't even know her name, but she fell out of a window or threw herself out of a window on the seventh floor and killed herself.'

Poirot's voice rose high and stern.

'And you never told me?' he said accusingly.

Mrs Oliver stared at him in surprise.

'I don't know what you mean.'

'What I mean? I ask you to tell me of a death. That is what I mean. *A death*. And you say there are no deaths. You can think only of an attempted poisoning. *And yet here is a death*. A death at — what is the name of those mansions?'

'Borodene Mansions.'

'Yes, yes. And when did it happen?'

'This suicide? Or whatever it was? I think — yes — I think it was about a week before I went there.'

'Perfect! How did you hear about it?'

'A milkman told me.'

'A milkman, *bon Dieu*!'

'He was just being chatty,' said Mrs Oliver.

'It sounded rather sad. It was in the daytime — very early in the morning, I think.'

'What was her name?'

'I've no idea. I don't think he mentioned it.'

'Young, middle-aged, old?'

Mrs Oliver considered. 'Well, he didn't say her exact age. Fifty-ish, I think, was what he said.'

'I wonder now. Anyone the three girls knew?'

'How can I tell? Nobody has said anything about it.'

'And you never thought of telling me.'

'Well, really, M. Poirot, I cannot say that it has anything to do with all this. Well, I suppose it may have — but nobody seems to have said so, or thought of it.'

'But yes, there is the link. There is this girl, Norma, and she lives in those flats, and one day somebody commits suicide (for that, I gather, was the general impression). That is, somebody throws herself or falls out of a seventh-floor high window *and is killed*. And then? Some days later this girl Norma, after having heard you talk about me at a party, comes to call upon me and she says to me that she is afraid that she may have committed a murder. Do you not see? A death — and not many days later someone who thinks she may have committed a murder. Yes, *this must be the murder.*'

Mrs Oliver wanted to say 'Nonsense' but she did not quite dare to do so. Nevertheless, she thought it.

'This then must be the one piece of knowledge that had not yet come to me. This ought to tie up the whole thing! Yes, yes, I do not see yet *how*, but *it must be so.* I must think. That is what I must do. I must go home and think until slowly the pieces fit together — because this will be the key piece that ties them all together . . . Yes. At last. At last I shall see my way.'

He rose to his feet and said, '*Adieu, chère Madame,*' and hurried from the room. Mrs Oliver at last relieved her feelings.

'Nonsense,' she said to the empty room. 'Absolute nonsense. I wonder if four would be too many aspirins to take?'

# 15

At Hercule Poirot's elbow was a tisane prepared for him by George. He sipped at it and thought. He thought in a certain way peculiar to himself. It was the technique of a man who selected thoughts as one might select pieces of a jigsaw puzzle. In due course they would be reassembled together so as to make a clear and coherent picture. At the moment the important thing was the selection, the separation. He sipped his tisane, put down the cup, rested his hands on the arms of his chair and let various pieces of his puzzle come one by one into his mind. Once he recognised them all, he would select. Pieces of sky, pieces of green bank, perhaps striped pieces like those of a tiger . . .

The painfulness of his own feet in patent-leather shoes. He started there. Walking along a road set on this path by his good friend, Mrs Oliver. A stepmother. He saw himself with his hand on a gate. A woman who turned, a woman bending her head cutting out the weak growth of a rose, turning and looking at him? What was there for him there? Nothing. A golden head, a golden head bright as a cornfield, with twists and loops of hair slightly reminiscent of Mrs Oliver's own in shape. He smiled a little. But Mary Restarick's hair was more tidily arranged than Mrs Oliver's ever was. A golden frame for her face that seemed just a little too large for her. He remembered that old Sir Roderick had said that she had to wear a wig, because of an illness. Sad for so young a woman. There was, when he came to think of it, something unusually heavy about her head. Far too static, too perfectly arranged. He considered Mary Restarick's wig — if it was a wig — for he was by no means sure that he could depend on Sir Roderick. He examined the possibilities of the wig in case they should be of significance. He reviewed the conversation they had had. Had they said anything important? He thought not. He remembered the room into which they had gone. A characterless room recently inhabited in someone else's house. Two pictures on the wall, the picture of a woman in a dove-grey dress. Thin mouth, lips set closely together. Hair that was greyish brown. The first Mrs Restarick. She looked as though she might have been older than her husband. His picture was on the opposite wall, facing her. Good portraits, both of them. Lansberger had been a good portrait painter. His mind dwelt on the portrait of the husband. He had not seen it so well that first day, as he had later in Restarick's office . . .

Andrew Restarick and Claudia Reece-Holland. Was there anything there? Was their association more than a merely secretarial one? It need not be. Here was a man who had come back to this country after years of absence, who had no near friends or relatives, who was perplexed and troubled over his daughter's character and conduct. It was probably natural enough that he should turn to his recently acquired eminently competent secretary and ask her to suggest somewhere for his daughter to live in London. It would be a favour on her part to provide that accommodation since she was looking for a Third Girl. Third girl . . . The phrase that he had acquired from Mrs Oliver always seemed to be coming to his mind. As though it had a second significance which for some reason he could not see.

His manservant, George, entered the room, closing the door discreetly behind him.

'A young lady is here, sir. The young lady who came the other day.'

The words came too aptly with what Poirot was thinking. He sat up in a startled fashion.

'The young lady who came at breakfast time?'

'Oh no, sir. I mean the young lady who came with Sir Roderick Horsefield.'

'Ah, indeed.'

Poirot raised his eyebrows. 'Bring her in. Where is she?'

'I showed her into Miss Lemon's room, sir.'

'Ah. Yes, bring her in.'

Sonia did not wait for George to announce her. She came into the room ahead of him with a quick and rather aggressive step.

'It has been difficult for me to get away, but I have come to tell you that I did not take those papers. I did not steal anything. You understand?'

'Has anybody said that you had?' Poirot asked. 'Sit down, Mademoiselle.'

'I do not want to sit down. I have very little time. I just came to tell you that it is absolutely untrue. I am very honest and I do what I am told.'

'I take your point. I have already taken it. Your statement is that you have not removed any papers, information, letters, documents of any kind from Sir Roderick Horsefield's house? That is so, is it not?'

'Yes, and I've come to tell you it is so. *He* believes me. *He* knows that I would not do such a thing.'

'Very well then. That is a statement and I note it.'

228

'Do you think you are going to find those papers?'

'I have other inquiries in hand,' said Poirot. 'Sir Roderick's papers will have to take their turn.'

'He is worried. He is very worried. There is something that I cannot say to him. I will say it to you. *He loses things.* Things are not put away where he thinks they are. He puts them in — how do you say it — in funny places. Oh I know. You suspect me. Everyone suspects me because I am foreign. Because I come from a foreign country and so they think — they think I steal secret papers like in one of your silly English spy stories. I am not like that. I am an intellectual.'

'Aha,' said Poirot. 'It is always nice to know.' He added: 'Is there anything else you wish to tell me?'

'Why should I?'

'One never knows.'

'What are these other cases you speak of?'

'Ah, I do not want to detain you. It is your day out, perhaps.'

'Yes. I have one day a week when I can do what I like. I can come to London. I can go to the British Museum.'

'Ah yes and to the Victoria and Albert also, no doubt.'

'That is so.'

'And to the National Gallery and see the pictures. And on a fine day you can go to Kensington Gardens, or perhaps as far as Kew Gardens.'

She stiffened . . . She shot him an angry questioning glance.

'Why do you say Kew Gardens?'

'Because there are some very fine plants and shrubs and trees there. Ah! you should not miss Kew Gardens. The admission fee is very small. A penny I think, or twopence. And for that you can go and see tropical trees, or you can sit on a seat and read a book.' He smiled at her disarmingly and was interested to notice that her uneasiness was increased. 'But I must not detain you, Mademoiselle. You have perhaps friends to visit at one of the Embassies, maybe.'

'Why do you say that?'

'No particular reason. You are, as you say, a foreigner and it is quite possible you may have friends connected with your own Embassy here.'

'Someone has told you things. Someone has made accusations against me! I tell you he is a silly old man who mislays things. That is all! And he knows nothing of importance. He has no secret papers or documents. He never has had.'

'Ah, but you are not quite thinking of what

you are saying. Time passes, you know. He was once an important man who did know important secrets.'

'You are trying to frighten me.'

'No, no. I am not being so melodramatic as that.'

'Mrs Restarick. It is Mrs Restarick who has been telling you things. She does not like me.'

'She has not said so to me.'

'Well, I do not like *her*. She is the kind of woman I mistrust. I think *she* has secrets.'

'Indeed?'

'Yes, I think she has secrets from her husband. I think she goes up to London or to other places to meet other men. To meet at any rate one other man.'

'Indeed,' said Poirot, 'that is very interesting. You think she goes to meet another man?'

'Yes, I do. She goes up to London very often and I do not think she always tells her husband, or she says it is shopping or things she has to buy. All those sort of things. He is busy in the office and he does not think of why his wife comes up. She is more in London than she is in the country. And yet she pretends to like gardening so much.'

'You have no idea who this man is whom she meets?'

'How should I know? I do not follow her. Mr Restarick is not a suspicious man. He

231

believes what his wife tells him. He thinks perhaps about business all the time. And, too, I think he is worried about his daughter.'

'Yes,' said Poirot, 'he is certainly worried about his daughter. How much do you know about the daughter? How well do you know her?'

'I do not know her very well. If you ask what I *think* — well, I tell you! I think she is mad.'

'You think she is mad? Why?'

'She says odd things sometimes. She sees things that are not there.'

'Sees things that are not there?'

'People that are not there. Sometimes she is very excited and other times she seems as though she is in a dream. You speak to her and she does not hear what you say to her. She does not answer. I think there are people who she would like to have dead.'

'You mean Mrs Restarick?'

'*And* her father. She looks at him as though she hates him.'

'Because they are both trying to prevent her marrying a young man of her choice?'

'Yes. They do not want that to happen. They are quite right, of course, but it makes her angry. Some day,' added Sonia, nodding her head cheerfully, 'I think she will kill herself. I hope she will do nothing so foolish, but that is the thing one does when one is much in love.' She shrugged her shoulders. 'Well — I go now.'

'Just tell me one thing. Does Mrs Restarick wear a wig?'

'A wig? How should I know?' She considered for a moment. 'She might, yes,' she admitted. 'It is useful for travelling. Also it is fashionable. I wear a wig myself sometimes. A *green* one! Or I did.' She added again, 'I go now,' and went.

# 16

'Today I have much to do,' Hercule Poirot announced as he rose from the breakfast table next morning and joined Miss Lemon. 'Inquiries to make. You have made the necessary researches for me, the appointments, the necessary contacts?'

'Certainly,' said Miss Lemon. 'It is all here.' She handed him a small briefcase. Poirot took a quick glance at its contents and nodded his head.

'I can always rely on you, Miss Lemon,' he said. '*C'est fantastique.*'

'Really, Monsieur Poirot, I cannot see anything fantastic about it. You gave me instructions and I carried them out. Naturally.'

'Pah, it is not so natural as that,' said Poirot. 'Do I not give instructions often to the gas men, the electricians, the man who comes to repair things, and do they always carry out my instructions? Very, very seldom.'

He went into the hall.

'My slightly heavier overcoat, Georges. I think the autumn chill is setting in.'

He popped his head back in his secretary's

room. 'By the way, what did you think of that young woman who came yesterday?'

Miss Lemon, arrested as she was about to plunge her fingers on the typewriter, said briefly, 'Foreign.'

'Yes, yes.'

'Obviously foreign.'

'You do not think anything more about her than that?'

Miss Lemon considered. 'I had no means of judging her capability in any way.' She added rather doubtfully, 'She seemed upset about something.'

'Yes. She is suspected, you see, of stealing! Not money, but papers, from her employer.'

'Dear, dear,' said Miss Lemon. 'Important papers?'

'It seems highly probable. It is equally probable though, that he has not lost anything at all.'

'Oh well,' said Miss Lemon, giving her employer a special look that she always gave and which announced that she wished to get rid of him so that she could get on with proper fervour with her work. 'Well, I always say that it's better to know where you are when you are employing someone, and buy British.'

Hercule Poirot went out. His first visit was to Borodene Mansions. He took a taxi.

Alighting at the courtyard he cast his eyes around. A uniformed porter was standing in one of the doorways, whistling a somewhat doleful melody. As Poirot advanced upon him, he said:

'Yes, sir?'

'I wondered,' said Poirot, 'if you can tell me anything about a very sad occurrence that took place here recently.'

'Sad occurrence?' said the porter. 'Nothing that I know of.'

'A lady who threw herself, or shall we say fell from one of the upper storeys, and was killed.'

'Oh, *that*. I don't know anything about that because I've only been here a week, you see. Hi, Joe.'

A porter emerging from the opposite side of the block came over.

'You'd know about the lady as fell from the seventh. About a month ago, was it?'

'Not quite as much as that,' said Joe. He was an elderly, slow-speaking man. 'Nasty business it was.'

'She was killed instantly?'

'Yes.'

'What was her name? It may, you understand, have been a relative of mine,' Poirot explained. He was not a man who had any scruples about departing from the truth.

'Indeed, sir. Very sorry to hear it. She was a Mrs Charpentier.'

'She had been in the flat some time?'

'Well, let me see now. About a year — a year and a half perhaps. No, I think it must have been about two years. No. 76, seventh floor.'

'That is the top floor?'

'Yes, sir. A Mrs Charpentier.'

Poirot did not press for any other descriptive information since he might be presumed to know such things about his own relative. Instead he asked:

'Did it cause much excitement, much questioning? What time of day was it?'

'Five or six o'clock in the morning, I think. No warning or anything. Just down she came. In spite of being so early we got a crowd almost at once, pushing through the railing over there. You know what people are.'

'And the police, of course.'

'Oh yes, the police came quite quickly. And a doctor and an ambulance. All the usual,' said the porter rather in the weary tone of one who had had people throwing themselves out of a seventh-storey window once or twice every month.

'And I suppose people came down from the flats when they heard what had happened.'

'Oh, there wasn't so many coming from the flats because for one thing with the noise of traffic and everything around here most of them didn't know about it. Someone or other said she gave a bit of a scream as she came down, but not so that it caused any real commotion. It was only people in the street, passing by, who saw it happen. And then, of course, they craned their necks over the railings, and other people saw them craning, and joined them. You know what an accident is!'

Poirot assured him he knew what an accident was.

'She lived alone?' he said, making it only half a question.

'That's right.'

'But she had friends, I suppose, among the other flat dwellers?'

Joe shrugged and shook his head. 'May have done. I couldn't say. Never saw her in the restaurant much with any of our lot. She had outside friends to dinner here sometimes. No, I wouldn't say she was specially pally with anybody here. You'd do best,' said Joe, getting slightly restive, 'to go and have a chat with Mr McFarlane who's in charge here if you want to know about her.'

'Ah, I thank you. Yes, that is what I mean to do.'

'His office is in that block over there, sir. On the ground floor. You'll see it marked up on the door.'

Poirot went as directed. He detached from his briefcase the top letter with which Miss Lemon had supplied him, and which was marked 'Mr McFarlane'. Mr McFarlane turned out to be a good-looking, shrewd-looking man of about forty-five. Poirot handed him the letter. He opened and read it.

'Ah yes,' he said, 'I see.'

He laid it down on the desk and looked at Poirot.

'The owners have instructed me to give you all the help I can about the sad death of Mrs Louise Charpentier. Now what do you want to know exactly, Monsieur' — he glanced at the letter again — 'Monsieur Poirot?'

'This is, of course, all quite confidential,' said Poirot. 'Her relatives have been communicated with by the police and by a solicitor, but they were anxious, as I was coming to England, that I should get a few more *personal* facts, if you understand me. It is distressing when one can get only official reports.'

'Yes, quite so. Yes, I quite understand that it must be. Well, I'll tell you anything I can.'

'How long had she been here and how did

she come to take the flat?'

'She'd been here — I can look it up exactly — about two years. There was a vacant tenancy and I imagine that the lady who was leaving, being an acquaintance of hers, told her in advance that she was giving it up. That was a Mrs Wilder. Worked for the BBC. Had been in London for some time, but was going to Canada. Very nice lady — I don't think she knew the deceased well at all. Just happened to mention she was giving up the flat. Mrs Charpentier liked the flat.'

'You found her a suitable tenant?' There was a very faint hesitation before Mr McFarlane answered:

'She was a satisfactory tenant, yes.'

'You need not mind telling me,' said Hercule Poirot. 'There were wild parties, eh? A little too — shall we say — gay in her entertaining?'

Mr McFarlane stopped being so discreet.

'There were a few complaints from time to time, but mostly from elderly people.'

Hercule Poirot made a significant gesture.

'A bit too fond of the bottle, yes, sir — and in with quite a gay lot. It made for a bit of trouble now and again.'

'And she was fond of the gentlemen?'

'Well, I wouldn't like to go as far as *that*.'

'No, no, but one understands.'

'Of course she wasn't so young.'

'Appearances are very often deceptive. How old would you have said she was?'

'It's difficult to say. Forty — forty-five.' He added, 'Her health wasn't good, you know.'

'So I understand.'

'She drank too much — no doubt about it. And then she'd get very depressed. Nervous about herself. Always going to doctors, I believe, and not believing what they told her. Ladies do get it into their heads — especially about that time of life — she thought that she had cancer. Was quite sure of it. The doctor reassured her but she didn't believe him. He said at the inquest that there was nothing really wrong with her. Oh well, one hears of things like that every day. She got all worked up and one fine day — ' he nodded.

'It is very sad,' said Poirot. 'Did she have any special friends among the residents of the flats?'

'Not that I know of. This place, you see, isn't what I call the matey kind. They're mostly people in business, in jobs.'

'I was thinking possibly of Miss Claudia Reece-Holland. I wondered if they had known each other.'

'Miss Reece-Holland? No, I don't think so. Oh I mean they were probably acquaintances, talked when they went up in the lift together, that sort of thing. But I don't think there was much social contact of any kind. You see, they would be in a different generation. I mean — ' Mr McFarlane seemed a little flustered. Poirot wondered why.

He said, 'One of the other girls who share Miss Holland's flat knew Mrs Charpentier, I believe — Miss Norma Restarick.'

'Did she? I wouldn't know — she's only come here quite recently, I hardly know her by sight. Rather a frightened-looking young lady. Not long out of school, I'd say.' He added, 'Is there anything more I can do for you, sir?'

'No, thank you. You've been most kind. I wonder if possibly I could see the flat. Just in order to be able to say — ' Poirot paused, not particularising what he wanted to be able to say.

'Well, now, let me see. A Mr Travers has got it now. He's in the City all day. Yes, come up with me if you like, sir.'

They went up to the seventh floor. As Mr McFarlane introduced his key one of the numbers fell from the door and narrowly avoided Poirot's patent-leather shoe. He hopped nimbly and then bent to pick it up. He replaced the spike which fixed it on the door very carefully.

'These numbers are loose,' he said.

'I'm very sorry, sir. I'll make a note of it. Yes, they wear loose from time to time. Well, here we are.'

Poirot went into the living-room. At the moment it had little personality. The walls were papered with a paper resembling grained wood. It had conventional comfortable furniture, the only personal touch was a television set and a certain number of books.

'All the flats are partly furnished, you see,' said Mr McFarlane. 'The tenants don't need to bring anything of their own, unless they want to. We cater very largely for people who come and go.'

'And the decorations are all the same?'

'Not entirely. People seem to like this raw wood effect. Good background for pictures. The only things that are different are on the one wall facing the door. We have a whole set of frescoes which people can choose from.

'We have a set of ten,' said Mr McFarlane with some pride. 'There is the Japanese one — very artistic, don't you think? — and there is an English garden one; a very striking one of birds; one of trees, a Harlequin one, a rather interesting abstract effect — lines and cubes, in vividly contrasting colours, that sort of thing. They're all designs by good artists. Our furniture is all the same. Two choices of colours, or of course people can add what

243

they like of their own. But they don't usually bother.'

'Most of them are not, as you might say, home-makers,' Poirot suggested.

'No, rather the bird of passage type, or busy people who want solid comfort, good plumbing and all that but aren't particularly interested in decoration, though we've had one or two of the do-it-yourself type, which isn't really satisfactory from our point of view. We've had to put a clause in the lease saying they've got to put things back as they found them — or pay for that being done.'

They seemed to be getting rather far away from the subject of Mrs Charpentier's death. Poirot approached the window.

'It was from here?' he murmured delicately.

'Yes. That's the window. The left-hand one. It has a balcony.'

Poirot looked out down below.

'Seven floors,' he said. 'A long way.'

'Yes, death was instantaneous, I am glad to say. Of course, it might have been an accident.'

Poirot shook his head.

'You cannot seriously suggest that, Mr McFarlane. It *must* have been deliberate.'

'Well, one always likes to suggest an easier possibility. She wasn't a happy woman, I'm afraid.'

'Thank you,' said Poirot, 'for your great courtesy. I shall be able to give her relations in France a very clear picture.'

His own picture of what had occurred was not as clear as he would have liked. So far there had been nothing to support his theory that the death of Louise Charpentier had been important. He repeated the Christian name thoughtfully. Louise . . . Why had the name Louise some haunting memory about it? He shook his head. He thanked Mr McFarlane and left.

# 17

Chief Inspector Neele was sitting behind his desk looking very official and formal. He greeted Poirot politely and motioned him to a chair. As soon as the young man who had introduced Poirot to the presence had left, Chief Inspector Neele's manner changed.

'And what are you after now, you secretive old devil?' he said.

'As to that,' said Poirot, 'you already know.'

'Oh yes, I've rustled up some stuff but I don't think there's much for you from that particular hole.'

'Why call it a hole?'

'Because you're so exactly like a good mouser. A cat sitting over a hole waiting for the mouse to come out. Well, if you ask me, there isn't any mouse in this particular hole. Mind you, I don't say that you couldn't unearth *some* dubious transactions. You know these financiers. I dare say there's a lot of hoky-poky business, and all that, about minerals and concessions and oil and all those things. But Joshua Restarick Ltd. has got a good reputation. Family business — or used to be — but you can't call it that now.

246

Simon Restarick hadn't any children, and his brother Andrew Restarick only has this daughter. There was an old aunt on the mother's side. Andrew Restarick's daughter lived with her after she left school and her own mother died. The aunt died of a stroke about six months ago. Mildly potty, I believe — belonged to a few rather peculiar religious societies. No harm in them. Simon Restarick was a perfectly plain type of shrewd business man, and had a social wife. They were married rather late in life.'

'And Andrew?'

'Andrew seems to have suffered from wanderlust. Nothing known against him. Never stayed anywhere long, wandered about South Africa, South America, Kenya and a good many other places. His brother pressed him to come back more than once, but he wasn't having any. He didn't like London or business, but he seems to have had the Restarick family flair for making money. He went after mineral deposits, things like that. He wasn't an elephant hunter or an archaeologist or a plant man or any of those things. All his deals were business deals and they always turned out well.'

'So he also in his way is conventional?'

'Yes, that about covers it. I don't know what made him come back to England after his brother died. Possibly a new wife — he's married again. Good-looking woman a good deal younger than he is. At the moment they're living with old Sir Roderick Horsefield whose sister had married Andrew Restarick's uncle. But I imagine that's only temporary. Is any of this news to you? Or do you know it all already?'

'I've heard most of it,' said Poirot. 'Is there any insanity in the family on either side?'

'Shouldn't think so, apart from old Auntie and her fancy religions. And that's not unusual in a woman who lives alone.'

'So all you can tell me really is that there is a lot of money,' said Poirot.

'Lots of money,' said Chief Inspector Neele. 'And all quite respectable. Some of it, mark you, Andrew Restarick brought into the firm. South African concessions, mines, mineral deposits. I'd say that by the time these were developed, or placed on the market, there'd be a very large sum of money indeed.'

'And who will inherit it?' said Poirot.

'That depends on how Andrew Restarick leaves it. It's up to him, but I'd say that there's no one obvious, except his wife and his daughter.'

'So they both stand to inherit a very large amount of money one day?'

'I should say so. I expect there are a good many family trusts and things like that. All the usual City gambits.'

'There is, for instance, no other woman in whom he might be interested?'

'Nothing known of such a thing. I shouldn't think it likely. He's got a good-looking new wife.'

'A young man,' said Poirot thoughtfully, 'could easily learn all this?'

'You mean and marry the daughter? There's nothing to stop him, even if she was made a ward of Court or something like that. Of course her father could then disinherit her if he wanted to.'

Poirot looked down at a neatly written list in his hand.

'What about the Wedderburn Gallery?'

'I wondered how you'd got on to that. Were you consulted by a client about a forgery?'

'Do they deal in forgeries?'

'People don't deal in forgeries,' said Chief Inspector Neele reprovingly. 'There *was* a rather unpleasant business. A millionaire from Texas over here buying pictures, and paying incredible sums for them. They sold him a Renoir and a Van Gogh. The Renoir was a small head of a girl and there was some query about it. There seemed no reason to believe that the Wedderburn Gallery had not bought it in the first place in all good faith. There was a case about it. A great many art experts came and gave their verdicts. In fact, as usual, in the end they all seemed to contradict each other. The gallery offered to take it back in any case. However, the millionaire didn't change his mind, since the latest fashionable expert swore that it was perfectly genuine. So he stuck to it. All the same there's been a bit of suspicion hanging round the gallery ever since.'

Poirot looked again at his list.

'And what about Mr David Baker? Have you looked him up for me?'

'Oh, he's one of the usual mob. Riff-raff — go about in gangs and break up night clubs. Live on purple hearts — heroin — Coke — Girls go mad about them. He's the kind they moan over saying his life has been so hard and he's such a wonderful genius. His painting is not *appreciated*. Nothing but good old sex, if you ask me.'

Poirot consulted his list again.

'Do you know anything about Mr Reece-Holland, MP?'

'Doing quite well, politically. Got the gift of the gab all right. One or two slightly peculiar transactions in the City, but he's wriggled out of them quite neatly. I'd say he was a slippery one. He's made quite a good deal of money off and on by rather doubtful means.'

Poirot came to his last point.

'What about Sir Roderick Horsefield?'

'Nice old boy but gaga. What a nose you have, Poirot, get it into everything, don't you? Yes, there's been a lot of trouble in the Special Branch. It's this craze for memoirs. Nobody knows what indiscreet revelations are going to be made next. All the old boys, service and otherwise, are racing hard to bring out their own particular brand of what they remember of the indiscretions of others! Usually it doesn't much matter, but some-times — well, you know, Cabinets change their policies and you don't want to afront someone's susceptibilities or give the wrong publicity, so we have to try and muffle the old boys. Some of them are not too easy. But you'll have to go to the Special Branch if you want to nose into any of that. I shouldn't think there was much wrong. The trouble is they don't destroy the papers they should. They keep the lot. However, I don't think there is much in that, but we have evidence that a certain Power is nosing around.'

Poirot gave a deep sigh.

'Haven't I helped?' asked the Chief Inspector.

'I am very glad to get the real low-down from official quarters. But no, I don't think there is much help in what you have told me.' He sighed and then said, 'What would be your opinion if someone said to you casually that a woman — a young attractive woman — wore a wig?'

'Nothing in that,' said Chief Inspector Neele, and added, with a slight asperity, 'my wife wears a wig when we're travelling any time. It saves a lot of trouble.'

'I beg your pardon,' said Hercule Poirot.

As the two men bade each other good-bye, the Chief Inspector asked:

'You got all the dope, I suppose, on that suicide case you were asking about in the flats? I had it sent round to you.'

'Yes, thank you. The official facts, at least. A bare record.'

'There was something you were talking about just now that brought it back to my mind. I'll think of it in a moment. It was the usual, rather sad story. Gay woman, fond of men, enough money to live upon, no particular worries, drank too much and went down the hill. And then she gets what I call the health bug. You know, they're convinced they have cancer or something in that line. They consult a doctor and he tells them they're all right, and they go home and don't believe him. If you ask me it's usually because they find they're no longer as attractive as they used to be to men. That's what's really depressing them. Yes, it happens all the time. They're lonely, I suppose, poor devils. Mrs Charpentier was just one of them. I don't suppose that any — ' he stopped. 'Oh yes, of course, I remember. You were asking about one of our MPs, Reece-Holland. He's a fairly gay one himself in a discreet way. Anyway, Louise Charpentier was his mistress at one time. That's all.'

'Was it a serious liaison?'

'Oh I shouldn't say so particularly. They went to some rather questionable clubs together and things like that. You know, we keep a discreet eye on things of that kind. But there was never anything in the Press about them. Nothing of that kind.'

'I see.'

'But it lasted for a certain time. They were seen together, off and on, for about six months, but I don't think she was the only one and I don't think he was the only one either. So you can't make anything of that, can you?'

'I do not think so,' said Poirot.

'But all the same,' he said to himself as he went down the stairs, 'all the same, it is a link. It explains the embarrassment of Mr McFarlane. It is a link, a tiny link, a link between Emlyn Reece-Holland, MP, and

Louise Charpentier.' It didn't mean anything probably. Why should it? But yet — 'I know too much,' said Poirot angrily to himself. 'I know too much. I know a little about everything and everyone but I cannot get my pattern. Half these facts are irrelevant. I want a pattern. A pattern. My kingdom for a pattern,' he said aloud.

'I beg your pardon, sir,' said the lift boy, turning a startled head.

'It is nothing,' said Poirot.

# 18

Poirot paused at the doorway of the Wedderburn Gallery to inspect a picture which depicted three aggressive-looking cows with vastly elongated bodies overshadowed by a colossal and complicated design of windmills. The two seemed to have nothing to do with each other or the very curious purple colouring.

'Interesting, isn't it?' said a soft purring voice.

A middle-aged man, who at first sight seemed to have shown a smile which exhibited an almost excessive number of beautiful white teeth, was at his elbow.

'Such *freshness*.'

He had large white plump hands which he waved as though he was using them in an arabesque.

'Clever exhibition. Closed last week. Claude Raphael show opened the day before yesterday. It's going to do well. Very well indeed.'

'Ah,' said Poirot and was led through grey velvet curtains into a long room.

Poirot made a few cautious if doubtful

remarks. The plump man took him in hand in a practised manner. Here was someone, he obviously felt, who must not be frightened away. He was a very experienced man in the art of salesmanship. You felt at once that you were welcome to be in his gallery all day if you liked without making a purchase. Sheerly, solely looking at these delightful pictures — though when you entered the gallery you might not have thought that they *were* delightful. But by the time you went out you were convinced that delightful was exactly the word to describe them. After receiving some useful artistic instruction, and making a few of the amateur's stock remarks such as 'I rather like that one,' Mr Boscombe responded encouragingly by some such phrase as:

'Now that's very interesting that you should say that. It shows, if I may say so, great perspicacity. Of course you know it isn't the ordinary reaction. Most people prefer something — well, shall I say slightly *obvious* like that' — he pointed to a blue and green striped effect arranged in one corner of the canvas — 'but this, yes, you've spotted the quality of the thing. I'd say myself — of course it's only my personal opinion — that that's one of Raphael's masterpieces.'

Poirot and he looked together with both their heads on one side at an orange lop-sided diamond with two human eyes depending from it by what looked like a spidery thread. Pleasant relations established and time obviously being infinite, Poirot remarked:

'I think a Miss Frances Cary works for you, does she not?'

'Ah yes. Frances. Clever girl that. Very artistic and very competent too. Just come back from Portugal where she's been arranging an art show for us. Very successful. Quite a good artist herself, but not I should say really creative, if you understand me. She is better on the business side. I think she recognises that herself.'

'I understand that she is a good patron of the arts?'

'Oh yes. She's interested in *Les Jeunes*. Encourages talent, persuaded me to give a show for a little group of young artists last spring. It was quite successful — the Press noticed it — all in a small way, you understand. Yes, she has her protégés.'

'I am, you understand, somewhat old-fashioned. Some of these young men — *vraiment*!' Poirot's hands went up.

'Ah,' said Mr Boscombe indulgently, 'you mustn't go by their appearances. It's just a fashion, you know. Beards and jeans or brocades and hair. Just a passing phase.'

'David someone,' said Poirot. 'I forget his

last name. Miss Cary seemed to think highly of him.'

'Sure you don't mean Peter Cardiff? He's her present protégé. Mind you, I'm not *quite* so sure about him as she is. He's really not so much *avant garde* as he is — well, positively reactionary. Quite — quite — Burne-Jones sometimes! Still, one never knows. You do get these reactions. She acts as his model occasionally.'

'David Baker — that was the name I was trying to remember,' said Poirot.

'He is not bad,' said Mr Boscombe, without enthusiasm. 'Not much *originality*, in my opinion. He was one of the group of artists I mentioned, but he didn't make any particular impression. A *good* painter, mind, but not striking. Derivative!'

Poirot went home. Miss Lemon presented him with letters to sign, and departed with them duly signed. George served him with an *omellette fines herbes* garnished, as you might say, with a discreetly sympathetic manner. After lunch, as Poirot was setting himself in his square-backed armchair with his coffee at his elbow, the telephone rang.

'Mrs Oliver, sir,' said George, lifting the telephone and placing it at his elbow.

Poirot picked up the receiver reluctantly. He did not want to talk to Mrs Oliver. He felt that she would urge upon him something which he did not want to do.

'M. Poirot?'

'*C'est moi.*'

'Well, what are you doing? What have you done?'

'I am sitting in this chair,' said Poirot. 'Thinking,' he added.

'Is that all?' said Mrs Oliver.

'It is the important thing,' said Poirot. 'Whether I shall have success in it or not I do not know.'

'But you must find that girl. She's probably been kidnapped.'

'It would certainly seem so,' said Poirot. 'And I have a letter here which came by the midday post from her father, urging me to come and see him and tell him what progress I have made.'

'Well, what progress *have* you made?'

'At the moment,' said Poirot reluctantly, 'none.'

'Really, M. Poirot, you really must take a grip on yourself.'

'You, too!'

'What do you mean, me too?'

'Urging me on.'

'Why don't you go down to that place in Chelsea, where I was hit on the head?'

'And get myself hit on the head also?'

'I simply don't understand you,' said Mrs

Oliver. '*I gave you a clue by finding the girl in the café. You said so.*'

'I know, I know.'

'What about that woman who threw herself out of a window? Haven't you got anything out of that?'

'I have made inquiries, yes.'

'Well?'

'Nothing. The woman is one of many. They are attractive when young, they have affairs, they are passionate, they have still more affairs, they get less attractive, they are unhappy and drink too much, they think they have cancer or some fatal disease and so at last in despair and loneliness they throw themselves out of a window!'

'You said her death was important — that it *meant* something.'

'It ought to have done.'

'Really!' At a loss for further comment, Mrs Oliver rang off.

Poirot leant back in his armchair, as far as he could lean back since it was of an upright nature, waved to George to remove the coffee pot and also the telephone and proceeded to reflect upon what he did or did not know. To clarify his thoughts he spoke out loud. He recalled three philosophic questions.

'What do I know? What can I hope? What ought I to do?'

He was not sure that he got them in the right order or indeed if they were quite the right questions, but he reflected upon them.

'Perhaps I *am* too old,' said Hercule Poirot, at the bottom depths of despair. 'What *do* I know?'

Upon reflection he thought that he knew too much! He laid that question aside for the moment.

'What can I hope?' Well, one could always hope. He could hope that those excellent brains of his, so much better than anybody else's, would come up sooner or later with an answer to a problem which he felt uneasily that he did not really understand.

'What ought I to do?' Well, that was very definite. What he ought to do was to go and call upon Mr Andrew Restarick who was obviously distraught about his daughter, and who would no doubt blame Poirot for not having by now delivered the daughter in person. Poirot could understand that, and sympathised with his point of view, but disliked having to present himself in such a very unfavourable light. The only other thing he could do was to telephone to a certain number and ask what developments there had been.

But before he did that, he would go back to the question he had laid aside.

'What do I know?'

He knew that the Wedderburn Gallery was under suspicion — so far it had kept on the right side of the law, but it would not hesitate at swindling ignorant millionaires by selling them dubious pictures.

He recalled Mr Boscombe with his plump white hands and his plentiful teeth, and decided that he did not like him. He was the kind of man who was almost certainly up to dirty work, though he would no doubt protect *himself* remarkably well. That was a fact that might come into use because it might connect up with David Baker. Then there was David Baker himself, the Peacock. What did he know about him? He had met him, he had conversed with him, and he had formed certain opinions about him. He would do a crooked deal of any kind for money, he would marry a rich heiress for her money and not for love, he might perhaps be bought off. Yes, he probably could be bought off. Andrew Restarick certainly believed so and he was probably right. Unless —

He considered Andrew Restarick, thinking more of the picture on the wall hanging above him than of the man himself. He remembered the strong features, the jutting out chin, the air of resolution, of decision. Then he thought of Mrs Andrew Restarick, deceased.

The bitter lines of her mouth . . . Perhaps he would go down to Crosshedges again and look at that portrait, so as to see it more clearly because there might be a clue to Norma in that. Norma — no, he must not think of Norma yet. What else was there?

There was Mary Restarick whom the girl Sonia said must have a lover because she went up to London so often. He considered that point but he did not think that Sonia was right. He thought Mrs Restarick was much more likely to go to London in order to look at possible properties to buy, luxury flats, houses in Mayfair, decorators, all the things that money in the metropolis could buy.

*Money* . . . It seemed to him that all the points that had been passing through his mind came to this in the end. Money. The importance of money. There was a great deal of money in this case. Somehow, in some way that was not obvious, money counted. Money played its part. So far there had been nothing to justify his belief that the tragic death of Mrs Charpentier had been the work of Norma. No sign of evidence, no motive; yet it seemed to him that there *was* an undeniable link. The girl had said that she 'might have committed a murder'. A death had taken place only a day or two previously. A death that had occurred in the building where she lived. Surely it would be too much of a coincidence that that death should not be connected in any way? He thought again of the mysterious illness which had affected Mary Restarick. An occurrence so simple as to be classic in its outline. A poison case where the poisoner was — must be — one of the household. Had Mary Restarick poisoned herself, had her husband tried to poison her, had the girl Sonia administered poison? Or had Norma been the culprit? Everything pointed, Hercule Poirot had to confess, to Norma as being the logical person.

'*Tout de même*,' said Poirot, 'since I cannot find anything, *et bien* then the logic falls out of the window.'

He sighed, rose to his feet and told George to fetch him a taxi. He must keep his appointment with Andrew Restarick.

# 19

Claudia Reece-Holland was not in the office today. Instead, a middle-aged woman received Poirot. She said that Mr Restarick was waiting for him and ushered him into Restarick's room.

'Well?' Restarick hardly waited until he had come through the door. 'Well, what about my daughter?'

Poirot spread out his hands.

'As yet — nothing.'

'But look here, man, there must be something — some clue. A girl can't just disappear into thin air.'

'Girls have done it before now and will do it again.'

'Did you understand that no expense was to be spared, none whatever? I — I can't go on like this.'

He seemed completely on edge by this time. He looked thinner and his red-rimmed eyes spoke of sleepless nights.

'I know what your anxiety must be, but I assure you that I have done everything possible to trace her. These things, alas, cannot be hurried.'

'She may have lost her memory or — or she may — I mean, she might be sick. Ill.'

Poirot thought he knew what the broken form of the sentence meant. Restarick had been about to say 'she may perhaps be dead'.

He sat down on the other side of the desk and said:

'Believe me, I appreciate your anxiety and I have to say to you once again that the results would be a lot quicker if you consulted the police.'

'No!' The word broke out explosively.

'They have greater facilities, more lines of inquiry. I assure you it is not only a question of money. Money cannot give you the same result as a highly efficient organisation can do.'

'Man, it's no use your talking in that soothing way. Norma is my daughter. My only daughter, the only flesh and blood I've got.'

'Are you sure that you have told me everything — everything possible — about your daughter?'

'What more *can* I tell you?'

'That is for you to say, not me. Have there been, for instance, any incidents in the past?'

'Such as? What do you mean, man?'

'Any definite history of mental instability.'

'You think that — that — '

'How do I know? How can I know?'

'And how do I know?' said Restarick, suddenly bitter. 'What do I know of her? All these years. Grace was a bitter woman. A woman who did not easily forgive or forget. Sometimes I feel — I feel that she was the wrong person to have brought Norma up.'

He got up, walked up and down the room and then sat down again.

'Of course I shouldn't have left my wife. I know that. I left her to bring up the child. But then at the time I suppose I made excuses for myself. Grace was a woman of excellent character devoted to Norma. A thoroughly good guardian for her. But was she? Was she really? Some of the letters Grace wrote to me were as though they breathed anger and revenge. Well, I suppose that's natural enough. But I was away all those years. I should have come back, come back more often and found out how the child was getting on. I suppose I had a bad conscience. Oh, it's no good making excuses now.'

He turned his head sharply.

'Yes. I did think when I saw her again that Norma's whole attitude was neurotic, indisciplined. I hoped she and Mary would — would get on better after a little while but I have to admit that I don't feel the girl was entirely normal. I felt it would be better for her to have a job in London and come home for weekends, but not to be forced into Mary's company the whole time. Oh, I suppose I've made a mess of everything. But where is she, M. Poirot? Where is she? Do you think she may have lost her memory? One hears of such things.'

'Yes,' said Poirot, 'that is a possibility. In her state, she may be wandering about quite unaware of who she is. Or she may have had an accident. That is less likely. I can assure you that I have made all inquiries in hospitals and other places.'

'You don't think she is — you don't think she's *dead?*'

'She would be easier to find dead than alive, I can assure you. Please calm yourself, Mr Restarick. Remember she may have friends of whom you know nothing. Friends in any part of England, friends whom she has known while living with her mother, or with her aunt, or friends who were friends of school friends of hers. All these things take time to sort out. It may be — you must prepare yourself — that she is with a boy friend of some kind.'

'David Baker? If I thought that — '

'She is not with David Baker. That,' said Poirot dryly, 'I ascertained first of all.'

'How do I know what friends she has?' He

sighed. 'If I find her, *when* I find her — I'd rather put it that way — I'm going to take her out of all this.'

'Out of all what?'

'Out of this country. I have been miserable, M. Poirot, miserable ever since I returned here. I always hated City life. The boring round of office routine, continual consultations with lawyers and financiers. The life I liked was always the same. Travelling, moving about from place to place, going to wild and inaccessible places. That's the life for me. I should never have left it. I should have sent for Norma to come out to me and, as I say, when I find her that's what I'm going to do. Already I'm being approached with various take-over bids. Well, they can have the whole caboodle on very advantageous terms. I'll take the cash and go back to a country that *means* something, that's *real*.'

'Aha! And what will your wife say to that?'

'Mary? She's used to that life. That's where she comes from.'

'To *les femmes* with plenty of money,' said Poirot, 'London can be very attractive.'

'She'll see it my way.'

The telephone rang on his desk. He picked it up.

'Yes? Oh. From Manchester? Yes. If it's Claudia Reece-Holland, put her through.'

He waited a minute.

'Hallo, Claudia. Yes. Speak up — it's a very bad line, I can't hear you. They agreed? . . . Ah, pity . . . No, I think you did very well . . . Right . . . All right then. Take the evening train back. We'll discuss it further tomorrow morning.'

He replaced the telephone on its rest.

'That's a competent girl,' he said.

'Miss Reece-Holland?'

'Yes. Unusually competent. Takes a lot of bother off my shoulders. I gave her pretty well *carte blanche* to put through this deal in Manchester on her own terms. I really felt I couldn't concentrate. And she's done exceedingly well. She's as good as a man in some ways.'

He looked at Poirot, suddenly bringing himself back to the present.

'Ah yes, M. Poirot. Well, I'm afraid I've rather lost my grip. Do you need more money for expenses?'

'No, Monsieur. I assure you that I will do my utmost to restore your daughter sound and well. I have taken all possible precautions for her safety.'

He went out through the outer office. When he reached the street he looked up at the sky.

'A definite answer to one question,' he said, 'that is what I need.'

# 20

Hercule Poirot looked up at the facade of the dignified Georgian house in what had been until recently a quiet street in an old-fashioned market town. Progress was rapidly overtaking it, but the new supermarket, the Gifte Shoppe, Margery's Boutique, Peg's Cafe, and a palatial new bank, had all chosen sites in Croft Road and not encroached on the narrow High Street.

The brass knocker on the door was brightly polished, Poirot noted with approval. He pressed the bell at the side.

It was opened almost at once by a tall distinguished-looking woman with upswept grey hair and an energetic manner.

'M. Poirot? You are very punctual. Come in.'

'Miss Battersby?'

'Certainly.' She held back the door. Poirot entered. She deposited his hat on the hall stand and led the way to a pleasant room overlooking a narrow walled garden.

She waved towards a chair and sat down herself in an attitude of expectation. It was clear that Miss Battersby was not one to lose time in conventional utterances.

'You are, I think, the former Principal of Meadowfield School?'

'Yes. I retired a year ago. I understand you wished to see me on the subject of Norma Restarick, a former pupil.'

'That is right.'

'In your letters,' said Miss Battersby, 'you gave me no further details.' She added, 'I may say that I know who you are, M. Poirot. I should therefore like a little more information before I proceed further. Are you, for instance, thinking of employing Norma Restarick?'

'That is not my intention, no.'

'Knowing what your profession is you understand why I should want further details. Have you, for instance, an introduction to me from any of Norma's relations?'

'Again, no,' said Hercule Poirot. 'I will explain myself further.'

'Thank you.'

'In actual fact, I am employed by Miss Restarick's father, Andrew Restarick.'

'Ah. He has recently returned to England, I believe, after many years' absence.'

'That is so.'

'But you do not bring me a letter of introduction from him?'

'I did not ask him for one.'

Miss Battersby looked at him inquiringly.

'He might have insisted on coming with me,' said Hercule Poirot. 'That would have hampered me in asking you the questions that I wish to ask, because it is likely that the answers to them might cause him pain and distress. There is no reason why he should be caused further distress than he is already suffering at this moment.'

'Has anything happened to Norma?'

'I hope not ... There is, however, a possibility of that. You remember the girl, Miss Battersby?'

'I remember all my pupils. I have an excellent memory. Meadowfield, in any case, is not a very large school. Two hundred girls, no more.'

'Why have you resigned from it, Miss Battersby?'

'Really, M. Poirot, I cannot see that that is any of your business.'

'No, I am merely expressing my quite natural curiosity.'

'I am seventy. Is that not a reason?'

'Not in your case, I should say. You appear to me to be in full vigour and energy, fully capable of continuing your headmistress-ship for a good many years to come.'

'Times change, M. Poirot. One does not always like the way they are changing. I will

273

satisfy your curiosity. I found I was having less and less patience with *parents*. Their aims for their daughters are short-sighted and quite frankly stupid.'

Miss Battersby was, as Poirot knew from looking up her qualifications, a very well-known mathematician.

'Do not think that I lead an idle life,' said Miss Battersby. 'I lead a life where the work is far more congenial to me. I coach senior students. And now, please, may I know the reason for your interest in the girl, Norma Restarick?'

'There is some occasion for anxiety. She has, to put it baldly, disappeared.'

Miss Battersby continued to look quite unconcerned.

'Indeed? When you say 'disappeared', I presume you mean that she has left home without telling her parents where she was going. Oh, I believe her mother is dead, so without telling her father where she was going. That is really not at all uncommon nowadays, M. Poirot. Mr Restarick has not consulted the police?'

'He is adamant on that subject. He refuses definitely.'

'I can assure you that I have no knowledge as to where the girl is. I have heard nothing from her. Indeed, I have had no news from her since she left Meadowfield. So I fear I cannot help you in any way.'

'It is not precisely that kind of information that I want. I want to know *what kind of a girl she is* — how you would describe her. Not her personal appearance. I do not mean that. I mean as to her personality and characteristics.'

'Norma, at school, was a perfectly ordinary girl. Not scholastically brilliant, but her work was adequate.'

'Not a neurotic type?'

Miss Battersby considered. Then she said slowly: 'No, I would not say so. Not more, that is, than might be expected considering her home circumstances.'

'You mean her invalid mother?'

'Yes. She came from a broken home. The father, to whom I think she was very devoted, left home suddenly with another woman — a fact which her mother quite naturally resented. She probably upset her daughter more than she need have done by voicing her resentment without restraint.'

'Perhaps it may be more to the point if I ask you your opinion of the late Mrs Restarick?'

'What you are asking me for is my private opinion?'

'If you do not object?'

'No, I have no hesitation at all in answering your question. Home conditions are very important in a girl's life and I have always studied them as much as I can through the meagre information that comes to me. Mrs Restarick was a worthy and upright woman, I should say. Self-righteous, censorious and handicapped in life by being an extremely stupid one!'

'Ah,' said Poirot appreciatively.

'She was also, I would say, a *malade imaginaire*. A type that would exaggerate her ailments. The type of woman who is always in and out of nursing homes. An unfortunate home background for a girl — especially a girl who has no very definite personality of her own. Norma had no marked intellectual ambitions, she had no confidence in herself, she was not a girl to whom I would recommend a career. A nice ordinary job followed by marriage and children was what I would have hoped for her.'

'You saw — forgive me for asking — no signs at any time of mental instability?'

'Mental instability?' said Miss Battersby. 'Rubbish!'

'So that is what you say. Rubbish! And *not* neurotic?'

'Any girl, or almost any girl, can be neurotic, especially in adolescence, and in her first encounters with the world. She is still immature, and needs guidance in her first encounters with sex. Girls are frequently attracted to completely unsuitable, sometimes even dangerous young men. There are, it seems, no parents nowadays, or hardly any, with the strength of character to save them from this, so they often go through a time of hysterical misery, and perhaps make an unsuitable marriage which ends not long after in divorce.'

'But Norma showed no signs of mental instability?' Poirot persisted with the question.

'She is an emotional but normal girl,' said Miss Battersby. '*Mental instability!* As I said before — rubbish! She's probably run away with some young man to get married, and there's nothing more normal than that!'

# 21

Poirot sat in his big square armchair. His hands rested on the arms, his eyes looked at the chimney-piece in front of him without seeing it. By his elbow was a small table and on it, neatly clipped together, were various documents. Reports from Mr Goby, information obtained from his friend, Chief Inspector Neele, a series of separate pages under the heading of 'Hearsay, gossip, rumour' and the sources from which it had been obtained.

At the moment he had no need to consult these documents. He had, in fact, read them through carefully and laid them there in case there was any particular point he wished to refer to once more. He wanted now to assemble together in his mind all that he knew and had learned because he was convinced that these things must form a pattern. There *must* be a pattern there. He was considering now, from what exact angle to approach it. He was not one to trust in enthusiasm for some particular intuition. He was not an intuitive person — but he did have *feelings*. The important thing was not the feelings themselves — but what might have caused them. It was the cause that was interesting, the cause was so often not what you thought it was. You had very often to work it out by logic, by sense and by knowledge.

What did he *feel* about this case — what *kind* of a case was it? Let him start from the general, then proceed to the particular. What were the salient facts of this case?

*Money* was one of them, he thought, though he did not know *how*. Somehow or other, *money* . . . He also thought, increasingly so, that there was *evil* somewhere. He knew evil. He had met it before. He knew the tang of it, the taste of it, the way it went. The trouble was that here he did not yet know exactly where it *was*. He had taken certain steps to combat evil. He hoped they would be sufficient. Something was happening, something was in progress, *that was not yet accomplished*. Someone, somewhere, was in *danger*.

The trouble was that the facts pointed both ways. If the person he *thought* was in danger was really in danger, there seemed so far as he could see no reason *why*. Why should that particular person be in danger? There was no motive. If the person he thought was in danger was *not* in danger, then the whole approach might have to be completely reversed . . . Everything that pointed one way he must turn round and look at from the complete opposite point of view.

He left that for the moment in the balance, and he came from there to the personalities — to the *people*. What pattern did *they* make? What part were they playing?

First — Andrew Restarick. He had accumulated by now a fair amount of information about Andrew Restarick. A general picture of his life before and after going abroad. A restless man, never sticking to one place or purpose long, but generally liked. Nothing of the wastrel about him, nothing shoddy or tricky. Not, perhaps, a strong personality? Weak in many ways?

Poirot frowned, dissatisfied. That picture did not somehow fit the Andrew Restarick that he himself had met. Not *weak* surely, with that thrust-out chin, the steady eyes, the air of resolution. He had been a successful business man, too, apparently. Good at his job in the earlier years, and he had put through good deals in South Africa and in South America. He had increased his holdings. It was a success story that he had brought home with him, not one of failure. How then could he be a *weak* personality? Weak, perhaps, only where *women* were concerned. He had made a mistake in his

marriage — married the wrong woman
... Pushed into it perhaps by his family? And
then he had met the other woman. Just that
one woman? Or had there been several
women? It was hard to find a record of that
kind after so many years. Certainly he had
not been a notoriously unfaithful husband.
He had had a normal home, he had been
fond, by all accounts, of his small daughter.
But then he had come across a woman whom
he had cared for enough to leave his home
and to leave his country. It had been a real
love affair.

But had it, perhaps, matched up with
any additional motive? Dislike of office work,
the City, the daily routine of London? He
thought it might. It matched the pattern.
He seemed, too, to have been a solitary type.
Everyone had liked him both here and
abroad, but there seemed no intimate friends.
Indeed, it would have been difficult for him
to have intimate friends abroad because he
had never stopped in any one spot long
enough. He had plunged into some gamble,
attempted a coup, had made good, then tired
of the thing and gone on somewhere else.
Nomadic! A wanderer.

It still did not quite accord with his own
picture of the man ... A *picture?* The word
stirred in his mind the memory of the picture

that hung in Restarick's office, on the wall behind his desk. It had been a portrait of the same man fifteen years ago. How much difference had those fifteen years made in the man sitting there? Surprisingly little, on the whole! More grey in the hair, a heavier set to the shoulders, but the lines of character on the face were much the same. A determined face. A man who knew what he wanted, who meant to get it. A man who would take risks. A man with a certain ruthlessness.

Why, he wondered, had Restarick brought that picture up to London? They had been companion portraits of a husband and wife. Strictly speaking artistically, they should have remained together. Would a psychologist have said that subconsciously Restarick wanted to dissociate himself from his former wife once more, to separate himself from her? Was he then mentally still retreating from her personality although she was dead? An interesting point . . .

The pictures had presumably come out of storage with various other family articles of furnishing. Mary Restarick had no doubt selected certain personal objects to supplement the furniture of Crosshedges for which Sir Roderick had made room. He wondered whether Mary Restarick, the new wife, had liked hanging up that particular pair of portraits. More natural, perhaps, if she had put the first wife's portrait in an attic! But then he reflected that she would probably not have had an attic to stow away unwanted objects at Crosshedges. Presumably Sir Roderick had made room for a few family things whilst the returned couple were looking about for a suitable house in London. So it had not mattered much, and it would have been easier to hang both portraits. Besides, Mary Restarick seemed a sensible type of woman — not a jealous or emotional type.

'*Tout de même*,' thought Hercule Poirot to himself, '*les femmes*, they are all capable of jealousy, and sometimes the one you would consider the least likely!'

His thoughts passed to Mary Restarick, and he considered her in turn. It struck him that what was really odd was that he had so few thoughts about her! He had seen her only the once, and she had, somehow or other, not made much impression on him. A certain efficiency, he thought, and also a certain — how could he put it? — artificiality? ('But there, my friend,' said Hercule Poirot, again in parenthesis, 'there you are considering her wig!')

It was absurd really that one should know so little about a woman. A woman who was efficient and who wore a wig, and who was good-looking, and who was sensible, and who could feel anger. Yes, she had been angry when she had found the Peacock Boy wandering uninvited in her house. She had displayed it sharply and unmistakably. And the boy — he had seemed what? Amused, no more. But she had been angry, very angry at finding him there. Well, that was natural enough. He would not be any mother's choice for her daughter —

Poirot stopped short in his thoughts, shaking his head vexedly. Mary Restarick was *not* Norma's mother. Not for her the agony, the apprehension about a daughter making an unsuitable unhappy marriage, or announcing an illegitimate baby with an unsuitable father! What *did* Mary feel about Norma? Presumably, to begin with, that she was a thoroughly tiresome girl — who had picked up with a young man who was going to be obviously a source of worry and annoyance to Andrew Restarick. But after that? What had she thought and felt about a stepdaughter who was apparently deliberately trying to poison her?

Her attitude seemed to have been the sensible one. She had wanted to get Norma out of the house, herself out of danger; and to co-operate with her husband in suppressing any scandal about what had happened. Norma came down for an occasional weekend to keep up appearances, but her life hence-forward was bound to centre in London. Even when the Restaricks moved into the house they were looking for, they would not suggest Norma living with them. Most girls, nowadays, lived away from their families. So that problem had been settled.

Except that, for Poirot, the question of who had administered poison to Mary Restarick was very far from settled. Restarick himself believed it was his daughter —

But Poirot wondered . . .

His mind played with the possibilities of the girl Sonia. What was she doing in that house? Why had she come there? She had Sir Roderick eating out of her hand all right — perhaps she had no wish to go back to her own country? Possibly her designs were purely matrimonial — old men of Sir Roderick's age married pretty young girls every day of the week. In the worldly sense, Sonia could do very well for herself. A secure social position, and widowhood to look forward to with a settled and sufficient income — or were her aims quite different? Had she gone to Kew Gardens with Sir Roderick's missing papers tucked between the pages of a book?

Had Mary Restarick become suspicious of her — of her activities, of her loyalties, of where she went on her days off, and of whom she met? And had Sonia, then, administered the substances which, in cumulative small doses, would arouse no suspicion of anything but ordinary gastroenteritis?

For the time being, he put the household at Cross-hedges out of his mind.

He came, as Norma had come, to London, and proceeded to the consideration of three girls who shared a flat.

Claudia Reece-Holland, Frances Cary, Norma Restarick. Claudia Reece-Holland, daughter of a well-known Member of Parliament, well off, capable, well trained, good-looking, a first-class secretary. Frances Cary, a country solicitor's daughter, artistic, had been to drama school for a short time, then to the Slade, chucked that also, occasionally worked for the Arts Council, now employed by an art gallery. Earned a good salary, was artistic and had bohemian associations. She knew the young man, David Baker, though not apparently more than casually. Perhaps she was in love with him? He was the kind of young man, Poirot thought, disliked generally by parents, members of the Establishment and also the police. Where the attraction lay for well-born girls

Poirot failed to see. But one had to acknowledge it as a fact. What did he himself think of David?

A good-looking boy with the impudent and slightly amused air whom he had first seen in the upper storeys of Crosshedges, doing an errand for Norma (or reconnoitring on his own, who should say?). He had seen him again when he gave him a lift in his car. A young man of personality, giving indeed an impression of ability in what he chose to do. And yet there was clearly an unsatisfactory side to him. Poirot picked up one of the papers on the table by his side and studied it. A bad record though not positively criminal. Small frauds on garages, hooliganism, smashing up things, on probation twice. All those things were the fashion of the day. They did not come under Poirot's category of evil. He had been a promising painter, but had chucked it. He was the kind that did no steady work. He was vain, proud, a peacock in love with his own appearance. Was he anything more than that? Poirot wondered.

He stretched out an arm and picked up a sheet of paper on which was scribbled down the rough heads of the conversation held between Norma and David in the café — that is, as well as Mrs Oliver could remember them. And how well was that? Poirot thought.

He shook his head doubtfully. One never knew quite at what point Mrs Oliver's imagination would take over! Did the boy care for Norma, really want to marry her? There was no doubt about her feelings for him. He had suggested marrying her. Had Norma got money of her own? She was the daughter of a rich man, but that was not the same thing. Poirot made an exclamation of vexation. He had forgotten to inquire the terms of the late Mrs Restarick's will. He flipped through the sheets of notes. No, Mr Goby had not neglected this obvious need. Mrs Restarick apparently had been well provided for by her husband during her lifetime. She had had, apparently, a small income of her own amounting perhaps to a thousand a year. She had left everything she possessed to her daughter. It would hardly amount, Poirot thought, to a motive for marriage. Probably, as his only child, she would inherit a lot of money at her father's death but that was not at all the same thing. Her father might leave her very little indeed if he disliked the man she had married.

He would say then, that David *did* care for her, since he was willing to marry her. And yet — Poirot shook his head. It was about the fifth time he had shaken it. All these things did not tie up, they did not make a satisfactory pattern. He remembered Restarick's desk, and the cheque he had been writing — apparently to buy off the young man — and the young man, apparently, was quite willing to be bought off! So that again did not tally. The cheque had certainly been made out to David Baker and it was for a very large — really a preposterous — sum. It was a sum that might have tempted any impecunious young man of bad character. And yet he had suggested marriage to her only a day before. That, of course, might have been just a move in the game — a move to raise the price he was asking. Poirot remembered Restarick sitting there, his lips hard. He must care a great deal for his daughter to be willing to pay so high a sum; and he must have been afraid too that the girl herself was quite determined to marry him.

From thoughts of Restarick, he went on to Claudia. Claudia and Andrew Restarick. Was it chance, sheer chance, that she had come to be his secretary? There might be a link between them. Claudia. He considered her. Three girls in a flat, Claudia Reece-Holland's flat. She had been the one who had taken the flat originally, and shared it first with a friend, a girl she already knew, and then with another girl, the third girl. *The third girl*, thought Poirot. Yes, it always came back to that. The third girl. And that is where *he* had come in the end. Where he had *had* to come. Where all this thinking out of patterns had led. To Norma Restarick.

A girl who had come to consult him as he sat at breakfast. A girl whom he had joined at a table in a café where she had recently been eating baked beans with the young man she loved. (He always seemed to see her at meal times, he noted!) And what did he think about her? First, what did other people think about her? Restarick cared for her and was desperately anxious about her, desperately frightened for her. He not only suspected — he was quite sure, apparently, that she had tried to poison his recently married wife. He had consulted a doctor about her. Poirot felt he would like dearly to talk to that doctor himself, but he doubted if he would get anywhere. Doctors were very chary of parting with medical information to anyone but a duly accredited person such as the parents. But Poirot could imagine fairly well what the doctor had said. He had been cautious, Poirot thought, as doctors are apt to be. He'd hemmed and hawed and spoken perhaps of medical treatment. He had not stressed too positively a mental angle, but had certainly suggested it or hinted at it. In fact, the doctor probably was privately sure that that was what *had* happened. But he also knew a good deal about hysterical girls, and that they sometimes did things that were not really the result of mental causes, but merely of temper, jealousy, emotion, and hysteria. He would not be a psychiatrist himself nor a neurologist. He would be a GP who took no risks of making accusations about which he could not be sure, but suggested certain things out of caution. A job somewhere or other — a job in London, later perhaps treatment from a specialist?

What did anyone else think of Norma Restarick? Claudia Reece-Holland? He didn't know. Certainly not from the little that he knew about her. She was capable of hiding any secret, she would certainly let nothing escape her which she did not mean to let escape. She had shown no signs of wanting to turn the girl out — which she might have done if she had been afraid of her mental condition. There could not have been much discussion between her and Frances on the subject since the other girl had so innocently let escape the fact that Norma had not returned to them after her weekend at home. Claudia had been annoyed about that. It was possible that Claudia was more in the pattern than she appeared. She had brains, Poirot thought, and efficiency . . . He came back to

Norma, came back once again to the third girl. What was *her* place in the pattern? The place that would pull the whole thing together. Ophelia, he thought? But there were two opinions to that, just as there were two opinions about Norma. Was Ophelia mad or was she pretending madness? Actresses had been variously divided as to how the part should be played — or perhaps, he should say, producers. They were the ones who had the ideas. Was Hamlet mad or sane? Take your choice. Was Ophelia mad or sane?

Restarick would not have used the word 'mad' even in his thoughts about his daughter. *Mentally disturbed* was the term that everyone preferred to use. The other word that had been used of Norma had been 'batty'. 'She's a bit batty.' 'Not quite all there.' 'A bit wanting, if you know what I mean.' Were 'daily women' good judges? Poirot thought they might be. There *was* something odd about Norma, certainly, but she might be odd in a different way to what she seemed. He remembered the picture she had made slouching into his room, a girl of today, the modern type looking just as so many other girls looked. Limp hair hanging on her shoulders, the characterless dress, a skimpy look about the knees — all to his old-fashioned eyes looking like an adult girl pretending to be a child.

'*I'm sorry, you are too old.*'

Perhaps it was true. He'd looked at her through the eyes of someone old, without admiration, to him just a girl without apparently will to please, without coquetry. A girl without any sense of her own femininity — no charm or mystery or enticement, who had nothing to offer, perhaps, but plain biological sex. So it may be that she was right in her condemnation of him. He could not help her because he did not understand her, because it was not even possible for him to appreciate her. He had done his best for her, but what had that meant up to date? What had he done for her since that one moment of appeal? And in his thoughts the answer came quickly. *He had kept her safe.* That at least. If, indeed, she needed keeping safe. That was where the whole point lay. *Did* she need keeping safe? That preposterous confession! Really, not so much a confession as an announcement: '*I think I may have committed a murder.*'

Hold on to that, because that was the crux of the whole thing. That was his métier. To deal with murder, to clear up murder, to *prevent* murder! To be the good dog who hunts down murder. Murder announced. Murder *somewhere*. He had looked for it and had not found it. The pattern of arsenic in the soup? A pattern of young hooligans stabbing each other with knifes? The ridiculous and sinister phrase, *bloodstains in the courtyard*. A shot fired from a revolver. At whom, and why?

It was not as it ought to be, a form of crime that would fit with the words she had said: 'I may have committed a murder.' He had stumbled on in the dark, trying to see a pattern of crime, trying to see where the third girl fitted into that pattern, and coming back always to the same urgent need to know what this girl was really like.

And then with a casual phrase, Ariadne Oliver had, as he thought, shown him the light. The supposed suicide of a woman at Borodene Mansions. *That* would fit. It was where the third girl had her living quarters. It *must* be the murder that she had meant. Another murder committed about the same time would have been too much of a coincidence! Besides there was no sign or trace of any other murder that had been committed about then. No other death that could have sent her hot-foot to consult him, after listening at a party to the lavish admiration of his own achievements which his friend, Mrs Oliver, had given to the world. And so, when Mrs Oliver had informed him in a casual manner of the woman who had thrown herself out of the window, it had seemed to him that at last he had got what he had been looking for.

Here was the clue. The answer to his perplexity. Here he would find what he needed. The why, the when, the where.

'*Quelle déception*,' said Hercule Poirot, out loud.

He stretched out his hand, and sorted out the neatly typed résumé of a woman's life. The bald facts of Mrs Charpentier's existence. A woman of forty-three of good social position, reported to have been a wild girl — two marriages — two divorces — a woman who liked men. A woman who of late years had drunk more than was good for her. A woman who liked parties. A woman who was now reported to go about with men a good many years younger than herself. Living in a flat alone in Borodene Mansions, Poirot could understand and feel the sort of woman she was, and had been, and he could see why such a woman might wish to throw herself out of a high window one early morning when she awoke to despair.

Because she had cancer or thought she had cancer? *But at the inquest, the medical evidence had said very definitely that that was not so.*

What he wanted was some kind of a link with Norma Restarick. He could not find it. He read through the dry facts again.

Identification had been supplied at the inquest by a solicitor. Louise Carpenter, though she had used a Frenchified form of her surname — Charpentier. Because it went better with her Christian name? Louise? Why was the name Louise familiar? Some casual mention? — a phrase? — his fingers riffled neatly through typewritten pages. Ah! there it was! Just that one reference. The girl for whom Andrew Restarick had left his wife had been a girl named Louise Birell. Someone who had proved to be of little significance in Restarick's later life. They had quarrelled and parted after about a year. The same pattern, Poirot thought. The same thing obtaining that had probably obtained all through this particular woman's life. To love a man violently, to break up his home, perhaps, to live with him, and then quarrel with him and leave him. He felt sure, absolutely sure, that this Louise Charpentier was the same Louise.

Even so, how did it tie up with the girl Norma? Had Restarick and Louise Charpentier come together again when he returned to England? Poirot doubted it. Their lives had parted years ago. That they had by any chance come together again seemed unlikely to the point of impossibility! It had been a brief and in reality unimportant infatuation. His present wife would hardly be jealous enough of her husband's past to wish to push his former mistress out of a window. Ridiculous! The only person so far as he could see who might have been the type to harbour a grudge over many long years, and wish to execute revenge upon the woman who had broken up her home, might have been the first Mrs Restarick. And that sounded wildly impossible also, and anyway, the first Mrs Restarick was dead!

The telephone rang. Poirot did not move. At this particular moment he did not want to be disturbed. He had a feeling of being on a trail of some kind . . . He wanted to pursue it . . . The telephone stopped. Good. Miss Lemon would be coping with it.

The door opened and Miss Lemon entered.

'Mrs Oliver wants to speak to you,' she said.

Poirot waved a hand. 'Not now, not now, *I pray you!* I cannot speak to her now.'

'She says there is something that she has just thought of — something she forgot to tell you. About a piece of paper — an unfinished letter, which seems to have fallen out of a blotter in a desk in a furniture van. A rather

incoherent story,' added Miss Lemon, allowing a note of disapproval to enter her voice.

Poirot waved more frantically.

'Not *now*,' he urged. 'I beg of you, not *now*.'

'I will tell her you are busy.'

Miss Lemon retreated.

Peace descended once more upon the
room. Poirot felt waves of fatigue creeping
over him. Too much thinking. One *must*
relax. Yes, one must relax. One must let
tension go — in relaxation the pattern would
come. He closed his eyes. There were all the
components there. He was sure of that now,
there was nothing more he could learn from
*outside*. It must come from *inside*.

★  ★  ★

And quite suddenly — just as his eyelids were
relaxing in sleep — *it came* . . .

It was all there — waiting for him! He
would have to work it all out. But he *knew*
now. All the bits were there, disconnected bits
and pieces, all fitting in. A wig, a picture,
5 am, women and their hair-dos, the Peacock
Boy — all leading to the phrase with which it
had begun:

*Third Girl* . . .

'*I may have committed a murder* . . . ' Of
course!

A ridiculous nursery rhyme came into his mind. He repeated it aloud.

*Rub a dub dub, three men in a tub*
*And who do you think they be?*
*A butcher, a baker, a candlestick maker . . .*

Too bad, he couldn't remember the last line.

A baker, yes, and in a far-fetched way, a butcher —

He tried out a feminine parody:

*Pat a cake, pat, three girls in a flat*
*And who do you think they be?*
*A Personal Aide and a girl from the Slade*
*And the Third is a —*

Miss Lemon came in.

'Ah — I remember now — '*And they all came out of a weenie POTATO.*''

Miss Lemon looked at him in anxiety.

'Dr Stillingfleet insists on speaking to you at once. He says it is *urgent.*'

'Tell Dr Stillingfleet he can — *Dr Stillingfleet,* did you say?'

He pushed past her, caught up the receiver. 'I am here. Poirot speaking! Something has happened?'

'She's walked out on me.'

'What?'

'You heard me. She's walked out. Walked out through the front gate.'

'You let her go?'

'What else could I do?'

'You could have stopped her.'

'No.'

'To let her go was madness.'

'No.'

'You don't understand.'

'That was the arrangement. Free to go at any time.'

'You don't understand what may be involved.'

'All right then, I don't. But I know what I'm doing. And if I don't let her go, all the work I've done on her would go for nothing. And I *have* worked on her. Your job and my job aren't the same. We're not out for the same thing. I tell you I was getting somewhere. Getting somewhere, so that I was quite sure she *wouldn't* walk out on me.'

'Ah yes. And then, *mon ami*, she did.'

'Frankly, I can't understand it. I can't see why the setback came.'

'Something happened.'

'Yes, but what?'

'Somebody she saw, somebody who spoke to her, somebody who found out where she was.'

'I don't see how that could have happened

300

. . . But what you don't seem to see is that she's a free agent. She had to be a free agent.'

'Somebody got at her. Somebody found out where she was. Did she get a letter, a telegram, a telephone call?'

'No, nothing of that kind. That I am quite sure of.'

'Then how — of course! Newspapers. You have newspapers, I suppose, in that establishment of yours?'

'Certainly. Normal everyday life, that's what I stand for in my place of business.'

'Then that is how they got at her. Normal, everyday life. What papers do you take?'

'Five.' He named the five.

'When did she go?'

'This morning. Half past ten.'

'Exactly. After she read the papers. That is good enough to start on. Which paper did she usually read?'

'I don't think she had any special choice. Sometimes one, sometimes another, sometimes the whole lot of them — sometimes only glanced at them.'

'Well, I must not waste time talking.'

'You think she saw an advertisement. Something of that kind?'

'What other explanation can there be? Goodbye, I can say no more now. I have to search. Search for the possible advertisement and then get on quickly.'

He replaced the receiver.

'Miss Lemon, bring me our two papers. The *Morning News* and the *Daily Comet*. Send Georges out for all the others.'

As he opened out the papers to the Personal advertisements and went carefully down them, he followed his line of thought.

He would be in time. He *must* be in time . . . There had been one murder already. There would be another one to come. But he, Hercule Poirot, would prevent that . . . If he was in time . . . He was Hercule Poirot — the avenger of the innocent. Did he not say (and people laughed when he said it), 'I do not approve of murder.' They had thought it an understatement. But it was not an understatement. It was a simple statement of *fact* without melodrama. He did not approve of murder.

George came in with a sheaf of newspapers.

'There are all this morning's, sir.'

Poirot looked at Miss Lemon, who was standing by waiting to be efficient.

'Look through the ones that I have searched in case I have missed anything.'

'The Personal column, you mean?'

'Yes. I thought there would be the name David perhaps. A girl's name. Some pet name or nickname. They would not use Norma. An appeal for help, perhaps, or to a meeting.'

Miss Lemon took the papers obediently with some distaste. This was not her kind of efficiency, but for the moment he had no other job to give her. He himself spread out the *Morning Chronicle*. That was the biggest field to search. Three columns of it. He bent over the open sheet.

A lady who wanted to dispose of her fur coat . . . Passengers wanted for a car trip abroad . . . Lovely period house for sale . . . Paying guests . . . Backward children . . . Home-made chocolates . . . '*Julia. Shall never forget. Always yours.*' That was more the kind of thing. He considered it, but passed on. Louis XVth furniture . . . Middle-aged lady to help run a hotel . . . '*In desperate trouble. Must see you. Come to flat 4.30 without fail. Our code Goliath.*'

He heard the doorbell ring just as he called out: 'Georges, a taxi,' slipped on his overcoat, and went into the hall just as George was opening the front door and colliding with Mrs Oliver. All three of them struggled to disentangle themselves in the narrow hall.

# 22

## I

Frances Cary, carrying her overnight bag, walked down Mandeville Road, chattering with the friend she had just met on the corner, towards the bulk of Borodene Mansions.

'Really, Frances, it's like living in a prison block, that building. Wormwood Scrubs or something.'

'Nonsense, Eileen. I tell you, they're frightfully comfortable, these flats. I'm very lucky and Claudia is a splendid person to share with — never bothers you. And she's got a wonderful daily. The flat's really very nicely run.'

'Are there just the two of you? I forget. I thought you had a third girl?'

'Oh, well, she seems to have walked out on us.'

'You mean she doesn't pay her rent?'

'Oh, I think the rent's all right. I think she's probably having some affair with a boy friend.'

Eileen lost interest. Boy friends were too

304

much a matter of course.

'Where are you coming back from now?'

'Manchester. Private view was on. Great success.'

'Are you really going to Vienna next month?'

'Yes, I think so. It's pretty well fixed up by now. Rather fun.'

'Wouldn't it be awful if some of the pictures got stolen?'

'Oh, they're all insured,' said Frances. 'All the really valuable ones, anyway.'

'How did your friend Peter's show go?'

'Not terribly well, I'm afraid. But there was quite a good review by the critic of *The Artist*, and that counts a lot.'

Frances turned into Borodene Mansions, and her friend went on her way to her own small mews house farther down the road. Frances said 'Good evening' to the porter, and went up in the lift to the sixth floor. She walked along the passage, humming a little tune to herself.

She inserted her key in the door of the flat. The light in the hall was not on yet. Claudia was not due back from the office for another hour and a half. But in the sitting-room, the door of which was ajar, the light *was* on.

Frances said aloud: 'Light's on. That's funny.'

She slipped out of her coat, dropped her overnight bag, pushed the sitting-room door farther open and went in . . .

Then she stopped dead. Her mouth opened and then shut. She stiffened all over — her eyes staring at the prone figure on the floor; then they rose slowly to the mirror on the wall that reflected back at her her own horror-stricken face . . .

Then she drew a deep breath. The momentary paralysis over, she flung back her head and screamed. Stumbling over her bag on the hall floor and kicking it aside, she ran out of the flat and along the passage and beat frenziedly at the door of the next flat.

An elderly woman opened it.

'What on earth — '

'There's someone dead — someone *dead*. And I think it's someone I know . . . David Baker. He's lying there on the floor . . . I think he's stabbed . . . he must have been stabbed. There's blood — blood everywhere.'

She began to sob hysterically. Miss Jacobs shoved a glass into her hand. 'Stay there and drink it.'

Frances sipped obediently. Miss Jacobs went rapidly out of the door along the passage and through the open door from which the light was pouring out. The living-room door was wide open and Miss

Jacobs went straight through it.

She was not the kind of woman who screams. She stood just within the doorway, her lips pursed hard together.

What she was looking at had a nightmarish quality. On the floor lay a handsome young man, his arms flung wide, his chestnut hair falling on his shoulders. He wore a crimson velvet coat, and his white shirt was dappled with blood . . .

She was aware with a start that there was a second figure with her in the room. A girl was standing pressed back against the wall, the great Harlequin above seeming to be leaping across the painted sky.

The girl had a white woollen shift dress on, and her pale brown hair hung limp on either side of her face. In her hand she was holding a kitchen knife.

Miss Jacobs stared at her and she stared back at Miss Jacobs.

Then she said in a quiet reflective voice, as though she was answering what someone had said to her:

'Yes, I've killed him . . . The blood got on my hands from the knife . . . I went into the bathroom to wash it off — but you can't really wash things like that off, can you? And then I came back in here to see if it was really *true* . . . But it *is* . . . Poor David . . . But I

307

suppose I *had* to do it.'

Shock forced unlikely words from Miss Jacobs. As she said them, she thought how ridiculous they sounded!

'Indeed? Why did you have to do anything of the kind?'

'I don't know . . . At least — I suppose I do — really. He was in great trouble. He sent for me — and I came . . . But I wanted to be free of him. I wanted to get away from him. I didn't really love him.'

She laid the knife carefully on the table and sat down on a chair.

'It isn't safe, is it?' she said. 'To hate anyone . . . It isn't safe because you never know what you might do . . . Like Louise . . . '

Then she said quietly, 'Hadn't you better ring up the police?'

Obediently, Miss Jacobs dialled 999.

## II

There were six people now in the room with the Harlequin on the wall. A long time had passed. The police had come and gone.

Andrew Restarick sat like a man stunned. Once or twice he said the same words. 'I can't believe it . . . ' Telephoned for, he had come from his office, and Claudia Reece-Holland had come with him. In her quiet way, she had been ceaselessly efficient. She had put through telephone calls to lawyers, had rung Crosshedges and two firms of estate agents to try and get in touch with Mary Restarick. She had given Frances Cary a sedative and sent her to lie down.

Hercule Poirot and Mrs Oliver sat side by side on a sofa. They had arrived together at the same time as the police.

Last of all to arrive, when nearly everyone else had gone, had been a quiet man with grey hair and a gentle manner, Chief Inspector Neele of Scotland Yard, who had greeted Poirot with a slight nod, and been introduced to Andrew Restarick. A tall red-haired young man was standing by the window staring down into the courtyard.

What were they all waiting for? Mrs Oliver wondered. The body had been removed, the photographers and other police officers had done their work, they themselves, after being herded into Claudia's bedroom, had been re-admitted into the sitting-room, where they had been waiting, she supposed, for the Scotland Yard man to arrive.

'If you want me to go,' Mrs Oliver said to him uncertainly —

'Mrs Ariadne Oliver, aren't you? No, if you have no objection, I'd rather you remained. I know it hasn't been pleasant — '

'It didn't seem real.'

Mrs Oliver shut her eyes — seeing the whole thing again. The Peacock Boy, so picturesquely dead that he had seemed like a stage figure. And the girl — the girl had been different — not the uncertain Norma from Crosshedges — the unattractive Ophelia, as Poirot had called her — but some quiet figure of tragic dignity — accepting her doom.

Poirot had asked if he might make two telephone calls. One had been to Scotland Yard, and that had been agreed to, after the sergeant had made a preliminary suspicious inquiry on the phone. The sergeant had directed Poirot to the extension in Claudia's bedroom, and he had made his call from there, closing the door behind him.

The sergeant had continued to look doubtful, murmuring to his subordinate, 'They *say* it's all right. Wonder who he is? Odd-looking little bloke.'

'Foreign, isn't he? Might be Special Branch?'

'Don't think so. It was Chief Inspector Neele he wanted.'

His assistant raised his eyebrows and suppressed a whistle.

After making his calls, Poirot had re-opened the door and beckoned Mrs Oliver from where she was standing uncertainly inside the kitchen, to join him. They had sat down side by side on Claudia Reece-Holland's bed.

'I wish we could *do* something,' said Mrs Oliver — always one for action.

'Patience, *chère* Madame.'

'Surely *you* can do something?'

'I have. I have rung up the people it is necessary to ring up. We can do nothing here until the police have finished their preliminary investigations.'

'Who did you ring up after the inspector man? Her father? Couldn't he come and bail her out or something?'

'Bail is not likely to be granted where murder is concerned,' said Poirot dryly. 'The police have already notified her father. They got his number from Miss Cary.'

'Where is she?'

'Having hysterics in the flat of a Miss Jacobs next door, I understand. She was the one who discovered the body. It seems to have upset her. She rushed out of here screaming.'

'She's the arty one, isn't she? Claudia would have kept her head.'

'I agree with you. A very — poised young woman.'

'Who *did* you ring up, then?'

'First, as perhaps you heard, Chief Inspector Neele of Scotland Yard.'

'Will this lot like his coming and meddling?'

'He is not coming to meddle. He has of late been making certain inquiries for me, which may throw light on this matter.'

'Oh — I see . . . Who else did you ring up?'

'Dr John Stillingfleet.'

'Who's he? To say that poor Norma is potty and can't help killing people?'

'His qualifications would entitle him to give evidence to that effect in court if necessary.'

'Does he know anything about her?'

'A good deal, I should say. She has been in his care since the day you found her in the Shamrock café.'

'Who sent her there?'

Poirot smiled. 'I did. I made certain arrangements by telephone before I came to join you at the café.'

'What? All the time I was so disappointed in you and kept urging you to *do* something — you *had* done something? And you never *told* me! Really, Poirot! Not a *word*! How could you be so — so *mean*.'

'Do not enrage yourself, Madame, I beg. What I did, I did for the best.'

'People always say that when they have done something particularly maddening. What else did you do?'

'I arranged that my services should be

retained by her father, so that I could make the necessary arrangements for her safety.'

'Meaning this Doctor Stillingwater?'

'Stilling*fleet*. Yes.'

'How on earth did you manage that? I shouldn't have thought for a moment that you would be the kind of person that her father would choose to make all these arrangements. He looks the kind of man who would be very suspicious of foreigners.'

'I forced myself upon him — as a conjurer forces a card. I called upon him, purporting to have received a letter from him asking me to do so.'

'And did he believe you?'

'Naturally. I showed the letter to him. It was typed on his office stationery and signed with his name — though as he pointed out to me, the handwriting was not his.'

'Do you mean you had actually written that letter yourself?'

'Yes. I judged correctly that it would awaken his curiosity, and that he would want to see me. Having got so far, I trusted to my own talents.'

'You told him what you were going to do about this Dr Stillingfleet?'

'No. I told no one. There was danger, you see.'

'Danger to Norma?'

'To Norma, or Norma was dangerous to someone else. From the very beginning there have always been the two possibilities. The facts could be interpreted in either way. The attempted poisoning of Mrs Restarick was not convincing — it was delayed too long, it was not a serious attempt to kill. Then there was an indeterminate story of a revolver shot fired here in Borodene Mansions — and another tale of flick-knives and bloodstains. Every time these things happen, Norma knows nothing about them, cannot remember, etcetera. She finds arsenic in a drawer — but does not remember putting it there. Claims to have had lapses of memory, to have lost long periods of time when she does not remember what she had been doing. So one has to ask oneself — is what she says *true*, or did she, for some reason of her own, *invent* it? Is she a potential victim of some monstrous and perhaps crazy plot — or is it she herself who is the moving spirit? Is she painting a picture of herself as a girl suffering from mental instability, or has she *murder* in mind, with a defence of diminished responsibility?'

'She was different today,' said Mrs Oliver slowly. 'Did you notice? *Quite* different. Not — not *scatty* any longer.'

Poirot nodded.

'Not Ophelia — Iphigeneia.'

A sound of added commotion outside in the flat diverted the attention of both of them.

'Do you think — ' Mrs Oliver stopped. Poirot had gone to the window and was looking down to the courtyard far below. An ambulance was drawn up there.

'Are they going to take It away?' asked Mrs Oliver in a shaky voice. And then added in a sudden rush of pity: 'Poor Peacock.'

'He was hardly a likeable character,' said Poirot coldly.

'He was very decorative . . . And so *young*,' said Mrs Oliver.

'That is sufficient for *les femmes*.' Poirot was opening the bedroom door a careful crack, as he peered out.

'Excuse me,' he said, 'if I leave you for a moment.'

'Where are you going?' demanded Mrs Oliver suspiciously.

'I understood that that was not a question considered delicate in this country,' said Poirot reproachfully.

'Oh, I beg your pardon.

'And that's not the way to the loo,' she breathed *sotto voce* after him, as she too applied an eye to the crack of the door.

She went back to the window to observe what was going on below.

'Mr Restarick has just driven up in a taxi,' she observed when Poirot slipped back quietly into the room a few minutes later, 'and Claudia has come with him. Did you manage to get into Norma's room, or wherever you really wanted to go?'

'Norma's room is in the occupation of the police.'

'How annoying for you. What are you carrying in that kind of black folder thing you've got in your hand?'

Poirot in his turn asked a question.

'What have you got in that canvas bag with Persian horses on it?'

'My shopping bag? Only a couple of Avocado pears, as it happens.'

'Then if I may, I will entrust this folder to you. Do not be rough with it, or squeeze it, I beg.'

'What is it?'

'Something that I hoped to find — and that I have found — Ah, things begin to pass themselves — ' He referred to increased sounds of activities.

Poirot's words struck Mrs Oliver as being much more exactly descriptive than English words would have been. Restarick, his voice loud and angry. Claudia coming in to telephone. A glimpse of a police stenographer on an excursion to the flat next door to take statements from Frances Cary and a mythical person called Miss Jacobs. A coming and going of ordered business, and a final departure of two men with cameras.

Then unexpectedly the sudden incursion into Claudia's bedroom of a tall loosely-jointed young man with red hair.

Without taking any notice of Mrs Oliver, he spoke to Poirot.

'What's she done? Murder? Who is it? The boy friend?'

'Yes.'

'She admits it?'

'It would seem so.'

'Not good enough. Did she say so in definite words?'

'I have not heard her do so. I have had no chance of asking her anything myself.'

A policeman looked in.

'Dr Stillingfleet?' he asked. 'The police surgeon would like a word with you.'

Dr Stillingfleet nodded and followed him out of the room.

'So that's Dr Stillingfleet,' said Mrs Oliver. She considered for a moment or two. 'Quite something, isn't he?'

# 23

Chief Inspector Neele drew a sheet of paper towards him, jotted one or two notes on it; and looked round at the other five people in the room. His voice was crisp and formal.

'Miss Jacobs?' he said. He looked towards the policeman who stood by the door. 'Sergeant Conolly, I know, has taken her statement. But I'd like to ask her a few questions myself.'

Miss Jacobs was ushered into the room a few minutes later. Neele rose courteously to greet her.

'I am Chief Inspector Neele,' he said, shaking hands with her. 'I am sorry to trouble you for a second time. But this time it is quite informal. I just want to get a clearer picture of exactly what you saw and heard. I'm afraid it may be painful — '

'Painful, no,' said Miss Jacobs, accepting the chair he offered her. 'It was a shock, of course. But no emotions were involved.' She added: 'You seem to have tidied up things.'

He presumed she was referring to the removal of the body.

Her eyes, both observant and critical,

passed lightly over the assembled people, registering, for Poirot, frank astonishment (What on earth is *this?*), for Mrs Oliver, mild curiosity; appraisement for the back of Dr Stillingfleet's red head, neighbourly recognition for Claudia to whom she vouchsafed a slight nod, and finally dawning sympathy for Andrew Restarick.

'You must be the girl's father,' she said to him. 'There's not much point to condolences from a total stranger. They're better left unsaid. It's a sad world we live in nowadays — or so it seems to me. Girls study too hard in my opinion.'

Then she turned her face composedly towards Neele.

'Yes?'

'I would like you, Miss Jacobs, to tell me in your own words exactly what you saw and heard.'

'I expect it will vary from what I said before,' said Miss Jacobs unexpectedly. 'Things do, you know. One tries to make one's description as accurate as possible, and so one uses more words. I don't think one is any more accurate; I think, unconsciously, one adds things that you think you may have seen or ought to have seen — or heard. But I will do my best.

'It started with screams. I was startled. I

thought someone must have been hurt. So I was already coming to the door when someone began beating on it, and still screaming. I opened it and saw it was one of my next-door neighbours — the three girls who live in 67. I'm afraid I don't know her name, though I know her by sight.'

'Frances Cary,' said Claudia.

'She was quite incoherent, and stammered out something about someone being dead — someone she knew — David Someone — I didn't catch his last name. She was sobbing and shaking all over. I brought her in, gave her some brandy, and went to see for myself.'

Everyone felt that throughout life that would be what Miss Jacobs would invariably do.

'You know what I found. Need I describe it?'

'Just briefly, perhaps.'

'A young man, one of these modern young men — gaudy clothes and long hair. He was lying on the floor and he was clearly dead. His shirt was stiff with blood.'

Stillingfleet stirred. He turned his head and looked keenly at Miss Jacobs.

'Then I became aware that there was a girl in the room. She was holding a kitchen knife. She seemed quite calm and self-possessed — really, most peculiar.'

Stillingfleet said: 'Did she say anything?'

'She said she had been into the bathroom to wash the blood off her hands — and then she said, 'But you can't wash things like that off, can you?''

'*Out, damnéd spot,* in fact?'

'I cannot say that she reminded me particularly of Lady Macbeth. She was — how shall I put it? — perfectly composed. She laid the knife down on the table and sat down on a chair.'

'What else did she say?' asked Chief Inspector Neele, his eyes dropping to a scrawled note in front of him.

'Something about *hate.* That it wasn't safe to *hate* anybody.'

'She said something about 'poor David', didn't she? Or so you told Sergeant Conolly. And that she wanted to be free of him.'

'I'd forgotten that. Yes. She said something about his making her come here — and something about Louise, too.'

'What did she say about Louise?' It was Poirot who asked, leaning forward sharply. Miss Jacobs looked at him doubtfully.

'Nothing, really, just mentioned the name. '*Like Louise,*' she said, and then stopped. It was after she had said about its not being safe to hate people . . . '

'And then?'

'Then she told me, quite calmly, I had better ring up the police. Which I did. We just — sat there until they came . . . I did not think I ought to leave her. We did not say anything. She seemed absorbed in her thoughts, and I — well, frankly, I couldn't think of anything to say.'

'You could see, couldn't you, that she was mentally unstable?' said Andrew Restarick. 'You could see that she didn't know what she had done or why, poor child?'

He spoke pleadingly — hopefully.

'If it is a sign of mental instability to appear perfectly cool and collected after committing a murder, then I will agree with you.'

Miss Jacobs spoke in the voice of one who quite decidedly did *not* agree.

Stillingfleet said:

'Miss Jacobs, did she at any time admit that she had killed him?'

'Oh yes. I should have mentioned that before — It was the very first thing she did say. As though she was answering some question I had asked her. She said, '*Yes. I've killed him.*' And then went on about having washed her hands.'

Restarick groaned and buried his face in his hands. Claudia put her hand on his arm.

Poirot said:

'Miss Jacobs, you say the girl put down the

322

knife she was carrying on that table. It was quite near you? You saw it clearly? Did it appear to you that the knife also had been washed?'

Miss Jacobs looked hesitantly at Chief Inspector Neele. It was clear that she felt that Poirot struck an alien and unofficial note in this presumably official inquiry.

'Perhaps you would be kind enough to answer that?' said Neele.

'No — I don't think the knife had been washed or wiped in any way. It was stained and discoloured with some thick sticky substance.'

'Ah.' Poirot leaned back in his chair.

'I should have thought you would have known all about the knife yourself,' said Miss Jacobs to Neele accusingly. 'Didn't your police examine it? It seems to me very lax if they didn't.'

'Oh yes, the police examined it,' said Neele. 'But we — er — always like to get corroboration.'

She darted him a shrewd glance.

'What you really mean, I suppose, is that you like to find out how accurate the observation of your witnesses is. How much they make up, or how much they actually see, or think they have seen.'

He smiled slightly as he said:

'I don't think we need have doubts about you, Miss Jacobs. You will make an excellent witness.'

'I shan't enjoy it. But it's the kind of thing one has to go through with, I suppose.'

'I'm afraid so. Thank you, Miss Jacobs.' He looked round. 'No one has any additional questions?'

Poirot indicated that he had. Miss Jacobs paused near the doorway, displeased.

'Yes?' she said.

'About this mention of someone called Louise. Did you know who it was the girl meant?'

'How should I know?'

'Isn't it possible that she might have meant Mrs Louise Charpentier? You knew Mrs Charpentier, didn't you?'

'I did not.'

'You knew that she recently threw herself out of a window in this block of flats?'

'I knew that, of course. I didn't know her Christian name was Louise, and I was not personally acquainted with her.'

'Nor, perhaps, particularly wished to be?'

'I have not said so, since the woman is dead. But I will admit that that is quite true. She was a most undesirable tenant, and I and other residents have frequently complained to the management here.'

'Of what exactly?'

'To speak frankly, the woman drank. Her flat was actually on the top floor above mine and there were continual disorderly parties, with broken glass, furniture knocked over, singing and shouting, a lot of — er — coming and going.'

'She was, perhaps, a lonely woman,' suggested Poirot.

'That was hardly the impression she conveyed,' said Miss Jacobs acidly. 'It was put forward at the inquest that she was depressed over the state of her health. Entirely her own imagination. She seems to have had nothing the matter with her.'

And having disposed of the late Mrs Charpentier without sympathy, Miss Jacobs took her departure.

Poirot turned his attention to Andrew Restarick. He asked delicately:

'Am I correct in thinking, Mr Restarick, that you were at one time well acquainted with Mrs Charpentier?'

Restarick did not answer for a moment or two. Then he sighed deeply and transferred his gaze to Poirot.

'Yes. At one time, many years ago, I knew her very well indeed . . . Not, I may say, under the name of Charpentier. She was Louise Birell when I knew her.'

'You were — er — in love with her!'

'Yes, I was in love with her . . . Head over ears in love with her! I left my wife on her account. We went to South Africa. After barely a year the whole thing blew up. She returned to England. I never heard from her again. I never even knew what had become of her.'

'What about your daughter? Did she, also, know Louise Birell?'

'Not to remember her, surely. A child of five years old!'

'But did she know her?' Poirot persisted.

'Yes,' said Restarick slowly. 'She knew Louise. That is to say, Louise came to our house. She used to play with the child.'

'So it is possible that the girl *might* remember her, even after a lapse of years?'

'I don't know. I simply don't know. I don't know what she looked like; how much Louise might have changed. I never saw her again, as I told you.'

Poirot said gently, 'But you *heard* from her, didn't you, Mr Restarick? I mean, you have heard from her since your return to England?'

Again there came that pause, and the deep unhappy sigh:

'Yes — I heard from her . . . ' said Restarick. And then, with sudden curiosity, he asked: 'How did you know that, M. Poirot?'

From his pocket, Poirot drew a neatly folded piece of paper. He unfolded it and handed it to Restarick.

The latter looked at it with a faintly puzzled frown.

*Dear Andy*
    *I see from the papers you're home again. We must meet and compare notes as to what we've both been doing all these years —*

It broke off here — and started again.

*Andy — Guess who this is from! Louise. Don't dare to say you've forgotten me! —*

*Dear Andy,*
    *As you will see by this letterhead, I'm living in the same block of flats as your secretary. What a small world it is! We must meet. Could you come for a drink Monday or Tuesday next week?*

*Andy darling, I must see you again . . . Nobody has ever mattered to me but you — you haven't really forgotten me, either, have you?*

'How did *you* get this?' asked Restarick of Poirot, tapping it curiously.

'From a friend of mine via a furniture van,' said Poirot, with a glance at Mrs Oliver.

Restarick looked at her without favour.

'I couldn't help it,' said Mrs Oliver, interpreting his look correctly. 'I suppose it was *her* furniture being moved out, and the men let go of a desk, and a drawer fell out and scattered a lot of things, and the wind blew this along the courtyard, so I picked it up and tried to give it back to them, but they were cross and didn't want it, so I just put it in my coat pocket without thinking. And I never even looked at it until this afternoon when I was taking things out of pockets before sending the coat to the cleaners. So it really wasn't my fault.'

She paused, slightly out of breath.

'Did she get her letter to you written in the end?' Poirot asked.

'Yes — she did — one of the more formal versions! I didn't answer it. I thought it would be wiser not to do so.'

'You didn't want to see her again?'

'She was the last person I wanted to see! She was a particularly difficult woman — always had been. And I'd heard things about her — for one that she had become a heavy drinker. And well — other things.'

'Did you keep her letter to you?'

'No, I tore it up!'

Dr Stillingfleet asked an abrupt question.

'Did your daughter ever speak about her to you?'

Restarick seemed unwilling to answer.

Dr Stillingfleet urged him:

'It might be significant if she did, you know.'

'You doctors! Yes, she did mention her once.'

'What did she say exactly?'

'She said quite suddenly: 'I saw Louise the other day, Father.' I was startled. I said: 'Where did you see her?' And she said: 'In the restaurant of our flats.' I was a bit embarrassed. I said: 'I never dreamed you'd remembered her.' And she said: 'I've never forgotten. Mother wouldn't have let me forget, even if I wanted to.''

'Yes,' said Dr Stillingfleet. 'Yes, that could certainly be significant.'

'And you, Mademoiselle,' said Poirot, turning suddenly to Claudia. 'Did Norma ever speak to you about Louise Carpenter?'

'Yes — it was after the suicide. She said something about her being a wicked woman. She said it in rather a childish way, if you know what I mean.'

'You were here in the flats yourself on the

night — or more correctly the early morning when Mrs Carpenter's suicide occurred?'

'I was not here that night, no! I was away from home. I remember arriving back here the next day and hearing about it.'

She half turned to Restarick . . . 'You remember? It was the twenty-third. I had gone to Liverpool.'

'Yes, of course. You were to represent me at the Hever Trust meeting.'

Poirot said:

'But Norma slept here that night?'

'Yes.' Claudia seemed uncomfortable.

'Claudia?' Restarick laid his hand on her arm. 'What *is* it you know about Norma? There's something. Something that you're holding back.'

'Nothing! What should I know about her?'

'You think she's off her head, don't you?' said Dr Stillingfleet in a conversational voice. 'And so does the girl with the black hair. And so do *you*,' he added, turning suddenly on Restarick. 'All of us behaving nicely and avoiding the subject and thinking the same thing! Except, that is, the chief inspector. He's not thinking anything. He's collecting the facts: mad or a murderess. What about *you*, Madam?'

'Me?' Mrs Oliver jumped. 'I — don't know.'

330

'You reserve judgment? I don't blame you. It's difficult. On the whole, most people agree on what they think. They use different terms for it — that's all. Bats in the Belfry. Wanting in the top storey. Off her onion. Mental. Delusions. Does *anyone* think that girl is sane?'

'Miss Battersby,' said Poirot.

'Who the devil is Miss Battersby?'

'A schoolmistress.'

'If I ever have a daughter I shall send her to that school . . . Of course I'm in a different category. *I know.* I know everything about that girl!'

Norma's father stared at him.

'Who is this man?' he demanded of Neele. 'What can he possibly *mean* by saying that he knows everything about my daughter?'

'I know about her,' said Stillingfleet, 'because she's been under my professional care for the last ten days.'

'Dr Stillingfleet,' said Chief Inspector Neele, 'is a highly qualified and reputable psychiatrist.'

'And how did she come into your clutches — without someone getting my consent first?'

'Ask Moustaches,' said Dr Stillingfleet, nodding towards Poirot.

'*You — you* . . .'

Restarick could hardly speak he was so angry.

Poirot spoke placidly.

'I had your instructions. You wanted care and protection for your daughter when she was found. I found her — and I was able to interest Dr Stillingfleet in her case. She was in danger, Mr Restarick, very grave danger.'

'She could hardly be in any more danger than she is now! Arrested on a charge of murder!'

'Technically she is not yet charged,' murmured Neele.

He went on:

'Dr Stillingfleet, do I understand that you are willing to give your professional opinion as to Miss Restarick's mental condition, and as to how well she knows the nature and meaning of her acts?'

'We can save the M'Naughten act for court,' said Stillingfleet. 'What you want to know now is, quite simply, if the girl is mad or sane? All right, I'll tell you. *That girl is sane* — as sane as any one of you sitting here in this room!'

# 24

## I

They stared at him.

'Didn't expect that, did you?'

Restarick said angrily: 'You're wrong. That girl *doesn't even know what she's done*. She's innocent — completely innocent. She can't be held responsible for what she doesn't know she's done.'

'You let *me* talk for a while. I know what I'm talking about. You don't. That girl is sane and responsible for her actions. In a moment or two we'll have her in and let her speak for herself. She's the only one who hasn't had the chance of speaking for herself! Oh yes, they've got her here still — locked up with a police matron in her bedroom. But before we ask her a question or two, I've got something to say that you'd better hear first.

'When that girl came to me *she was full of drugs*.'

'And *he* gave them to her!' shouted Restarick. 'That degenerate, miserable boy.'

'He started her on them, no doubt.'

'Thank God,' said Restarick. 'Thank God for it.'

'What are you thanking God for?'

'I misunderstood you. I thought you were going to throw her to the lions when you kept harping on her being sane. I misjudged you. It was the drugs that did it. Drugs that made her do things she would never have done of her own volition, and left her with no knowledge of having done them.'

Stillingfleet raised his voice:

'If you let *me* talk instead of talking so much yourself, and being so sure you know all about everything, we might get on a bit. First of all, *she's not an addict.* There are no marks of injections. She didn't sniff snow. Someone or other, perhaps the boy, perhaps someone else, was administering drugs to her without her knowledge. Not just a purple heart or two in the modern fashion. A rather interesting medley of drugs — LSD giving vivid dream sequences — nightmares or pleasurable. Hemp distorting the time factor, so that she might believe an experience has lasted an hour instead of a few minutes. And a good many other curious substances that I have no intention of letting any of you know about. Somebody who was clever with drugs played merry hell with that girl. Stimulants, sedatives, they all played their part in controlling her, and showing her *to herself* as a completely different person.'

Restarick interrupted: 'That's what I say. Norma wasn't responsible! Someone was hypnotising her to do these things.'

'You still haven't got the point! Nobody could make the girl do *what she didn't want to do*! What they *could* do, was make her *think* she had done it. Now we'll have her in and make her see what's been happening to her.'

He looked inquiringly at Chief Inspector Neele, who nodded.

Stillingfleet spoke over his shoulder to Claudia, as he went out of the sitting-room. 'Where'd you put that other girl, the one you took away from Jacobs, gave a sedative to? In her room on her bed? Better shake her up a bit, and drag her along, somehow. We'll need all the help we can get.'

Claudia also went out of the sitting-room.

Stillingfleet came back, propelling Norma, and uttering rough encouragement.

'There's a good girl . . . Nobody's going to bite you. Sit there.'

She sat obediently. Her docility was still rather frightening.

The policewoman hovered by the door looking scandalised.

'All I'm asking you to do is to speak the

truth. It isn't nearly as difficult as you think.'

Claudia came in with Frances Cary. Frances was yawning heavily. Her black hair hung like a curtain hiding half her mouth as she yawned and yawned again.

'You need a pick-me-up,' said Stillingfleet to her.

'I wish you'd all let me go to sleep,' murmured Frances indistinctly.

'Nobody's going to have a chance of sleep until I've done with them! Now, Norma, you answer my questions — That woman along the passage says you admitted to her that you killed David Baker. Is that right?'

Her docile voice said:

'Yes. I killed David.'

'Stabbed him?'

'Yes.'

'How do you know you did?'

She looked faintly puzzled. 'I don't know what you mean. He was there on the floor — dead.'

'Where was the knife?'

'I picked it up.'

'It had blood on it?'

'Yes. And on his shirt.'

'What did it feel like — the blood on the knife? The blood that you got on your hand and had to wash off — Wet? Or more like strawberry jam?'

'It was like strawberry jam — sticky.' She shivered. 'I had to go and wash it off my hands.'

'Very sensible. Well, that ties up everything very nicely. Victim, murderer — you — all complete with the weapon. Do you remember actually *doing* it?'

'No . . . I don't remember *that* . . . But I must have done it, mustn't I?'

'Don't ask me! I wasn't there. It's you are the one who's saying it. But there was another killing before that, wasn't there? An earlier killing.'

'You mean — Louise?'

'Yes. I mean Louise . . . When did you first think of killing her?'

'Years ago. Oh, years ago.'

'When you were a child.'

'Yes.'

'Had to wait a long time, didn't you?'

'I'd forgotten all about it.'

'Until you saw her again and recognised her?'

'Yes.'

'When you were a child, you hated her. Why?'

'Because she took Father, my father, away.'

'And made your mother unhappy?'

'Mother hated Louise. She said Louise was a really wicked woman.'

'Talked to you about her a lot, I suppose?'

'Yes. I wish she hadn't . . . I didn't want to go on hearing about her.'

'Monotonous — I know. Hate isn't creative. When you saw her again did you *really* want to kill her?'

Norma seemed to consider. A faintly interested look came into her face.

'I didn't, really, you know . . . It seemed all so long ago. I couldn't imagine myself — that's why — '

'Why you weren't sure you *had?*'

'Yes. I had some quite wild idea that I *hadn't* killed her at all. That it had been all a dream. That perhaps she really *had* thrown herself out of the window.'

'Well — why not?'

'Because I knew I had done it — I *said* I had done it.'

'You said *you* had done it? Who did you say that to?'

Norma shook her head. 'I mustn't . . . It was someone who tried to be kind — to help me. She said she was going to pretend to have known nothing about it.' She went on, the words coming fast and excitedly: 'I was outside Louise's door, the door of 76, just coming out of it. I thought I'd been walking in my sleep. They — she — said there had been an accident. Down in the courtyard. She

338

kept telling me it had been nothing to do with me. Nobody would ever know — And I couldn't remember what I had done — but there was stuff in my hand — '

'Stuff? What stuff? Do you mean *blood?*'

'No, not blood — torn curtain stuff. When I'd pushed her out.'

'You remember pushing her out, do you?'

'No, no. That's what was so awful. I didn't remember *anything*. That's why I *hoped*. That's why I went — ' She turned her head towards Poirot — 'to *him* — '

She turned back again to Stillingfleet.

'I *never* remembered the things I'd done, none of them. But I got more and more frightened. Because there used to be quite long times that were blank — quite blank — hours I couldn't account for, or remember where I'd been and what I'd been doing. But I found things — things I must have hidden away myself. Mary was being poisoned by *me*, they found out she was being poisoned at the hospital. *And I found the weed killer I'd hidden away in the drawer.* In the flat here there was a flick-knife. And I had a revolver that I didn't even know I'd bought! I *did* kill people, but I didn't remember killing them, so I'm not really a murderer — I'm just — *mad!* I realised that at last. I'm mad, and I can't help it. People can't blame you if you do

339

things when you are mad. If I could come here and even kill *David*, it *shows* I am mad, doesn't it?'

'You'd like to be mad, very much?'

'I — yes, I suppose so.'

'If so, why did you confess to someone that you had killed a woman by pushing her out of the window? Who was it you told?'

Norma turned her head, hesitated. Then raised her hand and pointed.

'I told Claudia.'

'That is absolutely untrue.' Claudia looked at her scornfully. 'You never said anything of the kind to me!'

'I did. I did.'

'When? Where?'

'I — don't know.'

'She told me that she had confessed it all to you,' said Frances indistinctly. 'Frankly, I thought she was hysterical and making the whole thing up.'

Stillingfleet looked across at Poirot.

'She could be making it all up,' he said judicially. 'There is quite a case for that solution. But if so, we would have to find the motive, a strong motive, for her desiring the death of those two people, Louise Carpenter and David Baker. A childish hate? Forgotten and done with years ago? Non-sense. David — just to be 'free of him'? It is not for that that girls kill! We want better motives than that. A whacking great lot of money — say! — Greed!' He looked round him and his voice changed to a conventional tone.

'We want a little more help. There's still one person missing. Your wife is a long time joining us here, Mr Restarick?'

'I can't think where Mary can be. I've rung up. Claudia has left messages in every place we can think of. By now she ought to have rung up at least from somewhere.'

'Perhaps we have the wrong idea,' said Hercule Poirot. 'Perhaps Madame is at least partly here already — in a manner of speaking.'

'What on earth do you mean?' shouted Restarick angrily.

'Might I trouble you, *chère* Madame?'

Poirot leaned towards Mrs Oliver. Mrs Oliver stared.

'The parcel I entrusted to you — '

'Oh.' Mrs Oliver dived into her shopping bag. She handed the black folder to him.

He heard a sharply indrawn breath near him, but did not turn his head.

He shook off the wrappings delicately and held up — a wig of *bouffant* golden hair.

'Mrs Restarick is not here,' he said, 'but *her wig is*. Interesting.'

'Where the devil did you get that, Poirot?' asked Neele.

'From the overnight bag of Miss Frances Cary from which she had as yet no opportunity of removing it. *Shall we see how it becomes her?*'

With a single deft movement, he swept aside the black hair that masked Frances's face so effectively. Crowned with a golden aureole before she could defend herself, she glared at them.

Mrs Oliver exclaimed:

'Good gracious — it *is* Mary Restarick.'

Frances was twisting like an angry snake. Restarick jumped from his seat to come to her — but Neele's strong grip restrained him.

'No. We don't want any violence from you. The game's up, you know, Mr Restarick — or shall I call you Robert Orwell — '

A stream of profanity came from the man's lips. Frances's voice was raised sharply:

'Shut up, you damned fool!' she said.

## II

Poirot had abandoned his trophy, the wig. He had gone to Norma, and taken her hand gently in his.

'Your ordeal is over, my child. The victim will not be sacrificed. You are neither mad, nor have you killed anyone. There are two

342

cruel and heartless creatures who plotted against you, with cunningly administered drugs, with lies, doing their best to drive you either to suicide or to belief in your own guilt and madness.'

Norma was staring with horror at the other plotter.

'My *father*. My *father*? He could think of doing that to *me*. His daughter. My father who loved me — '

'Not your father, *mon enfant* — a man who came here after your father's death, to impersonate him and lay hands on an enormous fortune. Only one person was likely to recognise him — or rather to recognise that this man *was not Andrew Restarick* — the woman who had been Andrew Restarick's mistress fifteen years ago.'

# 25

Four people sat in Poirot's room. Poirot in his square chair was drinking a glass of *sirop de cassis*. Norma and Mrs Oliver sat on the sofa. Mrs Oliver was looking particularly festive in unbecoming apple green brocade, surmounted by one of her more painstaking coiffures. Dr Stillingfleet was sprawled out in a chair with his long legs stretched out, so that they seemed to reach half across the room.

'Now then, there are lots of things I want to know,' said Mrs Oliver. Her voice was accusatory.

Poirot hastened to pour oil on troubled waters.

'But, *chère* Madame, consider. What I owe to you I can hardly express. All, but *all* my good ideas were suggested to me by you.'

Mrs Oliver looked at him doubtfully.

'Was it not you who introduced to me the phrase 'Third Girl'? It is there that I started — and there, too, that I ended — at the third girl of three living in a flat. Norma was always technically, I suppose, the Third Girl — but when I looked at things *the right way round* it

344

all fell into place. The missing answer, the lost piece of the puzzle, every time it was the same — the third girl.

'It was always, if you comprehend me, *the person who was not there*. She was a name to me, no more.'

'I wonder I never connected her with Mary Restarick,' said Mrs Oliver. 'I'd seen Mary Restarick at Crosshedges, talked to her. Of course the first time I saw Frances Cary, she had black hair hanging all over her face. That would have put anyone off!'

'Again it was you, Madame, who drew my attention to how easily a woman's appearance is altered by the way she arranges her hair. Frances Cary, remember, had had dramatic training. She knew all about the art of swift make-up. She could alter her voice at need. As Frances, she had long black hair, framing her face and half hiding it, heavy dead white *maquillage*, dark pencilled eyebrows and mascara, with a drawling husky voice. Mary Restarick, with her wig of formally arranged golden hair with crimped waves, her conventional clothes, her slight Colonial accent, her brisk way of talking, presented a complete contrast. Yet one felt, from the beginning, that she was not quite *real*. What kind of a woman *was* she? I did not know.

'I was not clever about her — No — I,

Hercule Poirot, was not clever at all.'

'Hear, hear,' said Dr Stillingfleet. 'First time I've ever heard *you* say that, Poirot! Wonders will never cease!'

'I don't really see why she wanted two personalities,' said Mrs Oliver. 'It seems unnecessarily confusing.'

'No. It was very valuable to her. It gave her, you see, a perpetual alibi whenever she wanted it. To think that it was there, all the time, before my eyes, and I did not see it! There was the wig — I kept being subconsciously worried by it, but not seeing *why* I was worried. Two women — never, at any time, seen together. Their lives so arranged that no one noticed the large gaps in their time schedules when they were unaccounted for. Mary goes often to London, to shop, to visit house agents, to depart with a sheaf of orders to view, supposedly to spend her time that way. Frances goes to Birmingham, to Manchester, even flies abroad, frequents Chelsea with her special coterie of arty young men whom she employs in various capacities which would not be looked on with approval by the law. Special picture frames were designed for the Wedderburn Gallery. Rising young artists had 'shows' there — their pictures sold quite well, and were shipped abroad or sent on exhibition with their frames stuffed with secret packets of heroin — Art rackets — skilful forgeries of the more obscure Old Masters — She arranged and organised all these things. David Baker was one of the artists she employed. He had the gift of being a marvellous copyist.'

Norma murmured: 'Poor David. When I first met him I thought he was wonderful.'

'That picture,' said Poirot dreamily. 'Always, always, I came back to that in my mind. Why had Restarick brought it up to his office? What special significance did it have for him? *Enfin*, I do not admire myself for being so dense.'

'I don't understand about the pictures.'

'It was a very clever idea. It served as a kind of certificate of identity. A pair of portraits, husband and wife, by a celebrated and fashionable portrait painter of his day. David Baker, when they come out of store, replaces Restarick's portrait with one of Orwell, making him about twenty years younger in appearance. Nobody would have dreamed that the portrait was a fake; the style, the brush strokes, the canvas, it was a splendidly convincing bit of work. Restarick hung it over his desk. Anyone who knew Restarick years ago, might say: 'I'd hardly have known you!' Or 'You've changed quite a lot,' would look up at the portrait, but would only think he himself had really forgotten what the other man had looked like!'

'It was a great risk for Restarick — or rather Orwell — to take,' said Mrs Oliver thoughtfully.

'Less than you might think. He was never a *claimant*, you see, in the Tichborne sense. He was only a member of a well-known City firm, returning home after his brother's death to settle up his brother's affairs after having spent some years abroad. He brought with him a young wife recently acquired abroad, and took up residence with an elderly, half blind but extremely distinguished uncle by marriage who had never known him well after his schoolboy days, and who accepted him without question. He had no other near relations, except for the daughter whom he had last seen when she was a child of five. When he originally left for South Africa, the office staff had had two very elderly clerks, since deceased. Junior staff never remains anywhere long nowadays. The family lawyer is also dead. You may be sure that the whole position was studied very carefully on the spot by Frances after they had decided on their coup.

'She had met him, it seems, in Kenya about two years ago. They were both crooks, though with entirely different interests. He went in

348

for various shoddy deals as a prospector — Restarick and Orwell went together to prospect for mineral deposits in somewhat wild country. There was a rumour of Restarick's death (probably true) which was later contradicted.'

'A lot of money in the gamble, I suspect?' said Stillingfleet.

'An enormous amount of money was involved. A terrific gamble — for a terrific stake. It came off. Andrew Restarick was a very rich man himself and he was his brother's heir. Nobody questioned his identity. And then — things went wrong. Out of the blue, he got a letter from a woman who, if she ever came face to face with him, would know at once that he wasn't Andrew Restarick. And a second piece of bad fortune occurred — David Baker started to blackmail him.'

'That might have been expected, I suppose,' said Stillingfleet thoughtfully.

'They didn't expect it,' said Poirot. 'David had never blackmailed before. It was the enormous wealth of this man that went to his head, I expect. The sum he had been paid for faking the portrait seemed to him grossly inadequate. He wanted more. So Restarick wrote him large cheques, and pretended that it was on account of his daughter — to prevent her from making an undesirable marriage. Whether he really wanted to marry her, I do not know — he may have done. But to blackmail two people like Orwell and Frances Cary was a dangerous thing to do.'

'You mean those two just cold-bloodedly planned to kill two people — quite calmly — just like that?' demanded Mrs Oliver.

She looked rather sick.

'They might have added you to their list, Madame,' said Poirot.

'Me? Do you mean that it was one of *them* who hit me on the head? Frances, I suppose? *Not* the poor Peacock?'

'I do not think it was the Peacock. But you had been already to Borodene Mansions. Now you perhaps follow Frances to Chelsea, or so she thinks, with a rather dubious story to account for yourself. So she slips out and gives you a nice little tap on the head to put paid to your curiosity for a while. You would not listen when I warned you there was danger about.'

'I can hardly believe it of her! Lying about in attitudes of a Burne-Jones heroine in that dirty studio that day. But why — ' She looked at Norma — then back at Poirot. 'They used *her* — deliberately — worked upon her, drugged her, made her believe that she had murdered two people. Why?'

'They wanted a *victim* . . . ' said Poirot.

He rose from his chair and went to Norma.

'*Mon enfant*, you have been through a terrible ordeal. It is a thing that need never happen to you again. Remember that now, you can have confidence in yourself always. To have known, at close quarters, what absolute evil means, is to be armoured against what life can do to you.'

'I suppose you are right,' said Norma. 'To think you are mad — really to *believe* it, is a frightening thing . . . ' She shivered. 'I don't see, even now, *why* I escaped — why *anyone* managed to believe that I hadn't killed David — not when even *I* believed I had killed him?'

'Blood was wrong,' said Dr Stillingfleet in a matter-of-fact tone. 'Starting to coagulate. Shirt was 'stiff with it', as Miss Jacobs said, not *wet*. You were supposed to have killed him not more than about five minutes before Frances's screaming act.'

'How did she — ' Mrs Oliver began to work things out. 'She had been to Manchester — '

'She came home by an earlier train, changed into her Mary wig and make-up on the train. Walked into Borodene Mansions and went up in the lift as an unknown blonde. Went into the flat where David was waiting for her, as she had told him to do. He

351

was quite unsuspecting, and she stabbed him. Then she went out again, and kept watch until she saw Norma coming. She slipped into a public cloakroom, changed her appearance, and joined a friend at the end of the road and walked with her, said goodbye to her at Borodene Mansions and went up herself and did her stuff — quite enjoying doing it, I expect. By the time the police had been called and got there, she didn't think anyone would suspect the time lag. I must say, Norma, you gave us all a hell of a time that day. Insisting on having killed everyone the way you did!'

'I wanted to confess and get it all over . . . Did you — did *you* think I might *really* have done it, then?'

'Me? What do you take me for? I know what my patients will do or won't do. But I thought you were going to make things damned difficult. I didn't know how far Neele was sticking his neck out. Didn't seem proper police procedure to me. Look at the way he gave Poirot here his head.'

Poirot smiled.

'Chief Inspector Neele and I have known each other for many years. Besides, he had been making inquiries about certain matters already. You were never really outside Louise's door. Frances changed the numbers.

She reversed the 6 and the 7 on your own door. Those numbers were loose, stuck on with spikes. Claudia was away that night. Frances drugged you so that the whole thing was a nightmare dream to you.

'I saw the truth suddenly. The only other person who could have killed Louise was the real 'third girl', Frances Cary.'

'You kept half recognising her, you know,' said Stillingfleet, 'when you described to me how one person seemed to turn into another.'

Norma looked at him thoughtfully.

'You were very rude to people,' she said to Stillingfleet. He looked slightly taken aback.

'Rude?'

'The things you said to everyone. The way you shouted at them.'

'Oh well, yes, perhaps I was . . . I've got in the way of it. People are so damned irritating.'

He grinned suddenly at Poirot.

'She's quite a girl, isn't she?'

Mrs Oliver rose to her feet with a sigh.

'I must go home.' She looked at the two men and then at Norma. 'What are we going to do with *her*?' she asked.

They both looked startled.

'I know she's staying with me at the moment,' she went on. 'And she says she's quite happy. But I mean there it is, quite a problem. Lots and lots of money because your father — the real one, I mean — left it all to you. And that will cause complications, and begging letters and all that. She *could* go and live with old Sir Roderick, but that wouldn't be fun for a girl — he's pretty deaf already as well as blind — and completely selfish. By the way, what about his missing papers, and the girl, and Kew Gardens?'

'They turned up where he thought he'd already looked — Sonia found them,' said Norma, and added, 'Uncle Roddy and Sonia are getting married — next week — '

'No fool like an old fool,' said Stillingfleet.

'Aha!' said Poirot. 'So the young lady prefers life in England to being embroiled in *la politique*. She is perhaps wise, that little one.'

'So that's that,' said Mrs Oliver with finality. 'But to go on about Norma, one has to be *practical*. One's got to make *plans*. The girl can't know what she wants to do all by *herself*. She's waiting for someone to *tell* her.'

She looked at them severely.

Poirot said nothing. He smiled.

'Oh, her?' said Dr Stillingfleet. 'Well, I'll tell you, Norma. I'm flying to Australia Tuesday week. I want to look around first — see if what's been fixed up for me is going to work, and all that. Then I'll cable you and you can join me. Then we get married. You'll have to take my word for it that it's not your money I want. I'm not one of those doctors who want to endow whacking great research establishments and all that. I'm just interested in *people*. I think, too, that you'd be able to manage *me* all right. All that about my being rude to people — I hadn't noticed it myself. It's odd, really, when you think of all the mess you've been in — helpless as a fly in treacle — yet it's not going to be *me* running *you*, it's going to be *you* running *me*.'

Norma stood quite still. She looked at John Stillingfleet very carefully, as though she was considering something that she knew from an entirely different point of view.

And then she smiled. It was a very nice smile — like a happy young nannie.

'All right,' she said.

She crossed the room to Hercule Poirot.

'*I* was rude, too,' she said. 'The day I came here when you were having breakfast. I said to you that you were too old to help me. That was a rude thing to say. *And it wasn't true . . .*'

She put her hands on his shoulders and kissed him.

'You'd better get us a taxi,' she said to Stillingfleet.

Dr Stillingfleet nodded and left the room.

Mrs Oliver collected a handbag and a fur stole and Norma slipped on a coat and followed her to the door.

'*Madame, un petit moment* — '

Mrs Oliver turned. Poirot had collected from the recesses of the sofa a handsome coil of grey hair.

Mrs Oliver exclaimed vexedly: 'It's just like everything that they make nowadays, no good at all! Hairpins, I mean. They just slip out, and everything falls off!'

She went out frowning.

A moment or two later she poked her head round the door again. She spoke in a conspiratorial whisper:

'Just tell me — it's all right, I've sent her on down — did you send that girl to this particular doctor on purpose?'

'Of course I did. His qualifications are — '

'Never mind his qualifications. You know what I mean. He and she — Did you?'

'If you must know, yes.'

'I thought so,' said Mrs Oliver. 'You do think of things, don't you.'

*The Agatha Christie Collection*
*Published by The House of Ulverscroft:*

THE MAN IN THE BROWN SUIT
THE SECRET OF CHIMNEYS
THE SEVEN DIALS MYSTERY
THE MYSTERIOUS MR QUIN
THE SITTAFORD MYSTERY
THE HOUND OF DEATH
THE LISTERDALE MYSTERY
WHY DIDN'T THEY ASK EVANS?
PARKER PYNE INVESTIGATES
MURDER IS EASY
AND THEN THERE WERE NONE
TOWARDS ZERO
DEATH COMES AS THE END
SPARKLING CYANIDE
CROOKED HOUSE
THEY CAME TO BAGHDAD
DESTINATION UNKNOWN
ORDEAL BY INNOCENCE
THE PALE HORSE
ENDLESS NIGHT
PASSENGER TO FRANKFURT
PROBLEM AT POLLENSA BAY
WHILE THE LIGHT LASTS

**MISS MARPLE**
THE MURDER AT THE VICARAGE
THE THIRTEEN PROBLEMS
THE BODY IN THE LIBRARY
THE MOVING FINGER

A MURDER IS ANNOUNCED
THEY DO IT WITH MIRRORS
A POCKET FULL OF RYE
4.50 FROM PADDINGTON
THE MIRROR CRACK'D
FROM SIDE TO SIDE
A CARIBBEAN MYSTERY
AT BERTRAM'S HOTEL
NEMESIS
SLEEPING MURDER
MISS MARPLE'S FINAL CASES

**POIROT**
THE MYSTERIOUS AFFAIR AT STYLES
THE MURDER ON THE LINKS
POIROT INVESTIGATES
THE MURDER OF ROGER ACKROYD
THE BIG FOUR
THE MYSTERY OF THE BLUE TRAIN
PERIL AT END HOUSE
LORD EDGWARE DIES
MURDER ON THE ORIENT EXPRESS
THREE ACT TRAGEDY
DEATH IN THE CLOUDS
THE ABC MURDERS
MURDER IN MESOPOTAMIA
CARDS ON THE TABLE
MURDER IN THE MEWS
DUMB WITNESS
DEATH ON THE NILE
APPOINTMENT WITH DEATH
HERCULE POIROT'S CHRISTMAS